SAVING
SILENCE

GINA BLAXILL lives in London. She
has an English degree from Cambridge
University and now works in schools
liaison, helping teenagers puzzle out
the mysteries of higher education.
Between the ages of eleven and fifteen
she wrote an epic thirty-six-part story
featuring over 1,000 characters – she
still remembers most of their names!

Saving Silence is Gina's third novel for
young adults.

SAVING SILENCE

GINA BLAXILL

MACMILLAN

ISBN 978-1-4472-0884-6

A CIP catalogue record for this book is available from
the British Library.

Printed and bound by CPI Group (UK) Ltd, Croydon CR0 4YY

To my aunt, Julia Blaxill,
for being my unofficial Dorset agent

IMOGEN

When I went out that night, I wasn't expecting to save someone's life. Let alone Sam Costello's.

There was a crowd of us including me, my boyfriend Ollie and my mate Nadina. After fifteen minutes of trawling the high street, we'd grabbed a table in Mmm Hot Chicken. It wasn't one of the nicer fast food joints Walthamstow had to offer but we liked it for three reasons. One, the owner was usually happy for us to hang out there all evening. Two, it was cheap. Three, the *E* and the *N* had fallen off the name sign on the front, making 'Mmm Hot Chick' a standing joke. I was ninety per cent certain they'd done this on purpose to draw attention.

This Saturday, Mmm Hot Chick was busy and poorly lit. The light over our table had blown so it was pure chance that I even spotted Sam step through the door. I watched him pause and glance past the queue of people waiting to be served. He was wearing what seemed to be his default outfit of a blazer, shirt and cord trousers – too smart for here. I'd never seen him in anything more casual, despite jeans or tracksuit bottoms being more or less unofficial uniform at our sixth form. Perhaps he dressed that way to make himself look older.

Right now, he was looking lost. Little wonder. From what

I knew of Sam, this wasn't his scene. He'd avoided people ever since he'd started our school in Year 10. Where he went at lunchtime I didn't know. It definitely wasn't the canteen. And he was always first out of the form room at the end of the day. If he had friends, they didn't go to our school. As form rep and then head prefect I'd done my bit to try to include him because it seemed the right thing to do. It hadn't worked. 'Give it a rest,' Nadina had told me. 'You can't be everyone's mate. He's just stuck up.' I wasn't convinced. Who would choose to be a loner? Perhaps he had a reason I couldn't work out. Something to do with his past. Sam came from somewhere up north and had arrived at our school rather suddenly. No one knew anything else about him.

So what was he doing here now? I soon knew, because Sam started walking in my direction. Then he froze. He was staring at something over my shoulder. I looked back but there wasn't anything out of the ordinary. Ollie had just come back from the loos, and everyone was laughing at something he had said.

'Save my seat,' I said. Nadina asked where I was going, but I was already making my way over to Sam.

'All right?' I asked when I was close enough.

Sam opened his mouth — but no words came out. It struck me how anxious he looked. There was sweat on his forehead and he was fiddling with the strap of his messenger bag. I gave him a friendly push.

'Earth to Sam!'

Sam's eyes fixed on mine. For a moment I wondered if he'd taken something. They looked glazed over, not quite in focus.

'Imogen,' he blurted. 'I need to talk to you.'

'Go ahead. Get a Coke and join us. We'll shove the chairs up and make space.'

'No. Not here. Outside.'

Without giving me a chance to reply, Sam hurried out. I called his name, but either he didn't hear me or didn't want to.

I felt a hand on my arm. It was Ollie.

'Why's he here? What's he want?'

I shrugged. 'To speak to me, so he says.'

'Why? You're not mates, Im. He's not your boyfriend. I'll have a word and stop him bothering you.' He started towards the door.

'Hey! It's OK. I'll go outside, see what he wants,' I said, grabbing Ollie's arm and pulling him round to face me. He looked really pissed off. Well, that explained why Sam had taken off so quickly. Ollie wasn't usually one of those aggressive types who grilled any guy that went near his girl, but right now he looked far from happy. I was surprised he'd reacted this way. Perhaps if he'd been at the table when Sam had arrived, Sam would never have come over at all.

'Call out a search party if I'm not back in five,' I said, grabbing my coat. I could feel Ollie's eyes burning into the back of my head as I walked out the door. For a moment I thought Sam had run off, but he was waiting there, hands in pockets, shoulders hunched against the cold. Everyone had been grumbling about the weather this year. There were rumours of snow next week. Whatever Sam had to say, he'd better make it quick. Why he thought talking here was more private was a mystery. We were right next to a group of smokers, and over the road people were milling about outside KFC. Around this time those neon fast-food signs were practically magnetic. Someone was shouting from inside the 24-hour mini-market. Music boomed out of a passing car. To an outsider this street might seem scary, and it was true that there had been some nasty break-ins at some local shops recently. But in the six years I'd been living in north-east London I'd always felt perfectly safe. Besides, I knew how to look after myself.

'So,' I said, 'what's up?'

'It's not easy to explain.' He didn't meet my eyes. 'I was going to put up and shut up, but I can't. It's too important. I'm sorry. Really sorry. You're not going to like this, but you need to know.'

He moved away from the smokers towards the bus stop, stepping out into the road to get past. I was about to follow when I heard an engine rev loudly and looked round. A car appeared out of nowhere. It was hurtling forward. Straight towards Sam.

I didn't think. I moved, crashing into Sam and pushing him aside. As we hit the pavement, I heard smashing glass. Someone shouted Sam's name, someone else screamed and pain whammed up my right side. My head swam before zipping into focus. We had to get away – fast. I scrambled up, pulling Sam with me. The car was backing away from the pavement and the bent bus-shelter post and what was left of Mmm Hot Chick's window, revving its engine.

Bright red blood was splattered all over Sam's neck and chest. He seemed to have lost the ability to function, staring at the car like a rabbit in the headlights.

'Run, stupid!' I shouted.

I grabbed his hand and dragged him out on to the road. I could see the bright lights of KFC and a ring of people outside. People meant safety. Headlights loomed and brakes squealed as a minicab swerved to avoid us. We made it across and through the doors. Warmth, faces, voices, overhead music – someone was trying to push us back, someone else was yelling about police. I fought my way through, focusing on getting to the back of the restaurant.

Noise erupted all around me. Realizing I was still holding Sam's hand, I dropped it and sat down heavily on the nearest chair.

'Move!' Nadina pushed through the people circling me

and Sam, Ollie close behind. She crushed me into a hug. Relieved to hold on to something solid, I hugged her back.

'Am I hallucinating or did that really just happen?' My voice sounded surprisingly calm.

'It bloody well did! You OK?'

'We need to call the police,' I said, taking out my phone. From the corner of my eye I could see Sam leaning against the wall with a dazed look on his face. Blood was dripping from his chin and soaking into his already sodden shirt. 'An ambulance too.'

'For the love of God! Let someone else do that.' Nadina snatched the phone. 'D'you realize what you just did, Im? Like, *seriously*!'

I stared at her. 'What?'

'Jesus!' Nadina waved a hand in front of my face. 'You concussed?'

'Stupid question,' Ollie said. 'She's hardly going to say, "Yeah, I'm concussed," is she?'

'Hey! Don't call me stupid. I've seen hospital dramas—'

'Knock it off, you two!' I snapped. 'I'm fine. OK?'

Ollie knelt in front of me and tentatively took my hands, giving them a squeeze. He'd been hanging behind Nads and only now did I see how ashen his face was. He was shaking his head as though he couldn't take this in, and he kept glancing over his shoulder. I'd never seen him frightened before.

'Did you see who did it?' he asked. I shook my head. 'You coulda been killed. Just sit here, yeah? We'll take care of the rest.'

I squeezed his hands back.

'Im, you saved Sam's life!' Nadina said, her expression earnest. 'It was him that car was heading for. He totally froze. He'd be *pulp* if it wasn't for you. Hear that? You're a bloody hero!'

Within minutes the emergency services arrived. While it was clear I hadn't sustained any physical injury, the paramedics still checked me over. Maybe I was in shock. I did feel as though I was passing in and out of reality. Sam was in a worse state. Someone had fetched some napkins to hold to his chin while we were waiting, but it hadn't stopped the bleeding. The paramedics were talking about stitches and plastics. They were worried about his wrist too. It was only after they'd taken him to A & E that I realized no one had gone with him.

Mmm Hot Chick's window was a mess. The police had put a cordon around the front. That's gonna need a lot of repair work, I thought. Ridiculously, I wondered if the owner would get the *E* and *N* on the sign replaced while he was at it. The police were keeping everyone who had witnessed the incident in KFC to interview. Ollie was reluctant to leave. He said something about 'looking after me', but the police didn't want too many people milling around. Only Nadina had been allowed to stay. Not that anyone could have stopped her if they'd tried.

A police officer came over to me. I told her what had happened, Nadina filling in the blanks.

'Sounds like you and your friend were just in the wrong place at the wrong time.' Even as the officer said the words I knew she was wrong. Everything had happened in such a blur it was hard to remember precisely, but someone had called Sam's name. Someone inside the car. I could've sworn it. And I'd instinctively shouted at him to run, feeling on a gut level that we were in danger.

So what did that mean? That this wasn't random? Was this a *murder* attempt? That was insane. Totally out there! This was Sam Costello we were talking about, for God's sake. Completely ordinary, if a bit secretive. A good kid. Not the type who got involved in violence.

Who on earth would want to kill him – and why?

SAM

SATURDAY 9 NOVEMBER

I hate hospitals. As in really, really hate hospitals. I spent far too much time in them when Mum was ill. All the whiteness and the serious-looking people marching down corridors, the horrible watery vending-machine coffee and the rattle of trolley wheels, and knowing that, nearby, people are dying and there's nothing you can do. Hospitals bring back a whole load of bad feelings, and remembering was the last thing I needed right now.

'Don't worry, Sam,' the paramedic kept saying as the ambulance sped towards Whipps Cross. 'We'll be at the hospital in a jiffy, and the doctors are going to patch up your chin. It's going to be OK.'

It wasn't my chin that I was worried about. I was a bit freaked by all the blood, and my wrist was throbbing – sprained, fractured, even broken? – but there was only so much I could take on board, and at this precise moment, I was far, *far* more worried about *them*.

There was no going back from here. They'd worked it all out. Who I was, what I'd seen. They knew. They'd tried to *kill* me. And if Imogen hadn't been there, the police would be scraping my remains off the pavement. I'd be chalked down as just another hit-and-run victim and at my funeral people would be saying things about what a short and tragic life I'd led.

Another even more frightening thought, one that turned

my entire body cold, crossed my mind.

They've tried to kill me once. What's to stop them trying again?

I hadn't thought tonight out properly. I'd thought I'd be safe. Next time I couldn't bank on getting away with it. Not with people this ruthless on my back.

Next time.

I might as well be dead.

'Where's my phone?' I struggled up from the stretcher-bed. 'Please. You need to give it to me.'

'I didn't see a phone in your bag, Sam,' the paramedic said.

Of course! I'd left it at home. My brain wasn't working properly, but the one thing I did know was that I had to say nothing, nothing at all, until I figured out what on earth I could do to get myself out of this mess. Myself, and Imogen too. She needed to know about what was going on. She wouldn't thank me for it, but she'd be safer if she knew.

I realized that there were tears in my eyes. I brushed them away angrily. I shouldn't be in this situation, on the way to hospital, stuck with this awful dilemma about what to do. As if I hadn't had enough crap to deal with over the past couple of years.

The ambulance finally arrived and the paramedic took me into A & E. She said something about plastic surgery and sedatives but all I could hear was the voice in my own head.

They tried to kill me and they'll try again.

IMOGEN

When I sat up in bed my whole body screamed. Man, these bruises were going to be a right pain. I scrabbled on the bedside table for my glasses. The display on my mobile showed midday. Great. So much for making my ten o'clock volleyball practice. I had — crazily — set my alarm. Maybe that was the kind of thing the ambulance staff had meant when they said I might be in shock.

We'd got home at about 2 a.m. 'We' meant me and Nads, who'd managed to wangle us a lift from one of the police officers. She'd called Mum on my behalf but Mum hadn't been able to make it over. Perhaps she hadn't understood what had happened or perhaps coming out that late had been too much bother. I wasn't surprised either way. This wasn't the first time.

My mobile also showed a text from Ollie.

U OK? Feeling better? Been worried. Proper glad u weren't hurt bad. Will come over later & cheer u up. X

Despite myself, I smiled. Ollie hadn't been so great at texting me recently. I'd wondered if he had something on his mind. Although we weren't usually soppy, it was nice to know he still cared.

I wondered if Sam was OK. I wondered what it was he'd come to tell me yesterday and why it was so important. Had someone really been trying to kill him? In the cold light of morning it seemed too insane to be true.

They were waiting in the kitchen when I finally made it downstairs, Mum, Nadina and Benno. From the number of cups on the table it looked as if they'd been waiting a while.

'Here's the hero!' Mum sang. I was almost surprised there weren't party poppers – but then there was hardly space for them. Though the open-plan kitchen/dining area was the biggest room in our tiny council house, it became full very quickly when more than two people crammed around the fold-out table. Not that it mattered. My family rarely ate meals together. Mum worked days and Dad worked nights, and even when they were in the house at the same time, they were too shattered to cook. Most of the time I put together meals for me and Benno, which usually meant sandwiches. As in the rest of the house, paint was beginning to flake off the walls, and the wooden cupboards crammed with mismatched plates and cutlery had seen better days.

'So how are you feeling?' Mum asked.

Wrecked, I thought. 'Fine,' I said.

'Let's get you some nice strong tea and toast. I know it's lunchtime, but never mind that. Benno, pop something in the toaster and fill the kettle, please.'

'I can make my own tea,' I said, though I knew no one would listen. 'Don't make a fuss.'

Mum squinted at me. 'Are you sure you feel fine?'

'Yes. Absolutely. Just ache a bit.'

'Hmm, paracetamol might be in order then. And honey. Honey's good for shock. We'll put a spoonful in your tea.'

I don't want honey in my tea, I thought. All this attention isn't making the fact that you didn't come to help last night any better. I needed you then, not now. You weren't there. I didn't say anything though. What was the point? Mum would only get self-righteous about how hard she worked and how tired she always was and how I ought to be able to look after myself. Sometimes I wondered how true that was. Mum managed to turn out pretty well for someone so overworked. She looked a good deal younger than forty, but not quite enough that people thought we were sisters, thank God. We did look very alike. I'd inherited Mum's slightly pointed chin and dark blonde hair which I usually also wore up. At least our glasses were a different shape. Mum's friends teasingly referred to me as her 'mini-me', which I couldn't stand. Benno was turning into a bit of a mini-Mum too, though he was a boy and only eleven.

Sometimes I felt sorry for Dad. His genes seemed to have got lost somewhere. But then in some ways Dad did seem like a bit of a nothing person. Thanks to his night shifts I didn't see much of him. Even when I did, he never had much to say. He was probably sleeping right now. For all I knew, he didn't even know what had happened yet.

I rolled my eyes at Nadina as Mum carried on fussing. She grinned. Sometimes I thought Nads liked my parents more than I did. Sometimes I thought my parents liked Nadina more than me too.

'Are the police going to get the bad guys?' Benno asked, bringing over my toast and tea. He'd put too much milk in and it was lukewarm. I didn't say anything though.

'Don't think they're optimistic.' Some big sisters would have lied and said yes just to make Benno feel safe, but we didn't do stuff like that in my family. 'No one got a decent look. Unless there's a star eyewitness with laser eyes that see through stuff, or magic CCTV, I have a feeling it might be difficult.'

'That officer said there were a lot of conflicting descriptions,' Nadina put in. 'Like, even you and me can't agree what colour the car was.'

'It was too dark to make out properly.' It was so frustrating. I normally had a good memory for facts and faces.

'Police never get to the bottom of anything like this,' Nadina said. 'You know what that officer said? That stuff like that wasn't unusual here, like Walthamstow was a ghetto or something.'

'Well, it's no Chelsea. Stuff does happen.'

'True, but we could do without the cynicism,' Mum said, and started talking about what she called 'the gang angle'. She had it all worked out. The guys in the car were gang members. We were on their patch and they'd been in the mood for trouble. Nadina joined in. I finished my breakfast-cum-lunch. Benno kept trying to get a word in – he loved crime stories – but after being talked over a couple of times he trailed into the living room and I heard him switch on the TV.

I sighed. I wasn't sure what to believe. Motiveless crime did happen, but not usually to kids like me and Sam. We weren't connected to any of the local gangs. At least, I assumed Sam wasn't in with a gang. Maybe he led a double life. It wouldn't surprise me. He hadn't let anyone at school get close to him. And I was pretty sure that someone in the car had called his name. I hadn't mentioned that to the police though. For some reason I hadn't wanted to. I remembered the nervous spark in Sam's eyes. Had he suspected someone might be after him or had he simply been anxious about talking to me? He'd had something to say that I 'wouldn't like'. But how could he know that? We were practically strangers.

And if Sam had known he was in danger . . . whatever it was had to be pretty damn important to risk leaving the house for.

When Nadina headed home I walked with her. I'd changed into my tracksuit so I could go for a run.

'You're not superwoman, y'know,' Nadina said as we

crossed the green towards the high street. Her family owned a shop there. 'Working out? Seriously? After what you've been through?'

'Need to do something. Running makes me feel better.'

'Chocolate does it for most people.'

'And Superdrug's haircare aisle does it for you.' Nadina's obsession with hairspray was a longstanding joke. I'd known Nads since Year 7. I had never, not once, seen her without her hair styled. She always carried a mirror and was never satisfied until it was perfect. Currently she was wearing it curled and tied to one side, her fringe dyed blonde. 'Making the most of what I got going for me, innit,' she had said when I'd asked why she bothered so much. This wasn't true – Nads had the kind of smile that lit up her face and a curvy figure that suited her perfectly. But I guess no one sees themselves as others do.

'Gotta shoot,' Nadina said, taking a packet of chewing gum from her jeans pocket and slipping a piece into her mouth. 'My cousins are coming over.'

I nodded. Nadina had a big extended family and spent a lot of time with them. She also helped out at the shop several days a week after sixth form. Sometimes that left me lonely, but I was used to it by now. 'Any news on Hamdi Gul?'

'Same, last I heard. Everyone in the mosque is praying, but it ain't doing much good, is it?'

I almost said I was sure things would be OK. But I wasn't sure and Nads knew it. Hamdi Gul was the son of a couple who ran a minimart a couple of roads from Nadina's family's shop. He was doing an IT degree at the local uni and worked in the shop part-time. I didn't really know him, but Nadina did. She knew everyone in the local Turkish community. Several nights ago some guys had run into the shop and demanded that Hamdi open up the till. Exactly what happened, no one knew, but there had been a scuffle and Hamdi had picked up a serious head injury. He'd been in hospital ever since. At first it had looked like he was going to regain consciousness, but his condition had worsened on Friday to critical.

Even thinking about it made me angry. It was so pointless! I couldn't get my head round why anyone would go so far for a couple of hundred quid and some bottles of booze. Hamdi was no threat and he'd already given them the cash. They'd just wanted to beat someone senseless.

Compared to Hamdi, Sam and I were well lucky. When I said so, Nadina half smiled.

'C'mon. Just cos there are worse things out there doesn't mean you've no right to feel chewed up. Way you talk sometimes, it's a surprise there's not a halo round your head. Cut yourself some slack.'

'Wasn't brought up to cut myself slack,' I said. 'There's no time for my unimportant problems.'

'Hey, your parents are OK, Im. Your mum cares, even if she's not that hands on.'

I ignored that. 'Are your parents scared? The kebab place two roads along got done the week before Hamdi's. All the shopkeepers must be on red alert.'

Nadina shrugged. 'Closing up's not an option. I told Dad he should keep a baseball bat behind the counter, but he just laughed. God, listen to us, Im!' She grinned. 'Prematurely old or what? We should be talking about manicures, not this heavyweight crap.'

I laughed. 'We suck, don't we? We're just not proper teenagers. Maybe we should embrace it. Get into knitting and stuff.'

'No chance. I'll take heavyweight crap over knitting any day. You meeting Ollie later?'

I nodded. Nadina hesitated a moment then said, 'Advance warning – he seemed pretty mad about you going outside like that with Sam. He tried to go out after you but I stopped him.'

I pursed my lips. 'I didn't have him down as the jealous type. OK. Thanks.'

'Just thought you oughta know. And now I really gotta go. See ya, grandma. Text if you need to.'

Waving her goodbye, I began my run. I started to feel more like myself again. Running felt so natural to me. When I was on my feet, nothing and no one could get me.

I could forget about all my worries. Running was what had made the worst patch in my life, when we'd lived in Kent, bearable. It was impossible to run away from who you were, but I felt I got close.

No point thinking about everything I didn't like in my life right now though. In just under two years I'd be able to escape to university and start over, away from all this grief.

Instead I thought about what Nads had said. It had been a joke, but she had a point. Nadina spent her free time working at the shop, on family commitments or volunteering. She wanted to be a social worker. My free time got eaten up by running, volleyball, babysitting Benno or stuff around the house. Teachers often complimented us on how responsible and mature we were. Until now I'd never thought we might be missing out.

By the time I'd worked up a sweat, I'd decided what to do. It was simple – speak to Sam. No doubt I was blowing Saturday out of proportion with these crazy notions that someone could have wanted him dead. I had questions. If anyone had answers, it was him.

'Hey, Im!'

I looked and saw Ollie waving from the other side of the green. I jogged over, wiping my forehead. I didn't look my best, but Ollie did sports too and didn't care about stuff like that. Today I could see that he was wearing a black hoody that said Devereux Hawks across the back. Ollie was proud of captaining the school basketball team. His hoody wasn't unlike my volleyball one. We made a right pair. But then we always had been a pair, even before we'd started going out at the end of Year 11. Ollie had been the male head prefect – prefects in our school were Year 11s, so sixth-formers could concentrate on their studies. Everyone had always acted like it was only a matter of time before we got together.

'Just like Im Maxwell to date a male version of herself,' one girl had mocked, to which I'd replied, 'Jealous?' That had shut her up. Ollie was the school pin-up – literally. His photo was plastered over the school prospectus and even on an advertisement at the station. No one complained. Ollie had his Colombian mum's olive complexion and dark hair, which he currently wore short on the sides and thick on top, and a weirdly symmetrical face. On someone else it might not have worked, but on him it did.

I was probably the least romantic girl in the whole year, but I liked having a boyfriend. Family always came first for Nadina so it was good to have someone else around.

'Your mum told me you were here,' Ollie said when I reached him. He leaned in to kiss me hello. When the kiss deepened, I pulled back in surprise. After Nads's warning I'd been braced for him to have a go at me about Sam.

'Wow, you really are relieved to see me out and about!' I joked. Ollie and me weren't normally too demonstrative in public. It was different in private, although we didn't go much further than making out. I didn't want more at the moment and he'd never pushed me. I liked that he respected me. We were together, sure, but first and foremost we were good mates.

'Obviously.' Ollie gave a small smile, not meeting my eyes. He seemed a little sheepish, and weirdly self-conscious. 'You could've been killed. Here.' He shoved a carrier bag at me. 'Thought you deserved a present. Seems a bit rubbish that invalids get grapes though, so I got you these.'

Inside the bag was a box of chocolates. It was a small one with Aldi branding. That explained his embarrassment – Ollie didn't have much spare cash and could be touchy about it. I gave him a peck on the cheek.

'Nice one. Who'd've known you were so thoughtful? Thanks!'

I changed the subject and we walked across the green discussing last night, hand in hand. After a while I said, 'I've had it up to here talking about yesterday. How about we do normal instead?'

Ollie hesitated, then said, 'Normal sounds good.' He felt inside his hoody pocket. 'Got just about enough to treat you at the falafel place. Fancy it?'

I laughed. 'Wow, falafel and chocolates! Lucky me.'

Ollie coloured slightly. 'Yeah, well, you should never have wound up in that accident. I'm just relieved you're OK.'

That explains why we're being so touchy-feely today, I thought as we headed off. Ollie was clearly still spooked by last night. It was sweet of him to show he cared like this. Whether it was being with Ollie, or deciding to speak to Sam, I felt better. Soon I would be back to being normal Imogen Maxwell, who didn't do doubts and had everything sorted.

SAM

After a few mind-numbingly empty hours waiting in A & E the anger I'd experienced in the ambulance had faded into a chilling *what am I going to do now* feeling. I even became desperate enough to drink one of the insult-to-real-coffee-coffees from the vending machines. By the time I got home what I was feeling had changed to – well, I don't even know what you'd call it. Denial? Disbelief? As I lay on my bed, surrounded by familiar things, it became a challenge to even get my head around what had happened, let alone that it had happened to me.

Tamsin had taken everything far more in her stride than I'd expected. When she'd teetered into A & E in her heels and enormous fluffy leopard-print coat I'd thought things were about to go from bad to worse, but apart from some dramatic hand-waving, she stayed pretty calm and didn't even appear pissed off at being dragged out so late. She was far less horrified by the fact that I'd almost been killed than by my chin, which, by the time the doctor had finished stitching it up, looked like it belonged on Frankenstein's monster.

'He's going to be scarred for life!' She had cried. 'Isn't there something else you can do? Didn't someone say something about plastic surgery?'

'The stitches will do the job just fine,' the doctor said. I'd noticed him checking Tamsin out when we'd entered. As usual she seemed oblivious to it. 'A week and they can come out. The cut's underneath the chin. He'll barely notice the scar in a few months. And his wrist is only lightly sprained; all things considered, Sam's pretty lucky.'

I didn't feel lucky. As Tamsin drove home I pretended to be sleepy to avoid answering her questions. As we drew up in front of the house I tried to sort my head out. I didn't think they knew where I lived – surely they'd have tried to get me before now. I did wonder how they'd found me last night, but there was no way they could have followed me – I'd only decided to go out last minute. No, it must just have been bad luck. Maybe they'd been hanging round the high street anyway. I'd been meaning to speak to Imogen for a while before Saturday but she was never alone at school, and unless you're one of the cool kids you don't just approach girls like her in public. More importantly, I was afraid of who might see us.

Then I'd overheard her talking to Nadina Demir about a girls' night out on the high street, so I knew where she'd be on Saturday night. If I'd've known that the girl's night out had turned into a big night out, guys included, I'd never have gone. But by the time I'd clocked that Imogen was with a massive gang of people including her boyfriend, it was too late to back out.

At least I was home. I didn't feel at all at ease, but it was the safest place right now – Dad had installed an expensive security system last year after the house next door had been burgled, so there was that to rely on. And there was Jessie too – she rarely left my side, though greyhounds weren't really much use as guard dogs.

My phone was under my pillow where I'd hidden it. It was a smartphone with a green cover, new last birthday, with unlimited texts, calls and Internet. 'So you can keep in the loop with your mates,' Dad had said, and I'd smiled and said it was an amazing present and didn't mention that it had smacked home just how much of a loner I was these days. Before Mum had got ill I had lots of friends, but as time went on I'd ended up cutting them out. They hadn't understood what I was dealing with and it was just painful being around happy people. The only people that still contacted me were my cousin Mia and Harrison, my old neighbour. Stupid phone! So much for it being *smart*; all it ever did was make me feel bad. And now it had got me into serious trouble too.

Mia had texted last night asking what I was up to. I texted back, then wished I hadn't. Mia would wonder why I was replying at such a funny time. My cousin was only thirteen but looked and behaved like she was older, plus she was sharp enough to pick up on things you'd rather she didn't. Mia knew a little about what was going on and I was determined that she wouldn't find out any more. Thinking about her made me realize just how on my own I was. I definitely wasn't going to tell Tamsin what had happened, Dad was in Copenhagen for work, and I couldn't see any way that Mia's parents could help.

I could only think of one other person I might be able to trust. Her number was in my phone, though by rights I shouldn't actually have it. Nadina had left her mobile behind after science back in Year 11, and because I was loitering so I didn't have to leave the classroom with everyone else, I was the only person left to pick it up and return it to her after break. I didn't look at any of her messages. All I'd done was take Imogen's number because – well, I didn't really know why. I often didn't know why I did things; they just made sense at the time, even if they made a total lack of sense later. The point was, I had it, and I could ring her now and tell her what I'd been going to say last night and then maybe between us we could do the right thing, whatever the right thing was . . .

But then I thought back and saw car headlights rushing towards me and knew I couldn't. Imogen had put herself out enough for me already. If I could protect Mia by keeping quiet, the least I could do was the same for Imogen, right? This was *my* problem and I could sort it out myself. That's what real men did, like the blokes in the old-fashioned films I used to watch with Mum. If you were stupid enough to put yourself in danger, it was up to you to fix it.

Near the end, that was all Mum and I had really done –
work our way through box sets of DVDs, submerging
ourselves in classic films and TV shows, pretending that
reality wasn't knocking on the door. The steroids she was
on meant she was always hungry, and although she was too
weak to cook, I'd make her whatever she wanted, whenever
she wanted it. Cooking was about the only useful thing I
could do to actually help her, to distract her from the pain.
When I couldn't sleep I'd stay up late into the night, working
my fear and anger into dough so there would be fresh bread
for Mum in the morning.

None of these things were what fourteen-year-old boys
usually did in their spare time, but there isn't much space for
normal when you know your mum's dying of cancer. I'd
thought a lot of Mum's films were silly at first, unrealistic
nonsense about people in costumes, but I'd gone along with
them for her sake. Later on I changed my mind. The stories
were so outside real life that I started looking forward to
escaping into other people's made-up worlds. When we sat
down in front of *It's A Wonderful Life*, or *The Third Man*, I
knew that for the next two hours or so I could escape the
crushing reality of the here and now.

'The men in these films, they're what real men ought
to be like,' Mum had said one day when we'd just finished
watching *Casablanca*. 'Stoic, reliable, brave. Grow up like
them, Sammy, and I can leave knowing I brought you up

right. Do the right thing. Treat the people you care about like they're precious. Protect them at all costs. It's a good way to live.' Maybe I was just suggestible, but I'd taken that to heart. I hadn't wanted to let Mum down, though now I was older I did half wonder if that had been her medication talking.

Either way, her words had struck a chord — must have, else I wouldn't have made the decision I just had. The problem was, just shutting up didn't feel brave at all.

IMOGEN
MONDAY 11 NOVEMBER

Today, everything was worse.

While I'd known the story of Saturday night would spread, I'd seriously underestimated the stir it would cause. Even before I reached school I was mobbed by people wanting to know details.

'For God's sake! Can you at least wait until I drop my little brother off?' I snapped when someone asked whether it was true that there'd been a gunfight. Benno had taken my arm, which told me the questions were upsetting him. Usually he stood a little way back, trying to look as though he wasn't being walked to school. I suspected this was more because he thought that was the done thing than because I actually embarrassed him.

I managed to snatch a moment to say goodbye. Benno was wearing the horrible mauve uniform I'd had to put up with for five years before moving on to sixth form. The blazer was my old one and too big. Benno almost vanished within it. I felt annoyed with Mum for recycling. Starting big school in your sister's leftovers, great idea. Benno might as well be wearing a label saying: 'Please pick on me.' Luckily he seemed to have fitted in just fine.

'Don't be surprised if you get nosy idiots pestering you,' I told him. 'Just tell anyone who asks what happened and then leave it. If they give you grief, text me and I'll pop across to the lower school at lunchtime and sort them out.'

Benno hesitated. 'You know the guy you saved? Do you think he'll be in school today?'

'Sam? It depends how he's feeling, I guess. Why?'

'Just wanted to know if he was OK.' When Benno saw my confused expression he said almost defensively. 'He's my reading tutor at after-school club. He's nice.'

Benno was dyspraxic. He'd been really self-conscious until about a month ago when the school reading club had changed everything for him. His reading tutor had done a great job getting him enthusiastic about words. So that had been Sam! To have turned things around like that for Benno was really impressive.

'Oh, OK,' I said, trying not to look surprised. 'Never knew Sam did that kind of thing. I'll let you know if I hear anything, OK? Now off you go.' I gave him a friendly push. 'See you later, soldier.'

In the sixth-form common room I faced the music.

'It wasn't a big deal,' I said, banging the kettle down on the sideboard hard enough to splash my hand. We had a tiny little kitchen area for making hot drinks. It could only fit three people – we'd tested that one – though the common room itself had plenty of chairs. 'The car came along. I pushed Sam out the way. End of.'

'Why were you and Sam even outside in the first place? Has anyone told Ollie?' There were some nasty giggles. Deciding I'd had enough, I poured my half-made tea down the sink. As I left, I heard someone call, 'Too up yourself to speak to us? You get all the good stuff, Little Miss Perfect — and now you're a lifesaver too. Everything comes easy to you. Ever wondered what it's like to have to work for things?'

Outside I almost collided with Ms Paul, the head teacher. Oh help, I thought, as she started congratulating me loudly on my sharp thinking. All this praise would have been embarrassing even if half the year weren't listening in. I hotfooted it to the loos as soon as I could, locking myself in a cubicle and ignoring the girls preening into mirrors. It's like I'm a scared Year 7 in her first week, I thought, sitting down on the seat. Get a grip, Imogen! You saved Sam. That's a good thing. No need to get all hot and bothered.

But I *was* hot and bothered, and not just because of Ms Paul embarrassing me. That remark about me 'getting all the good stuff' stung — because it was true.

If I wasn't me, I could really hate me. The realization was so startling that I winced. I'd never thought about how others saw me. I preferred not to think when I didn't have to. My life was pretty sorted. I knew where I fitted in and where I was going and I liked it that way. No thinking. Just doing.

Now I saw myself through everyone else's eyes. It was

totally surreal, almost as though I was looking in a mirror. Imogen Maxwell, who'd been head prefect in Year 11, liked by all the teachers. Organizer of the school cabaret two years running, head of the Amnesty Student Action Group, two A*s, seven As and one B in her GCSEs. Captain of the Walthamstow youth volleyball team and the fastest sprinter in the year. Girlfriend to Ollie, the sixth-form poster boy. And now a lifesaver on top of everything else.

It must seem like all the good stuff just fell into my lap. It kind of had. I found lessons and sports fairly easy, and when I tried something new, I usually did it well. It must make others sick. It made me a little sick. There were so many people I knew who had so much less.

So if I did have it all, why didn't I enjoy it more? Why did I feel empty inside? Christ. Here I was being ungrateful. Even worse!

I slammed my foot into the cubicle door, feeling a surge of impatience. I didn't do this soul-searching crap! Last week everything had been fine. *Normal.* Why did I have to start asking questions about my life and not liking the answers? Why did it feel like I'd suddenly woken up?

Sam didn't share any lessons with me and so I didn't get a chance to sound him out until lunchtime. A once-over of the buildings told me he wasn't in. Not surprising, I guessed. Even if he was feeling OK, he was probably wary of being the centre of attention.

Ollie met me for lunch on the picnic benches outside the sports hall. It was chilly there, but it was quiet so I didn't care. I sat on the table and opened a packet of crisps. Ollie perched beside me and took one when I offered.

'OK?' he asked.

'Been better,' I said. 'Did you get that sports science homework finished?'

Ollie rolled his eyes. 'Look, you don't have to pretend everything's normal.'

'There's nothing to say. What happened happened. End of.'

'It's not end of though, is it? Nothing's resolved. I've been thinking, Im, and I've got questions. Why did you follow Sam outside? What was he saying to you? You don't even know him, *do you*? Unless there's something you're not telling me . . .'

'Whoa, cool it!' After what Nads had said I wasn't surprised that we were having this conversation, but I *was* taken aback by the anger in his voice. Very different from the touchy-feely, sensitive, almost embarrassed Ollie of yesterday. Clearly relief at having me safe had worn off quickly. 'Nothing's going on. He wanted to talk, that's all.'

'Yeah, *away* from everyone else. Away from your *actual* boyfriend. You seemed pretty happy to go outside in the freezing cold with him. Obviously you know each other a lot better than you've let on. Everyone's been gossiping about you two today and it's really humiliating! Are you cheating on me?'

I groaned. 'You *are* joking, right?'

'Do I look like I'm joking?' Ollie really didn't. His lower lip had a dissatisfied twist to it which told me how pissed off he was.

'No, you look like you want to punch something.'

My bad joke didn't lift the mood. I sighed, laying the crisp packet down in my lap. I felt a speck of rain fall on to my palm. 'Take a chill pill, Ollie. Me and Sam? He's *really* not my type. What he wanted – your guess is as good as mine. I don't fancy him, OK? Come on, stupid.' I gave Ollie a gentle push. 'Why would I want him when I've got you?'

He didn't smile. 'You've always liked him. When he started here you went way beyond what was needed to be friendly to him, even after he threw it back in your face. Remember that? So stop lying to me! How many times have you seen him on the sly?'

Annoyed now, I said, 'None! I'm not lying. Like I said: I've got you. And unless you're trying to use what happened on Saturday night as some lame excuse to break up with me, I'm happy with that.'

'I wish I believed you.'

'*Ollie!*' I cried in frustration. 'Sam doesn't even like me!

You said it; he's thrown every attempt I ever made to be friendly back in my face.'

'So what was he saying?'

'*I don't know!*' I felt like yelling, but just about managed to keep my voice calm. 'I never got the chance to find out.'

Ollie looked as though he wanted to say something else. Instead he glanced away. I put a hand on his arm. 'What do I need to do to convince you I'm telling the truth?'

'Dunno.' Ollie slid off the bench.

I grabbed his hand. 'I'm not leaving things like this. It's a stupid misunderstanding. You're the only guy in my life, Ollie. Not Sam.'

The buzzer went for the end of break. Ollie sighed. After a moment he said, 'Fine, whatever you say. I'll see you later. You are OK after Saturday though, seriously?'

'Yeah,' I said, relieved that I seemed to have got through to him. 'I'm always OK, aren't I?'

'Hard to tell with you.'

Ollie headed off. I wondered what he meant. It didn't feel as if we had patched things up, exactly. Ollie still seemed reluctant to believe me. It was weird. Why would a popular, confident guy like Ollie feel so threatened by a loner like Sam?

My mind wasn't on business studies that afternoon. I zoned in and out, doodling on the corner of my notepad. The conversation with Ollie had thrown up a problem. Before lunchtime I'd been all set on visiting Sam. Calling wasn't an option as I didn't have his number, but I did know where he lived. There'd been an episode last year about Sam's dad wanting to build an extension and neighbours complaining and it had been in the local paper. They had only mentioned the road, not the exact address, but I'd recognize the house from the photograph when I saw it. Going round didn't feel right now. Ollie being jealous was stupid, but I didn't want to rub him up the wrong way.

Then again, what about me? Didn't I have a right to do what I wanted?

In the end I went for the good-girl option. I dropped Benno home, made us something to eat and went to volleyball as usual, turning over in my head all the questions I hadn't asked Sam.

But the next day, when Sam wasn't in again, I knew I couldn't wait any longer.

Sometimes a girl's gotta do what a girl's gotta do, I thought. What Ollie doesn't know can't hurt him. Tuesday was Benno's reading club day so I didn't need to pick him up after school. Sam wouldn't be there obviously, but there were other tutors. So I was free to go to Sam's place straight from sixth form. Luckily the bus to his also passed the high street, so if anyone did mention it to Ollie it wouldn't arouse suspicion. Not that anyone would.

Imogen gets on a bus! Hardly a newsflash.

Sam's place was one of those Edwardian houses with big gardens, up near Lee Valley Nature Reserve. It was quiet there. Almost like not being in London at all. I couldn't help but feel a little excited. I knew so little about Sam and now I was going to see where he lived.

A woman wearing a dressing gown answered the door when I knocked. She had a very pretty face, but it was her hair that made an impact. It was waist length, exceedingly thick and a red-brown colour that had to have come out of a bottle. This house ain't the only thing with extensions, I thought. Behind her I could see a greyhound wearing a fluorescent collar.

'Hi, I'm Imogen,' I said. 'Came to see how Sam is.'

The woman blinked at me sleepily. She looked a bit young to be Sam's mum. Perhaps she was his sister, though her accent said London rather than the North. 'That's nice. He's in the kitchen.'

She drifted back into the house, leaving the door open. Feeling a bit uncomfortable, I stepped inside. The interior was pretty grand compared to what I was used to, all marble floors, furniture that definitely wasn't Argos or Ikea and modern art on the walls. So Sam's folks were well off.

I wasn't sure whether the woman meant me to follow her, but I could smell baking wafting from the direction she was heading so I followed. We entered the kind of kitchen you see in TV adverts. It had plush wooden units, an enormous fridge and an island in the centre with a stylish low-hanging light. Sam was standing there up to his elbows in flour. In front of him was a ball of dough. As I watched he smacked it against the surface, kneading it with an anger that took me aback. Clearly his bandaged wrist wasn't giving him too much grief. To his side was some sort of loaf and a line of biscuits. From the cracked eggs and open packets on the sideboard I guessed they were freshly baked. When Sam saw me he stopped dead.

'Sam, your friend's here,' The woman picked up one of the biscuits, then wandered out the way we'd come. I wasn't sure what to make of her. Out of the corner of my eye I noticed the dog settle down on a blanket in the corner with an elderly-sounding sigh.

I looked at Sam. He didn't look at me. Now I was here, it felt surreal. Disconcerting. In just a few minutes I'd discovered more about Sam than I had in two years. He had a dog. He made bread. From the vibes I was getting off this place, his home life might not be so great.

And it was so weird to see him like this. Sam always dressed really smartly. It was a look that suited him, but he never seemed entirely comfortable. Was what I was seeing now, a guy in an old T-shirt and sweats and covered in flour, the real Sam?

'Hi,' I said.

Sam gathered up the dough and slammed it down one last time. He then rolled it into a ball and set it aside, rubbing the dough off his fingers. I could see a line of blue stitches just underneath his chin. It was a surprisingly square chin. Macho even. It looked like it had been stolen from someone else's face — strange I hadn't noticed before. The muscles on his arms were more defined than I'd anticipated too. He looked wiry, but strong. Maybe making bread was more of a workout than I'd realized? I'd always looked at Sam and just seen someone with smart clothes and a funny accent, but actually he was pretty good-looking. And as it happened, I rather liked the way he spoke. It was different.

'Just baking,' he replied, finally looking me in the eye.

'I noticed. I wouldn't want to be that dough! You were kneading it like you wanted to kill it.'

'It needs a bit of force else it won't rise properly. I don't do this stuff much any more.' Sam moved the flour packets so they were next to each other, then placed the bottle of olive oil at a right angle. I seemed to be hitting a nerve.

'How are you?' I asked. 'We missed you at school.'

'Who's we?' For a second Sam half smiled. 'I didn't feel like coming in and Tamsin didn't make me. I'm OK. Thanks for asking.'

'Did the stitches hurt?'

'They look worse than they are.' Sam paused. 'I know, classic line but it's true. The nurse said it would scar but I

39

figure that's OK. Scars are sort of cool, right? Shame they didn't need to call the plastic surgeons in the end. I could've got them to make me look like Robert Pattinson.'

Despite myself, I laughed. 'Would that have made what happened worth it?'

'Would you like one?'

It took me a moment to realize he meant the biscuits.

'Sure,' I said. The biscuit was lukewarm and golden brown, and I could see that it had some kind of nuts in it. I took a bite. Spice and sugar – strong but not too strong – filled my mouth.

'Wow,' I said. 'These are really good. What are they?'

I could have sworn Sam blushed slightly. Perhaps he didn't get too many compliments. 'They're called biscotti. You sound like Gregg from *MasterChef*; he always goes for the sweets and he makes funny expressions too. I saw an episode when someone made a lemon pavlova and he looked like he was about to pass out.'

'I've not seen *MasterChef*,' I said. Sam started rearranging his ingredients again. Could he still be in shock? Then it hit me. This was probably the first time someone from sixth form had dropped round. Maybe he didn't want anyone to know anything about the real him. And I'd stepped right in it.

'You can take some biscuits, if you'd like.' Sam broke the silence. 'For your brother, I mean. And the sourdough loaf. All this won't get eaten otherwise.'

'How's sourdough different to normal bread?' I wondered out loud.

Sam explained that you needed something called a 'starter', which you added to the flour – apparently this was some gloopy wild-yeast mixture he kept in a jar in the fridge and 'fed' with rye flour when it was hungry. For the first time Sam seemed animated, and I found myself liking him more and more. Despite saying he didn't do it any more, baking bread was clearly something he was enthusiastic about. Sure it was an unexpected hobby for a guy his age. But it was certainly interesting.

'I never get time to do things like this.' I said. 'Always seems to be something more important that needs doing.'

'It's dead easy.' He grinned and part of me couldn't help noticing how attractive he looked when he smiled.

All this had left me feeling a little jealous. Of what exactly, I wasn't sure. 'Maybe I can bake something with my bro. He'll be well pleased with your biscuits; he even thinks the school muck's amazing.'

'Gross!' Sam laughed. 'I *really* don't rate that canteen. They use fake cheddar in everything. Of all the cheeses in all the world, they choose processed stuff that tastes of nothing . . .'

'Processed stuff'll be cheaper,' I said.

Sam's grin vanished and for a moment he looked

embarrassed. 'I didn't think of that.' He hesitated. 'Is he OK? Your brother, I mean.'

'Yeah,' I said, taken aback. 'There a reason he wouldn't be?'

'It's just . . . well . . . he's being picked on.'

I blinked. 'What? Did he say something to you at reading club?'

Sam looked surprised. 'You know about that?'

'It's hardly a big secret. Benno seems OK to me. Are you sure about this?'

'He made me promise not to tell you, but I'm worried about him. I just thought you should know.'

I couldn't help but feel a bit hurt. Why would Benno confide in Sam when he had me? I was his *sister*. OK, maybe we didn't spend tons of time together, but he had to know I was there for him. Sam implying I'd missed something this important really got under my skin.

It also reminded me of why I had come.

'Was this what you were trying to tell me on Saturday?'

Something jangled. The dog, who I'd thought was asleep, was on her feet. She went over and nudged Sam's hand with her nose.

'Yeah,' he said, avoiding looking directly at me. 'Sorry if you thought it was something more interesting.'

'Bit overdramatic, don't you think? All that speaking outside and it being something I'm not going to "like",' I said, raising an eyebrow. 'Well, thanks, I guess.'

'I need to feed Jessie now. See you at sixth form tomorrow, maybe.'

I didn't take the hint. 'What about the car, Sam? I know what I saw. I know what I *heard*. It seemed pretty deliberate to me. Are you in some kind of trouble?'

Sam turned away. 'Why would you think that?'

'I heard them call your name. They wanted to hurt you. Maybe even kill you!'

'Don't be stupid. The police said it was random.' Sam's body language was defensive now. 'I was in the wrong place at the wrong time.'

'You can't lie to my face and expect me to swallow it. I could help you, Sam. Whatever it is. You've helped me with Benno and I owe you. I don't do sympathy, but I'm not a bad person to have around if you're in trouble.'

He shrugged.

'What are you afraid of?' I said more softly. 'I won't tell anyone.'

'Nothing,' Sam said quietly. 'I need to feed the dog.'

'Sam. Tell me.'

'Look.' His head snapped up. His eyes met mine, and there was sudden steel in them. 'It was a random accident. Leave me alone, Imogen.'

With that he opened the cupboard, took out a bag of dog mixer and dumped it on the counter. I stared at his back, completely thrown. There was a faint patch of sweat on his T-shirt between his shoulder blades that hadn't been there when I'd come in, and his hands were shaking.

'Sam—'

'Go away! I mean it.'

I wasn't going to get anywhere. Forceful hadn't worked and neither had the softly-softly approach. And I'd thought Sam was one of those quiet sensitive types! He wasn't. He was bloody stubborn.

'Fine.' I'd given him the opportunity to speak up and he hadn't. 'Can't help you if you won't help yourself.'

Sam opened a drawer and took out a metal spoon, making an unnecessary amount of noise. I took my cue and left, grabbing a handful of biscuits on the way out.

Outside it was dark and beginning to rain. As I waited for the bus I felt glum and uncomfortable.

There was no big mystery. Just Sam tipping me off about Benno. Weirdly I felt disappointed. I'd built it up – and him up – to be something far more interesting. But then again, the way he'd acted had made me more certain than ever that the people in the car really had intended to hurt him. Not that it was my business. Sam didn't want my help. He hadn't when he'd started school and I'd tried to be friendly and he didn't now. You couldn't force someone to like you.

My phone rang. Damn, what if it was Ollie? What if he'd

found out I'd been at Sam's? I whipped out my mobile. To my relief the screen said 'Home'.

'Are you nearby?' Dad asked when I picked up.

'Depends on where you are,' I said, only a little sarcastically. It was rare for Dad to call rather than Mum – she was probably still at work. 'What's up?'

'Could you come home? There's someone who wants to speak to you.'

SAM

Jessie looked at me as I mixed her food, her expression saying, 'What the hell's wrong with you?'

'Who knows?' I sighed as I laid down her dinner. 'Tamsin thinks I'm still concussed and she might be right. What do you think?'

Jessie ignored me and stuck her head in the bowl. Straightening up, I looked round the kitchen. What must Imogen have thought of me, plastered with flour and wearing battered old clothes? I picked up a biscuit, paused a moment, then put it down. I hadn't baked in ages. I'd only done it today because . . . I didn't even know why. Working my anger into dough hadn't stopped Mum dying. It was hardly going to keep me safe now.

Imogen had come to my house, actually come in, stood there, asked how I was, and I didn't think she was mocking me either. I felt both dazed-happy and dazed-disturbed. I was sure that someone like Ollie Moreno wouldn't be such an idiot over this. He'd probably always had girlfriends. I used to think he was effortlessly cool and super slick. Not any more. At least Imogen had bought my bluff. The stuff about Benno was true. But it wasn't the thing I'd come to tell her on Saturday. The thing that almost got me — and her — killed.

I hoped Imogen would leave this well alone now. I especially hoped she wouldn't discuss it with Ollie. I could hide in the kitchen as long as I liked, but that wasn't going to make the danger go away.

This was a life-or-death situation now.

IMOGEN

SCHOOLGIRL HERO SAVES CLASSMATE.

I stood staring at the *Walthamstow Chronicle* billboard feeling as if I wanted to go and shove my head in a bucket of very icy water, lock myself in my wardrobe or jump in front of the 123 bus. Anything to get away from the smiling picture of me in my school uniform staring back at me from the front page. Ugh! Of all the photos Dad could have chosen to give to the reporter he'd called me home to speak to yesterday!

There is so much wrong with this, I thought. Point one, I resent being called schoolgirl. The word is 'student'. Two, Sam isn't my classmate any more. We do different subjects. Three, hero is fast becoming my least-favourite word in the English language.

I'd tried telling Dad that I didn't want a fuss. He'd been half asleep and I'd have got my own way if it hadn't been for the bossy reporter. In the end I'd agreed to say a few words to shut her up. Fatal error. Far from shutting anyone up, the report was there, and it was glowing.

'Im?' Benno said.

I snapped back to reality. 'Let's get to school, eh?'

'You looked like you were going to cry.'

'Me cry? As if! Everything's just fine and dandy.' Changing

the subject, I said, 'How was reading club yesterday without Sam?'

'Fine.' Benno said, pushing his glasses up the bridge of his nose. He didn't look at me. If it wasn't for what Sam had said, I'd believe you, I thought. I hadn't got a proper chance to speak to Benno last night, with the reporter visiting.

'You didn't go, did you?'

'I didn't want to if Sam wasn't there. I don't know the other tutors.'

I sighed. 'You should've texted me. You know Mum doesn't like you walking home alone.'

'I was OK. I got a lift home.'

'Oh yeah? Who with?'

'Er . . . someone in my class.'

I laid my hand on his shoulder. 'Benno, I hope you know you can tell me stuff. Anything. I look out for you and I care. More importantly, I'm not Mum and Dad.'

'Yeah, yeah.' Now Benno was doing a poor job of hiding how uncomfortable he felt. I let out a groan. 'You idiot! Why didn't you tell me you were being bullied?'

'I'm not.' Benno said in a tone that clearly said he was. 'What would you know about that anyway?'

'This stuff happens, kiddo. There's no shame in it. But keeping quiet's really not the way to fix this. Tell me everything. We'll sort it.'

Benno pulled away. 'Didn't want to say cos other people have it worse.'

Benno shouldn't have to be thinking about these things at his age! If someone was making him unhappy, he should feel safe enough to speak out, not lie. And he had lied, a heck of a lot. I realized I'd never met these mates he claimed to have made. Whenever I picked Benno up from the gates, he was always waiting by himself. So what had my brother been doing those times he'd told us he was round his so-called friends' houses – mooching round the high street, hiding in shops, knocking about with dodgy types who befriended lonely kids? Was that what he thought his family expected from him? Mum and Dad were on Planet Zog most of the time, but I was horrified that he hadn't told me.

'I thought you'd think I was weedy.' Benno's voice wobbled. 'You're tough. I wanted to be like you. And you're always busy like Mum and Dad.'

'I love you, stupid!' He'd got it so badly wrong that it made me hurt. Did he really see me as someone that *uncaring*? And was I? 'Do none of the teachers know?'

Benno shook his head, sniffing. I fumbled in my bag for a tissue and didn't tell him it was gross when he blew his nose then wiped his eyes with it.

'We'll go out after school, just you and me. Maccy D's, or the Turkish cafe or something. We'll talk. I'm not angry, OK? Think you can get through today all right?'

Benno nodded. And then Nadina's voice said from behind us, 'Enjoy the front page while it lasts. You're not gonna be on it next week.'

I turned and got out the first syllable of 'hello'. Nadina looked like she'd been chewed up and spat out. She had eyeliner trails down her cheeks. Even her hair looked flat. It *must* be bad.

I threw my arms around her. 'What happened, babe?'

'Not me it's happened to,' Nadina said. Benno offered her his snotty tissue. 'Y'know Hamdi?'

It took me a moment to connect the name to the guy who'd been attacked in the shop. 'Oh Christ. He's not . . .'

Nadina nodded. 'There was me thinking he'd pull though. My parents heard from his about an hour ago.' She nodded at the newspaper front page. 'You be glad you've given people good news. Cos next edition, it's all going to be about catching the bastards who did this.'

I'd never liked circuses when I was little. Not because they weren't fun, but because you just got a taste of every act. I preferred detail, knowing something through and through. Maybe that was why I found multitasking difficult. And today was all about multitasking: Benno, Nadina, Sam. Actually learning though, that was bottom of my priority list. There wasn't time to think about Sam, who still wasn't in, and Benno I'd talk to later, so for the rest of the school day I concentrated on supporting Nads.

'Nothing you can say's gonna make it better,' she told me as she splashed her face with water in the toilets. 'Hamdi was a good guy. He wanted to set up an IT business. He had a girlfriend. He was going places.'

Nadina finished earlier than I did on Wednesdays so we said goodbye in the corridor before she headed home. I bumped into Ollie on the way to my next lesson.

'Did you hear the news about Hamdi?' I asked. Ollie nodded. 'It's awful. Nads says he was a really nice guy.'

'Yeah.' Ollie fiddled with the strap to his sports bag. He seemed in an even stranger mood than he had been on Monday. Still brooding about Sam, clearly. 'I'll see you later, OK? Gotta run, else I'll be late.'

'OK,' I said, watching him hurry off in the direction of the sports block. Obviously we needed another talk. Now wasn't the time though.

When lessons finished, I met Benno and we set off. As I pressed the button at the crossing outside school I caught sight of a figure on the other side of the road, looking at us.

Sam! He was bundled up in a scarf and winter coat, but it was obviously him. Suddenly he walked away rapidly, towards the bus stop. The 123 rolled past as the lights turned red. By the time Benno and I were across, he was gone.

What was that about? I wondered. Feeling my pocket vibrate, I took out my mobile. The screen showed a text from an unknown number.

Sorry, it said. **Sam**.

If I'd thought Sam would pick up, I would have called him. Never mind how he got my number. But Benno was here. I wasn't going to fob him off when he needed me. If Sam wanted to play weird games with me, tough. I wasn't playing. Not right now anyway.

'Are we going? I'm really thirsty,' said Benno, taking my arm.

Dropping the phone into my pocket, I smiled and gave his shoulders a squeeze.

Looking back, I know I probably made the wrong decision. There could only be one reason Sam had been outside sixth form. He wanted to talk. Maybe this time I could've got answers? But Benno's comment about me always being too busy for him had got to me. He needed me right now.

In the Turkish cafe, over some sweet tea and baklava, Benno and I talked – really talked. I realized how out of touch I was. Once upon a time I'd've known which mangas he liked and what cool gadgets he wanted. When had I stopped paying attention? It turned out there was a particular boy in his class who was making Benno's life a misery. The others were simply joining in to avoid getting picked on themselves. I felt relieved. This was nothing that couldn't be sorted out.

I will be a better sister, I thought. And to make good on it, I took him home via the DVD rental shop and we watched one of the Iron Man films together. Dad stuck his head round the door as he left for his shift.

'Nice to see you doing something together,' he commented. 'You could go and see that new superhero film at the cinema too, the one advertised on all the buses. I'll treat you.'

I smiled and said it would be nice. I knew it wouldn't happen. Dad never remembered stuff like this. Still, he'd been right about one thing. Doing something with my brother felt good.

Sam and his mysterious games could wait until tomorrow.

But as it turned out, tomorrow was too late.

SAM

On the bus I felt angry at myself. What the hell was I doing, leaving the house and going to sixth form, somewhere I knew for a fact wasn't safe? I took a seat. My eyes met the hostile gaze of a guy wearing a beanie hat on the opposite side of the bus. I looked away quickly. Then I sidled a glance back. He was still looking at me. What if he was one of them? I rammed my finger on the stop button, jumping off as soon as the doors opened and running down the nearest side road.

If the guy had followed there was no way I'd've been fast enough to escape, but he hadn't. He was still on the bus and was probably just a normal guy who didn't like the look of me. Or maybe he hadn't given me a funny look at all and I was just starting to go crazy with stress, seeing threats where there were none.

It was the first time I'd left the house since Saturday and I felt like I was falling apart. I can't carry on like this, I thought. I have a life, and yeah, it could be better, but I want it back. I *have* to do something to sort this out.

Yesterday I'd been resolved not to involve Imogen. I'd been congratulating myself on throwing her off, trying to make out I was some . . . I don't know, brave heroic character from one of Mum's films. Ditto Mia. But it just didn't work in real life.

This morning I realized how wrong it all was. I knew stuff that Imogen ought to know and I couldn't get away from that. It wasn't fair that I was in a position to change her life. Having that kind of power over someone's future was horrible, but Imogen was a doer, someone who liked facts, someone who was almost brutally practical. She'd rather know, I was sure, and better it came from me than from someone else. And maybe she'd help me figure out what I ought to do too.

But when I saw her with Benno I bottled it. There was no way I could speak freely with him there. He was just a kid – I didn't want him getting involved in this, especially now I'd got to know him.

For a moment I did consider going to the police. They were there to help, theoretically, but it was dangerous to accuse anyone of anything around here, unless you knew beyond a shadow of a doubt they'd get convicted. I'd heard about so many revenge attacks that I knew there was no chance I'd be safe. I remembered reading about a builder who'd reported a couple of guys for breaking into his neighbour's house. A couple of nights later the man was walking his kids home from school when a bunch of guys jumped out and beat him up in front of them. He'd ended up on life support. I didn't want that happening to me.

I'd had enough of faffing about. It was time for a new plan.

IMOGEN

THURSDAY 14 NOVEMBER

For the first time ever I considered bunking school. What was the point of sitting in lessons when I couldn't concentrate? Learning about cash flow and business plans – whatever! I pictured Sam's earnest face and I wondered what was going on under that too-thick head of hair, that hidden world I'd completely failed to get through to.

I couldn't vent my frustration on Nadina, not when she wasn't herself. I was impressed she'd made it in at all. 'What else was I gonna do?' she asked, pushing soggy fries round her plate at lunchtime. We were sitting in our usual spot behind the cutlery counter in the canteen, which with its peachy-orange walls looked as though it had a bad case of fake tan. Kimmie and Justyna, two mates of ours, were next to us arguing about *X Factor*. 'It's doom and gloom back home. Doing my head in.'

'I can come over,' I said. 'Or you're welcome to stop by mine. Might do you good to get away.'

'Cheers, but there ain't anything you can do.'

I decided to change the subject and told her that I was going to pop round to Sam's. It would upset Ollie if he found out – he was still being distant – but it was the only thing I could think to do. So after school I took Benno home and then caught the bus over.

The same woman as last time opened the door. This time she was wearing a baggy sweater over leggings. She looked pale, but at the sight of me her eyes lit up.

'Thank goodness! Someone who might know.'

'Eh?' I said, thrown off balance.

The woman gave me a look that said it should be obvious what she meant. 'Do you know where Sam is?'

'Isn't he here?'

'I've no idea where he is!'

'What?' I said, confused.

'Maybe you can help me . . .' The woman held the door open. I hesitated before entering.

Inside the house was as pristine as it had been on Tuesday – but silent. I followed the woman into the kitchen. This time the counter was spotlessly shiny. There was a sheet of paper in the centre, very white and conspicuous. The woman pushed it at me. The handwriting was big and clear and reminded me of Benno's.

Dear Tamsin, it read.

I don't want you to worry or think I'm missing or have run away or anything. I want a break so I've gone away for a bit. I'm not living rough and I'll be perfectly safe and I'll come back soon. Please don't stress out and no need to let Dad know. I'm fine and will give you a call later.

Bye. Sam.

I looked at the woman, who I guessed was Tamsin. Her face fell when she realized I was as clueless as she was.

'He's never done anything like this before.' She sounded like she was about to cry. 'He says he's safe, but Sam would say that even if he was being dangled over a crocodile pit. He's far too polite, and he hates to bother people with his problems.'

That sounded familiar. Funny, I'd never have put Sam and I down as being on the same page there. I read the note again. One phrase jumped out as odd.

'What is it he needs a break from?'

'I don't know!' Tamsin flung up her hands. I wondered if she was an actress. She was certainly glam enough to be, and it might explain why she was knocking round the house in the middle of the day when most people were out at work. 'I don't understand the way Sam's mind works. I'm only the stepmother. *I* don't understand anything.'

You and me both, I thought. I wondered what had happened to Sam's real mum. Perhaps Sam's dad was one of those men who had affairs with younger, prettier women and then divorced their wives for them. Somehow I'd always pictured Sam as a bit of a mummy's boy. Wrong again, clearly.

'What's his dad think?' I asked.

'I've not said anything. Phil's in Copenhagen right now. Business. Very important.'

'I'm sure Sam is OK. He's definitely weighed up what

he's doing, else he wouldn't have left a note.'

'Left a note! God, it sounds like we're talking about a suicide.' Tamsin laughed, sounding slightly hysterical. 'I'm not so sure. He's really been affected by this accident.'

'It's probably just shock.' I knew how I'd felt on Sunday – weird and dislocated and slightly outside the world. 'Has he done anything else out of the ordinary lately? Other than pulling this vanishing trick?'

Tamsin perched on the counter. 'Sam's been a creature of habit ever since he came here. Up at the same time every morning, breakfast at half seven, goes to school, comes back, does his homework, goes jogging with the dog, then mostly stays in his room. But about two weeks ago he changed. His cousin Mia was visiting from Yorkshire. He was out late with her on Saturday night and he seemed fine when they left. But the next morning, after Mia went home, he seemed so jumpy. After that he stopped going running. He even asked if I could start dropping him off at school, and Sam . . . well, Sam's not hot on spending time with me, or putting people out of their way . . .'

She went quiet. I felt a little relieved. Tamsin going full steam was almost as overwhelming as sitting in the front row when Ms Paul was booming speeches in assembly. 'Did you ask what was up?'

'I just hoped he'd tell me in his own time.'

'Do you think Sam's in trouble?'

'Imogen . . .' Tamsin said quietly. I was surprised she'd remembered my name. It made me like her suddenly. 'If you know anything, even if it means betraying Sam's confidence . . .'

Tamsin had very intense hazel eyes. Right now I felt they were burning into me. 'Sam's never let me in.' I said. 'Sorry.'

Tamsin sighed heavily. 'There's no one else I can think to ask. I was glad when you came the other day, you know. I thought, good, he does have friends.'

I winced. Way to make me feel bad! I glanced round the kitchen, picturing Sam, happy to chat about rubbish like baking, but defensive when it came to what was really important.

'He's running scared,' I said, everything becoming clear. Sam in Mmm Hot Chick, looking wild. Saying he hadn't wanted to do this, but that he had to tell me something. The car speeding towards us. Sam, too scared to go into school. Switching stories, trying to throw me off. Now he was hiding – but from what?

'Do you think this is serious?' Tamsin asked, looking frightened and suddenly little girl-like.

'You've tried calling, right?'

'Obviously! As far as I know he took his mobile, but it just went to voicemail.'

There could be lots of reasons for that. Some less pleasant than others. Christ, Sam, I thought. If you were lying about what you really came to tell me on Saturday, does that mean I'm in danger now? You said you knew something about me. Is it connected to what's happening to you? How do I even begin to find out?

I took Sam's dog for a walk. Maybe it was a weird thing to do, but Jessie had strolled up while I was with Tamsin and I realized that with Sam away she'd probably not gone out all day.

I glanced at Jessie as we walked through the gates to the park. She gave me a weary look that almost made her seem human. She wasn't spritely on her feet. From the grey muzzle, I guessed she'd been with Sam growing up. He probably spent more time with her than with actual people.

The air was chilly and it was starting to drizzle. No one seemed to be about. Still, I wasn't going to palm Jessie off with a short walk. Deciding to warm up, I began to jog, Jessie trotting beside me on the lead. As we crossed on to the central path, I saw that I wasn't alone after all. Two people were slouched on a bench about two hundred metres ahead. They were too far away for me to really make out, but I was almost sure that they were looking my way.

Whatever, I thought, carrying on. But when I got closer and saw that they definitely were looking at me, I became concerned.

Then they stood up. One wore a cap and a heavy khaki

coat, the other a black hoody. Scarves were drawn up high over their faces. They were totally anonymous. There was a path branching off to my right, just before I reached their bench. I decided to take it. When I looked back, I saw that they weren't standing still any longer.

They were running. After me.

Panic kicked in. I broke into a sprint. I felt Jessie's lead tug. She was doing her best with the sudden change of pace, but I knew it wasn't enough. She was too old to sprint for longer than a few minutes. The guys weren't as fast as I could be, but thanks to Jessie they were gaining on me.

One of them yelled out. The words were lost on the wind. Did they have knives? Did they want to hurt me? I couldn't see. The gates looked impossibly far away. But beyond was a busy road. There I'd be safe. Jessie's lead cut into my hand.

'Phone!'

They were closer. Close enough for me to hear what they were shouting. 'Phone, phone, phone . . .' – again and again. Seeing them almost on my heels, I did it. I dropped Jessie's lead. I heard her yelp but I didn't look back. I bolted towards the exit. It felt as if I'd never run so fast. Every second, every moment, I was sure I'd feel a hand grab my arm. But there was nothing. When I did turn round, they'd given up. If they were still shouting, I couldn't hear.

I'd lost them.

I'd also lost Jessie.

★

It was only once I'd reached the nearby shopping street that I was able to think again, surrounded by familiar sights and smells and people. I crashed down on a bench at the bus station, drawing long, ragged breaths.

If I hadn't let Jessie go, I'd have been toast. What had they wanted? Just to nick my phone?

The timing was almost funny. In fact I did start to laugh. I stopped when some schoolkids looked at me like I was a nutter. I half wanted to explain that I was perfectly sane, only I bloody well had enough on my plate this week without getting mugged. Talk about coincidences! Someone up there was having a right joke with me.

A nutter, I thought. Yeah, that's what I am now. Whatever happened to normal?

The answer was, normal hadn't gone anywhere. It was all around. Buses were drawing in, people were pushing forward to get seats and teenagers were hanging about eating chips. I just wasn't part of normal any more.

All my life I'd felt safe where I lived. People talked about the dark side of north-east London, but I'd never experienced it. But now things were different. I was different. Because I knew I had reason to feel afraid.

I'd never felt so alone.

SAM

On the tube everyone seemed to be looking at me. They weren't of course — it was hardly as though the sight of a teenager with a rucksack and a stitched-up chin was jaw-droppingly spectacular. My imagination was just running riot. It felt as if I had a neon sign saying 'Running away from home' flashing above my head. Not that I was running away, not really. I'd tried to do it as well as I could, leaving Tamsin the note, and I would call her later, and it wasn't as though I was planning on staying away forever. I didn't have much with me. Nothing had seemed that important when push came to shove, only some clothes, cash from my savings account and my not-very-smart phone. I definitely wasn't leaving that.

I'd thought so much about what to do that now I was doing it I really didn't know if it was right any more. But then, when things got to this stage, did right and wrong even matter any more?

It's your fault, Mum, I thought. 'Be a real man — protect the people you care about, no matter what.' It's all very well you telling me this; it sounds great on paper. You never mentioned how difficult it is in practice.

I hadn't wanted to come down to London when Mum died. I'd have been happy staying in Yorkshire, but my grandparents would've struggled and my aunt and uncle didn't have the money to provide for me. I hated the idea of being a burden on people, even family. When Dad stepped in and actually seemed to want me, it seemed like the easiest solution.

On the surface, Dad is all teeth and tan and flash suits and business calls and he drives a Mercedes. He's easy to stereotype. People were often surprised when I told them that he'd been OK with me, visiting every so often and sending regular cheques. He and Mum even got on reasonably well. Their relationship had been pretty short and they'd never been married, so I guess there wasn't so much to feel bitter about. He wasn't affectionate, but that was fine – Mum more than made up for it. She could be clingy though. When I was younger, this had annoyed me, but when everything changed I forgave her for it.

Dad didn't really engage with Mum being ill. I'm sure he felt guilty. Maybe taking me in was his way of dealing with that. Even now I wasn't really sure where I stood with Dad or what he thought of me. I'd learned that he could be quite old-fashioned and that he was surprisingly sentimental, especially about Walthamstow, which was where he grew up. I liked both these qualities, but it didn't make building a relationship any easier. At the start he tried to do 'father–son activities' like going fishing on the nature reserve, but they weren't my kind of thing – or his, I suspected. The only thing we really had in common was we both liked stories – Dad worked in TV, developing scripts and concepts. And when the weight I'd piled on looking after Mum towards the end fell off, he'd been hot on buying me new gear – smart, older-looking stuff. I felt weird wearing it, but then I'd've felt weird wearing anything new, so I let him have his way. Eventually we slipped into a relationship where we talked but didn't really talk, and as Dad was so busy with work, I guessed that was the best I could expect.

At first I'd thought I was taking moving in with Dad pretty well. I couldn't help being off with Tamsin – no one wants a stepmum who's younger, prettier and healthier than the mum you've just lost – but I managed to find things to like about the house. My room was fine, the kitchen was great and the area wasn't too bad, with the old houses and nature reserve where I could take Jessie, who Dad had been cool with taking in. It was on the first day of school that I realized how out of my depth I was.

For starters, there was a big hefty security guy at the door who checked kids and their bags for *weapons*. Coming from a sleepy town in Yorkshire, I'd always assumed that this kind of thing only happened in films. It turned out I was wrong. Then there was my tutor group, which I couldn't help but notice was incredibly multiracial. Where I'd lived before almost everyone had been white. Not that race bothers me, but it was a bit overwhelming and I was terrified of accidentally saying something that could be taken the wrong way. Later I realized that despite all their different backgrounds, the kids weren't so different after all. Even the kids for whom English was a second language seemed to speak in the same aggressive-sounding London way, and they all dressed the same outside school and hung out together.

What I was aware of was how I came across to them. The first time I'd spoken, someone went, 'Ohmy*days*!' and the others laughed. A girl had asked, 'Which country you from then?' and I hadn't known how to answer. My accent wasn't that Northern, and yet these kids acted like I was impossible to understand.

When a tall blonde girl who spoke in a way that said she was something marched up at break and announced that she was going to show me round, I was stressed out enough to be sure this was a joke. It didn't make it easier that the girl was pretty, though not the in-your-face way lots of the others were, with their long nails and bling jewellery.

I let her take me on the tour because she wouldn't take no for an answer, but the more I saw, the more out of place I felt. Everyone seemed tough and loud and upfront and grown-up, talking about people and things I'd never heard of in slang that made no sense to me. They made me feel immature and somehow empty. How could I connect with anyone when most of them laughed at my accent every time

I opened my mouth? The stuff I enjoyed – reading books, watching classic old films and making good food – didn't seem to matter here. Forget up north; I might as well have been an alien.

By the time Imogen Maxwell – the bossy blonde girl – rounded up a group and took me to lunch in the canteen, I'd had enough.

'Thanks for the offer, but I've got a phone call to make.' It was the first excuse I could think of.

'No mobiles allowed.' Imogen's wry tone told me this wasn't a popular rule. 'Keep it on silent and in your bag, OK?'

Frustrated, I tried, 'I'm really not hungry.'

'Hey, the canteen food's not *that* bad! There's no rule that says you've got to eat. Just sit and chill instead.'

What did she think I was going to find to talk about with her and her mates for a whole hour? It was already clear we were worlds apart. Imogen's assumption that I wanted to hang out, like I should be grateful for her time, really got my back up. It was my choice who I did or didn't make friends with, and it was my choice if I wanted to be alone. Who was she to decide I needed looking after, when I'd done a perfectly good job looking after myself and Mum for so long?

'I said no, thanks,' I snapped. Imogen called something I didn't catch as I walked away, but I didn't bother turning back. I spent lunchtime in an empty classroom playing games on my phone, trying to convince myself I was better off on my own. During my afternoon lessons I pointedly avoided making eye contact with anyone. I was hoping that English literature last thing would at least give me the opportunity to lose myself in a book for an hour or so, but the teacher had to fight with the rowdy class to get them to pay any attention at all to William Blake's poems. Shame really - if they'd just shut up long enough to actually read one, they might realize how brilliant they were.

The next day I felt even less like being around people. At break I was wandering the corridors looking for somewhere quiet where I could read when Imogen and Nadina found me.

'Need a hand finding anything?' Imogen asked, rather pointedly.

'I'm fine, thanks.' I said.

She tilted her head to one side, folding her arms. 'So, what kind of things are you into?'

After English yesterday, I thought it better not to mention books. I'd only have the piss taken out of me. And saying that I liked classic old films and was good at cooking were both a definite no-no. I shrugged and said something about having a dog. Nadina snorted.

'Ain't no dog-walking club here. She's asking cos she wants to see what you might want to join.'

'What makes you think I want to join one of your clubs?' I said, more rudely than I'd meant to. Did this girl even realize how bossy she was? After a silence that went on a bit too long, Imogen said coolly, 'We'll leave you to it then,' and left. A week down the line, no one was bothering with me at all. They'd written me off and I was glad. Being a nobody, a loner, was something I was comfortable with.

A nobody to everybody but Imogen, that was. I caught her frowning at me in lessons, like I was some kind of equation that she couldn't quite solve.

Well, I don't get you either, and I don't know why you're so interested, I thought. For one of the in-crowd, Imogen was pretty odd. She genuinely seemed to care about school stuff, like charity sales and shows and sports day, things cool kids always take the mick out of. But Imogen simply steamrolled over the mick-taking and acted as if they were the weirdos. She was very businesslike about it all. Was she really a good person or just going through the motions? I couldn't tell. Everyone had a story that made them who they were. What was hers?

IMOGEN

I walked back to Sam's, wondering what to say to Tamsin. So much for a good turn! I thought of Jessie, with her placid, world-weary air, and my stomach twisted. I should go back to the park. She could still be there. But I was scared. What if those guys were still hanging about? What if they were trying to find me?

I *can't*, I thought. Now that I was OK my limbs were doing the jelly-like shaking thing I recognized from Saturday night. If I went back and got into more trouble I wasn't even sure I'd be able to run.

Jessie would turn up. Someone might have found her already. I hadn't looked at her collar, but it probably had a tag on or perhaps she was microchipped. Or she might have tried to get home on her own. Though there was that bloody busy road between the park and Sam's. Unless she was lucky, she'd never make it. Christ! If she got run over, it would be on my head.

As I neared Sam's, I half expected to see a dog-shaped mound in the gutter. When I turned the final corner I froze. There it was. A dark shape by the edge of the road. Not moving.

A yap from ahead startled me. I looked up and there she was, standing at the front door of the house. The 'body' was a bin bag. I raced over, choked with relief.

'Jessie!'

She wagged her tail, then looked pointedly at the front door. Against the odds, she'd crossed that road. Man, for all I knew, she'd waited for the green man at the traffic lights! I didn't care how she'd done it. I was just bloody glad she had.

Back home no one was in. Dad usually left around now, but Mum and Benno should have been here. It was only when I was done showering that I remembered. Mum had an office party tonight. She'd mentioned she'd be popping home to get changed after work, but I was supposed to stay in to babysit Benno!

Sorry, bro, I thought. He'd be none too pleased at having to sit in the corner at Mum's work while she and her colleagues drank cheap wine. Wrapping myself in a towel, I rifled through my jeans to check my phone. Sure enough, Mum had called several times. I deleted her voicemails. I didn't feel like listening to a ticking-off.

Phone. That was what the guys in the park had wanted. Now that I was thinking straight . . . it was weird for me to run into a random mugging, given everything else that had happened. I mean – what were the chances?

'Let it go, freak,' I said out loud. 'It's not connected. Just bad luck.'

★

I settled down in the living room. Being home alone wasn't something that happened often. I wasn't sure how to kill the time. I didn't fancy doing homework or watching TV. Normally on an evening like this I'd hang out with Nadina or Ollie, but Nads had enough crap on her plate right now and Ollie would go spare if he knew I'd been to Sam's, not once, but twice.

Where are you, Sam? I thought. He didn't have friends that I knew of. Tamsin would've tried family. Was Sam afraid of putting people in danger? Was that why he'd kept everything from me? I'd tried texting him, with no response. Clearly he had decided to stop talking to me altogether.

My phone vibrated. I was surprised enough to drop it. Jesus, I really was jumpy. Picking it up, I saw it was a text from an unknown number.

We saw you both there. Give us the phone.

I stared at those nine words. Slowly, then more rapidly, my heart began to pound. My thoughts leaped to the guys in the park.

Phone, phone, phone.

'How did they get my number?' I whispered.

Why would someone want my phone? It wasn't new. There was nothing special on there. At least I didn't think there was. I checked my messages and pictures. They were all regular things I couldn't see being of interest to anyone but me. Could this text be for someone else?

Not likely. Not after the park.

I went to the front door and bolted it. Then I pulled the living-room curtains closed. If anyone was outside I didn't want them to see me.

We saw you both there. Give us the phone.

OK, I thought. Three questions: Where is there? Who is both? And who is us? Actually, make that four. What the hell is so important about my phone?

The doorbell rang. I shrank back, my breath catching in my throat. When it rang again I went to the living-room door, inching it open so I could see the front door. A shadow flickered behind the glass. One person. Someone tall.

My phone vibrated. This time it was ringing. It was Ollie.

'Hi,' I whispered.

'Hey,' Ollie said. 'Where are you?'

'Home. Ollie, there's someone outside —'

'Duh! That's me!' I felt my muscles ease up. 'Who did you think it was?'

I opened up. Ollie stood outside, wearing a striped scarf. He didn't look too happy, and at the sight of me his frown deepened.

'You look like a wreck.' He said, leaning in with a hug. He smelt of ash. I wondered who he'd been with. Far as I knew, none of Ollie's friends smoked.

'You say the nicest things,' I replied. We went to the kitchen and I poured him a pineapple juice. Ollie didn't do hot drinks. He took the glass, looking at me quizzically as I leaned against the sideboard.

'Someone bothered you? Need me to sort 'em out?'

'I'm in one piece. Which, given tonight, is something.' I waved my phone at him. 'What do you make of this?'

Ollie read the text. I took back the phone and told him what had happened in the park. I pretended I'd been walking the terrier from over the road rather than Jessie.

Ollie frowned, massaging my shoulder with his free hand. It felt good. Comforting even. And he looked worried, more worried than I'd expected. It reminded me of how he'd been that afternoon when he'd given me chocolates. Perhaps we could get things back in that zone rather than all this stupid suspicion.

'Do you think these guys got the wrong person?' I asked.

'Let me look.' Ollie held out his hand. I handed my phone over.

'I'm sure I'd know if there was something significant there,' I said. 'Anyway, you know what's on there. You were messing round with it the other night and there's nothing new since.'

Ollie went into the videos folder, which was empty, then into the texts inbox. I saw the text from Sam at the same time he did.

'So you don't know each other,' Ollie said, looking at me. 'Right.'

Crap, I thought. I took a breath. 'There's only one text there,' I said. 'All it says is "sorry". I don't know what he means or how he got my number. It doesn't mean anything.'

'I want to believe you,' Ollie said. I reached out and took my phone from his hand, placing it in my pocket. Then I did the only thing I could think of. I leaned in and kissed him. At first I thought he was going to draw back, but after a moment he responded. I shifted into a better position, drawing my arms underneath his coat. He deepened the kiss. There was an intensity to it that was new to me. Did he want to move our relationship on from the comfortable normality we'd fallen into? I felt Ollie's hand slip to the small of my back. Then I heard voices outside, Mum's, mingling with the fainter um–mmm belonging to Benno. I drew back and Ollie muttered in annoyance. By the time Mum entered, we were standing as though we'd just been chatting. Footsteps from the hallway told me Benno had gone upstairs. Mum threw me a dirty look.

I cleared my throat. 'How was tonight?'

'It would have been more successful if I hadn't had to bring your brother along,' Mum said. 'What happened to you, Imogen? It's not like you to let me down.'

'I needed help with coursework.' Ollie spoke before I could. 'Like, emergency help. Im gave me a hand.'

It was a rubbish lie, but Mum liked Ollie, and he knew it. To her mind, having a boyfriend clearly meant I was a normal, happy teenager. 'At least you were making yourself useful,' she said drily. 'All right. Immy, just make sure you apologize to Benno.'

I nudged Ollie, silently thanking him. We spent a few minutes making small talk with Mum before Ollie made his excuses.

'You don't have to go,' I said, leading him to the door. 'We could watch a movie or something.'

'I'm meant to have urgent coursework to do,' Ollie pointed out. 'Anyway, I've got something on.'

I didn't ask if I could go with him. That would just sound needy. But I felt miffed all the same. Much as I didn't like admitting it, I could do with a bit more comfort. Why had Ollie even come over if he had to dash? And what about us? I'd been trying to prove something to him in the kitchen. I wasn't sure the message had got through.

'About Sam,' Ollie looked over his shoulder as he stepped out. This time the smile was completely gone. 'If you're telling me the truth, why did you go round his house? Twice?'

'I only went to see how he was. This accident – I think it's linked to me somehow.'

'How much do you know about Sam?'

'Nothing! And that's what's so frustrating. He won't tell me anything.'

Ollie shook his head and walked away. I watched him

cross the road, wishing I hadn't messed up. I couldn't blame him for not believing me. I knew it looked bad.

Then a thought struck me. How had Ollie even known I'd been to Sam's? There was only one person I could think of who could have told him.

At eleven, just as I was getting into bed, my mobile went again. Before I even picked it up, I knew it would be another message from *them*.

If you don't give us the phone we'll hurt your brother.

I spaced out for a moment. Then I sank on to my bed, heart racing.

SAM

There were severe delays so I had to wait ages at Liverpool Street Station for the train I needed. Something about a 'shopping trolley' obstructing the line. Who does that kind of thing? I wondered, then realized that was a really stupid question. Vandalizing train lines was nothing compared to what the guys I was up against had tried to do.

I was hungry so I went to M&S and filled a basket with sandwiches, brownies and chocolate. It was only when I was queuing up to pay that I realized I'd picked up far too much food for one person. What was I doing? I didn't need to eat all that crap. I dumped the basket and left, angry at myself. All I seemed to be doing these days was screwing up. The only good I'd done at all recently had been with Benno.

It had been a little weird meeting him properly. It was my first time mentoring at the school reading club. It wasn't something I'd really wanted to do at first. My English teacher suggested it one day when I was helping her carry some books to her car, more because I had nothing better to do than because I was trying to be teacher's pet.

'We've got a few kids who find reading difficult and need some encouragement,' she said. 'I want to get a mentoring scheme going – buddy them up with sixth-formers who can give them more help and attention than they get in class. I thought you'd be perfect. Patient and kind, with a genuine love of reading.'

It's not every day you get told you're perfect for something, so of course I said yes. Reading club might not be the coolest place to be, but I had nothing to lose and I liked the idea of being able to help people. The club took place after school in one of the English classrooms. Ms Taylor picked up a range of books from the library, many of which seemed far too basic even for Year 7s. When Benno sat down with me and started to read aloud, I realized just how wrong I'd got it. Just because I found reading easy, didn't mean it was the same for others. He stuttered over every word, even short ones, which shocked me because he was quite articulate when he spoke. My heart really went out to him. I made sure to praise Benno as much as I corrected him and I tried my best not to be patronizing. I must have been OK, because by week three his reading was a lot more fluent. I couldn't help feeling chuffed – with Benno, and also with me.

'You're really good at this now.' I said. 'Maybe you could try reading to your parents sometime. I bet they'll be impressed.'

I was a bit taken aback by his scowl. 'They wouldn't care. They don't even know I do this club.'

I asked him what he meant. And that was when I clocked he was Imogen's brother, because out it all came –

resentment about how uncared for he felt and how his parents were never around. When I asked if he'd spoken to his sister, Benno said, 'She's a robot. She doesn't feel anything. No one would ever pick on her.'

'I think we'd all know if your sis really was a robot.' I grinned. Then, 'Hang on. Benno, are you being picked on?'

That was how I found out that Benno was being bullied. I don't really know what it was that made him feel he could confide in me. Perhaps I've just got one of those faces.

'I really think you should tell your sister,' I said. 'She used to be head prefect here – if anyone knows how to deal with this, it's definitely her.'

Benno went quiet. 'She's busy. She'll think this is silly.'

'You're a tough one, aren't you?' I said. 'You're wrong. Definitely. Just because she isn't all fluffy and cuddly doesn't mean she doesn't care. As a matter of fact, I know that your sister hates bullies.'

Benno looked interested for the first time.

'Let me tell you a story about your sis.' I said. 'When I came to this school, I was in a bit of a bad place. For lots of reasons I didn't want to make friends or join in with stuff, and people got the idea I thought I was too good for them. I got Facebooked by people saying I should "go back home".' And nastier stuff, I thought, remembering the post from HotGirl1998:

Y don't u just go and kill urself now, world will b beta without u.

'It was cyber-bullying, basically. I didn't tell anyone because I didn't think anyone could help. It went on for months. I don't know how your sister found out but she gave the people doing it hell. She even told the head teacher. A couple of kids got suspended, and one girl who was on a warning already even got expelled. Takes real guts to go to the teachers. It doesn't exactly make you popular. Imogen risked a lot doing that – for me, and I'd not been very nice to her.'

'What did she say about it?'

'To me? Nothing. She's not even aware I know what she did. Maybe she just saw it as a head prefect's duty. But that's how I know she's kind, or at least fair. Even if she seems a bit of an ice queen.'

Benno fingered the spine of the book we'd been reading. 'So why doesn't she notice me?'

'It's easy to ignore the people who are right under your nose. Trust her. What've you got to lose, hey?'

Benno gave me a look that said he didn't believe me. He made me swear I'd keep everything secret. I promised, knowing full well I was going to break it.

I really hoped Imogen had sorted things out for him. Maybe I'd find out when I went home. When – if – this nightmare was all over.

IMOGEN
FRIDAY 15 NOVEMBER

My mood that morning must have been obvious, because when I came down to breakfast Benno, who was sitting at the table with a bowl of Shreddies, stared at me.

'You look like you want to kill someone,' he said. 'Like a superhero. It's cool.'

'I don't know about cool,' I said, 'but believe me, I feel pretty bloodthirsty.' I skirted a look at Dad, who was reading the paper. He was never normally around at this time. I asked him if he had the day off. He nodded.

'Nice of you to mention it to us,' I said.

Dad frowned. 'Should I have done? You've your own things going on.'

My own things, which you have absolutely no idea about, I thought. Dad never asked what I was up to, and I doubted Mum filled him in. He probably didn't even know which A levels I was taking. Or maybe I was just getting at Dad because I was in a bad mood and he was an easy target. I had briefly considered telling my parents about the text, but they'd just complicate everything. Mum would huff about me bothering her and tell me the threat wasn't worth taking seriously. Dad might say we should go to the police, but what could they do? We had no idea who'd threatened me and no way of finding out, as far as I could see.

Deciding to ignore Dad, I perched on the side of the table by Benno. 'Hey, what have you got on today after school? Stay safe, OK?'

Benno gave me a strange look. 'Just playing computer games at home.'

'Good,' I said, and picked up a bowl. I hadn't forgotten last night's text. What had happened in the park guaranteed that I was going to take the threat to hurt Benno seriously.

I'd arranged to have lunch with Nadina in Greggs. She had free periods on Fridays and usually only came in for the afternoon. We could have met in the sixth-form canteen, but what I had to say wasn't something I wanted others overhearing.

Nads was waiting at one of the breakfast-bar seats by the window, sandwiches and doughnuts spread out in front of her.

'Hey you,' she said as I stepped in. 'Got you your favourite chilli chicken bloomer. Last one left. There was this bloke eyeing it so I nabbed it. Thoughtful, eh?'

I felt a pang inside and ignored it. I slid into the seat next to her.

Nads frowned. 'Whoa, who pissed you off?'

'Let me tell you a story,' I said, and filled her in about what had happened with Jessie. I showed her the texts.

Nads swore. 'What d'you think's going on?'

'Who knows? What I do know is that I've enough crap to deal with without Ollie going mental cos he knows I've been going round Sam's!'

Nadina didn't even flinch. 'You can't blame him,' she said. 'I'd be pissed off too if my girlfriend had been going round another guy's house. You have been kinda obsessed with Sam since the accident.'

'I wouldn't have this problem if *you* hadn't told him!'

'Eh?' Nadina looked flabbergasted. 'I never said anything to Ollie.'

'Yeah, right. It wouldn't be the first time you've spilled secrets.'

Nadina reddened. She knew exactly what I was talking about. Two years back, I'd told her about a boy I'd fancied. Within a week everyone knew – including the boy. I'd never been vulnerable like that at school before. I'd hated it. 'I only told Kimmie and Justyna,' Nads had admitted. Like that had made it better! She just couldn't resist gossiping. Why hadn't I learned from that?

Nadina pushed her half-eaten lunch to one side. 'Well, I didn't blab this time! I'm your best mate, Im. I've learned my lesson.'

I crushed my napkin into a ball. I hadn't intended to get this angry or be so mean but somehow I couldn't help myself. 'Most of the time I don't call you on gossiping. Usually it doesn't matter. But this time it does. I don't know why Sam bugs Ollie so much, but I don't want to lose him over this, because I *do not* fancy Sam. I'm just interested in him, which is entirely different. This is getting blown up all out of proportion!'

Nadina leaned forward. Slowly and emphatically she said, '*I. Didn't. Tell.*'

'So how did Ollie find out?'

Nadina grabbed her bag. 'Y'know what? I've had a tough week and I ain't sitting here listening to this. I don't know how this got out, but it's a nice world when your own best friend won't trust you!'

The words stung. 'You're a fine one to talk about trust. Past evidence speaks for itself.'

'Past *evidence*?' Nadina raised her voice. 'You just love your facts and figures, don't you? Here's some news: they ain't always right! Sometimes you gotta go with what your heart tells you. Even if the facts say otherwise.'

'You saw those messages. Maybe I wouldn't be so mad if I wasn't freaked out!'

'So bloody what? I'm scared about what happened to Hamdi, about my family getting attacked, lots of things, and I'm not bitching at you! What's happening to you ain't so special. And this ain't school any more, where you stamp your foot and everyone stands to attention.'

'You are totally missing the point.'

'The point is, you're *not* acting like my mate. And until

you gimme a bit more respect, you can get outta my face.'

Nadina stalked out without looking back. I looked down at the bloomer in my hands. Chilli chicken. My favourite. The last one left.

Oh, screw that! I thought. I wasn't about to let a sandwich make me feel guilty. Nadina blowing up in my face had shaken me even though I partly deserved it. I still believed I was right though. She could give me that rubbish about listening to my heart. But this wasn't some cheesy Hollywood movie. This was real life. Facts and figures were usually right.

That didn't explain why I felt so bad though.

I rang Ollie because I wanted to see where we stood. I caught him in the middle of playing basketball. He wasn't mad at me, but he didn't quite sound himself.

'Just don't like lies,' he said. 'I don't want to get all serious, but it's like I don't know who you are any more.'

Serious, I thought. That was exactly what we seemed to be now – was this growing up? Ollie and me had never done this deep and meaningful stuff before. We just worked together at school and then enjoyed ourselves outside it, doing normal stuff like watching matches, films and hanging out. I missed that. It was fun and it was easy. I was half minded to go and watch him playing basketball, but maybe it was smarter to give him space.

Going to Sam's again was the last thing I should do, given the trouble it had caused. It probably made me a bad girlfriend. But the damage had already been done with Ollie and I couldn't help wondering if anything else had happened. For some reason I felt self-conscious as I rang the bell. This made the third visit in a week.

Tamsin opened the door. Her face fell when she saw me. I smiled. 'Hey. Just passing by. Any news?'

'Yes, actually,' She was wearing the dressing gown again, her hair wrapped in a towel. 'Sam phoned yesterday.'

I was a bit taken aback by how relieved I felt. 'What did he say?'

'Apparently he's fine. Didn't tell me where he was or what he was doing, just that I shouldn't worry.' She gave a little shrug. 'If I thought they'd take it seriously, I'd call the police. I can't though, can I? He's not *missing*.'

Yeah, he's well aware of that, I thought. Smart move, Sam. I was about to go when Tamsin said, 'This is a little cheeky, but how would you feel about minding the house for a few hours tomorrow? I'd make it worth your while. Normally I wouldn't bother for an evening, but I'd rather someone was here in case Sam rings. I'm not convinced he'd try my mobile if I didn't pick up.' She gave me an apologetic look. 'I hope you don't think I'm being a wicked stepmother for going out, but it's my dad's sixtieth and I don't want to let him down.'

It wasn't the most thrilling Saturday night I could imagine, but I could do with the cash. And it might be an opportunity to find out more about Sam.

Tamsin asked me to come over at six. Half an hour before I was due to leave, Ollie texted, asking me to hang out.

I dithered over how to reply. I wanted to patch things up with him, but now was definitely not a good time. There was no way I could tell him the real reason I couldn't meet up. In the end I said my parents were taking me and Benno to dinner for a treat. A crap lie – when had they ever done that? I asked if we could meet up tomorrow instead. After a few tense minutes' wait Ollie texted back:

Sure why not?

I got on the bus to Sam's feeling like I'd dodged a bullet.

After running through where I could find things, Tamsin left. I watched the lights from her car head away from the front-room window. She'd promised to be back no later than eleven. That gave me bags of time, but I decided to wait half an hour, just in case. I sat on the sofa in front of the telly, scrolling through channels. Jessie settled on the rug by the window. She didn't look up when I called her name. Perhaps she was missing Sam. Or maybe she just was an emo dog.

As I went upstairs I told myself that what I was about to do wasn't prying. It wasn't like I'd broken in or anything.

I had to admit though that I was kind of intrigued to know more about Sam.

On the upstairs landing I had to open a couple of doors to find the right one. It was pretty tidy for a boy's room – more than Ollie's or Benno's anyway. I wasn't surprised to see that Sam had his own TV, games console and computer. The walls were bare apart from a pinboard, but the bookshelf was full of cookbooks and tons of novels, the kind we'd studied for GCSE English. Did he actually enjoy reading this stuff? Judging from the DVDs by the telly, I guessed yes. Old black-and-white movies, titles I recognized as classics – he must be quite a film buff. On the desk was a pile of school textbooks. Man, I didn't even know which A levels Sam was taking.

Sam had planned to disappear, but that didn't mean he wouldn't have left clues. OK, I thought, if I was running away, where would I go? Out of town, definitely. Not to family. Too easy to trace. Friends? Sam had only started at Devereux in Year 10. He was a loner here, but for all I knew he had mates up north wherever it was he'd come from. How could I find that out?

My eyes fell on the pinboard. It was covered with Post-it notes, but there were also photos, one of Jessie and another of a younger-looking Sam and a woman. They looked comfortable together. His mum, I guessed. She didn't look entirely right, somehow. Like she was ill. Sam had never said anything about his mum. Had she died?

What struck me more though was how different Sam looked. There was no way of hiding it – he'd been overweight. That square jaw of his was hard to make out. He must have lost a massive amount of weight before coming here. Perhaps that was why he seemed ashamed of being able to cook. He'd dressed entirely differently too, in baggy T-shirts and trackies that didn't suit him nearly as well as the image he'd got going now.

Then something else caught my eye. Another photo, right at the bottom of the board – it was *me*. What the hell? But when I leaned in for a closer look I realized how completely wrong I was. It was some other blonde girl with similar-shaped glasses; that was all. Guess I'm still feeling a bit jumpy, I thought.

Feeling guilty for intruding, I booted up Sam's computer. Luckily it wasn't password protected. The desktop picture was Jessie sitting by a lake. I opened My Pictures. Inside were about twenty folders.

'I am not a stalker,' I told myself. 'I have good reasons for doing this.'

I clicked on one titled 'Summer'. Most of the photos inside were of a grassy place I didn't recognize. There were a few of people – Sam, Tamsin, a tanned man with very white teeth I knew was Sam's dad, a middle-aged couple and the blonde girl. She also appeared in the next folder I checked, as did the couple. Either they're friends or family,

I thought. The girl and Sam were clearly friendly. Could he have gone to hers? But if they were close, or related, Tamsin would have rung her already.

Then I heard footsteps on the stairs.

I was for it now! I looked round. There was nothing I could do and nowhere to hide. But Tamsin wasn't due for hours yet. The front door was locked. Whoever this was must have a key. Sam's dad? Sam? If they came in here –

The door tilted open. A grey muzzle appeared round the edge.

I let out a nervous laugh. Jessie looked at me like I was stupid and climbed on the bed.

When I turned back to the computer, something had popped on to the screen. I realized it was an online chat window. Sam must have Messenger configured to log in automatically.

The person messaging was called Mia.

Sam! Where r u?

As I moved the mouse to click close, Mia said:

Tamsin rang Mum. R u OK? Is it the other night?

Could Mia mean last Saturday? I opened up the conversation box. I recognized Mia's user picture instantly. She was the blonde girl from the photos.

I knew what I was going to do even before my hands settled on the keyboard.

Hi, I typed. Imagining how Sam would sound was

beyond me. I kept it neutral. *I'm OK.*

Where r u? People are worried! Texted u but u didnt reply.

Just with friends. Needed to get away.

OMG they did see us! But how could they know who we are? Did they track u down? Am I OK?

Could I have stumbled upon the reason why Sam was so afraid? And had Mia been with him? Problem was, now I was pretending to be him, there was only so much I could ask.

Sam, I'm serious. U said it was OK. Were u lying to make me feel better?

Think, Imogen! What might Sam say?

You're OK, I typed. *I don't think they saw us. But it got a bit too much for me.*

U could have come here! U didn't need to disappear.

Didn't want to bother you.

I must have got something right, because Mia replied:

So typical! U always try to go it alone! Like you're some old skool film hero! I could have come to police with u. Well u cant hide things from me. I did detective work, I read online that the shop man died. Did they find who did it?

'What?' I said out loud. Was I reading correctly? Unless there was a massive coincidence, Mia meant Hamdi Gul. Sam was connected to that?

It was time to chance my arm.

Not yet, I wrote.

I know I said for you not to get involved but I need to ask. Did you see anything? Anything I might have forgotten?

A pause.

U know I didn't. I was getting the table in the diner while u went in the shop. I only knew something had happened when I saw u running.

There was an American-style diner across the road from the Guls' that did burgers and fries. It was more upmarket than most of the other fast-food joints in the area and very popular.

You didn't see anything at all?

I said no! What's up, Sam? I thought u went to the police, told them what u saw. U said u were going to.

Now I was lost. I'd no idea what Sam had or hadn't done. As I dithered, Mia said:

Where r u? Seriously you need to say.

I can't.

Mia went quiet. I was halfway through typing a new message when she said:

Im going to call u.

A few seconds later she logged out of the conversation.

'Brilliantly handled!' I leaned back in the chair, rolling my shoulders. They'd tensed up while I'd been concentrating.

So Sam – and Mia – knew something about the robbery and the attack on Hamdi Gul. Sam had gone in the shop.

Could he have seen the attackers? Had they seen him? Had he gone to the police?

My hunch was Sam hadn't and had lied to Mia. Tamsin would have known. While I wasn't sure she was the sharpest tool in the shed, she'd definitely have connected this to Sam's disappearance.

So Sam had kept quiet. Why?

Tamsin returned bang on eleven and immediately asked if there had been any calls. Apart from a couple of unimportant ones, there hadn't been. I'd spent the evening in front of the telly, unable to find anything else. I was all set to take the bus back but Tamsin insisted on giving me a lift.

'I'm fine to drive, if that's what you're thinking,' she said with a smile. 'All the drinking tonight was done by my parents. Funny role reversal, isn't it? Anyway, giving you a lift's the least I can do.'

Her being kind made me feel extra bad about sneaking round the house. The route back took us along the high street. As we turned on to it Tamsin had to brake sharply. Two police cars and an ambulance zoomed past, sirens wailing.

'More drama!' Tamsin said. 'What is it about Saturday nights? I'll take a different route.'

As Tamsin indicated to turn off, I frowned. The police cars were pulling over further up, just by the green.

Right where Nadina's family's shop was.

'Tamsin,' I said, 'do you mind driving that way, please? My mate – it's just, her family have a shop there. Probably just being jumpy but . . .'

The rest of the sentence choked me up. Tamsin opened her mouth, then closed it. She turned off the indicator. As we drew near, I saw the paramedics rushing in with a stretcher. My dread turned to panic.

'Oh God,' I whispered. 'Oh God, oh God, oh God. Please no.'

The shop they were running into was Nadina's. There was a hole in the front window and the vegetable racks outside were overturned. As I stared, I heard a new siren. A second ambulance raced up.

Oh God. Two ambulances.

I couldn't see Nadina or her parents anywhere.

Tamsin said something as I opened the door and bolted out, but I didn't hear her. As I got to the front of the crowd I remembered how Nadina had pushed her way to my side last weekend.

'Keep back, please. This is a crime scene.' A police officer barred my way.

'This is my friend's shop!' I yelled.

Then the paramedics reappeared with the stretcher. Someone was on it. I knew even before I saw it that the body was Nadina.

SAM
SATURDAY 16 NOVEMBER

I was sitting outside, wishing I was warmer and wondering how much longer I should stay out, when my phone rang. I wasn't exactly sure what I'd been expecting when I'd arrived, but today had passed quietly and I'd started feeling better. I was even wondering whether I could take the bandage off my wrist, which felt more or less OK. Right now I was sitting on a bench in some kind of park. It was too dark to see much except the lights of tall blocks of flats in the distance. My nose felt icy enough to drop off and I hadn't eaten for what seemed like forever. Every so often people passed by. No one bothered me, which was, after all, exactly why I'd come all this way.

I'd thought Mia might call. She'd texted several times already – Tamsin had contacted her parents, desperate for clues as to where I might be. Imogen had texted too. I'd ignored both of them. Whether it was cold, boredom or just the need to hear another voice, I decided to answer.

'Hi, Mia.'

'Sam!' Mia's voice always sounded high-pitched over the phone. 'What was that weird IM all about?'

'What IM?'

'Just now, asking what I saw.'

'Not me.' The by now familiar feeling of fear rose in

my gut. 'I'm sitting on a bench in the middle of nowhere. Someone else must be using my account!'

'Oh God. I must have been talking to them online. This is beyond creepsville! Sam, what's going on? I know this is about what happened when I was staying with you. Did you really tell the police what you saw?'

Suddenly glaring flaws were appearing in my hiding-away plan. Either you disappear completely or you don't; this halfway house of taking calls and ringing Tamsin to let her know I was OK just didn't work.

'Of course I went to the police,' I lied. 'As for what's going on, I'm not sure. But if someone's impersonating me, what did you tell them?'

'Nothing, at least I don't think so.' Mia sounded even more high-pitched now. 'Let me check. I've got the window open. Hmm . . . no, I just said about me going to the cafe, the shop man being dead—'

'*Dead?*'

'Didn't you know? There was nothing on the main news here, but it's all over the Internet. He died in hospital a few days ago. It's terrible.'

I stared into the darkness. All the time I'd been out of my mind with worry about myself, and I hadn't even thought about seeing if Hamdi Gul – I wasn't even sure that was his name – had pulled through. I suppose it must have been all over the *Metro* and maybe local news websites too, but I hadn't picked up a paper or thought to look anything up. I felt small and selfish.

I hadn't just witnessed an armed robbery any more. I could write that off, pretend it didn't really matter – I mean, people nicked stuff all the time. Carrying knives wasn't uncommon either. No, I'd witnessed a *murder*.

And suddenly it all made so much more sense. Of course they'd tried to kill me! They must have known that there was a chance Hamdi wasn't going to make it, that they'd beaten him up too badly. They needed to clean up the evidence. In other words, me.

The thought that they were afraid of what I'd seen and might do – afraid of me – was beyond weird.

'Mia,' I said, 'don't worry about me and don't say anything, please. I'll ring later.'

I ended the call. Mia immediately rang back but I ignored her. Think and don't panic, I told myself. Who was impersonating me online, pumping Mia for information? Whoever it was would need my login details. Either they'd hacked my Messenger account or they were on my computer. I felt uncomfortable as I remembered how lazy I was with online security – it was just so much easier to get web pages to remember your passwords . . .

. . . which meant whoever it was could be in my house right now.

And oh my God! What if it was *them*?

Now I really did freak out. Tamsin was in terrible danger! They might have hurt her already! I wasn't her biggest fan, but I didn't want that to happen.

If it was them, it meant they knew that Mia had been there too. It wouldn't be hard to find where she lived, not if they were in my room. Mia was just a kid! She wouldn't be able to protect herself if they came after her. They might try to kill her too!

And I couldn't do anything to stop them. In a panic, I did the only thing I could think of. I dialled the home line.

It rang and rang. What was I expecting? These guys to play receptionist and pick up? Or Tamsin to answer, everything as normal? I was about to give up when I heard the click of the receiver.

'Hello?' It was a girl's voice. She didn't sound rough or hostile. In fact she sounded familiar . . .

I put on an accent. It came out a funny mix between northern and Cockney, very unconvincing, but enough, I hoped, to disguise my voice. 'Can I speak to Tamsin, please?'

'She's not here. Can I take a message?'

'No, I'll ring back later.' I rang off. That had been *Imogen*! What was she doing at my house? Had it been her pretending to be me on Messenger? Given the timing, it seemed likely. At least that meant Mia was safe. But it also meant that she hadn't been taken in by my bluffing in the kitchen the other day after all.

Is she doing this by herself or are her friends helping? Perhaps Ollie had been there, listening in . . . I really needed to know if she was alone or not. It could change everything, especially as Imogen was asking questions that very much looked like she was getting close to the truth . . .

IMOGEN
SUNDAY 17 NOVEMBER

The police wouldn't let me go to the hospital. They gave me crap about 'understanding I was upset but there was nothing I could do'. I screamed at them. I couldn't help it. One of them took me aside and told me that getting mad wasn't going to help Nadina. And then I looked at the glass in the doorway of the shop and realized there was a pool of blood and the nausea was so overpowering that I doubled up and threw up.

It could only have been about five minutes later that another police officer came over, but it seemed like a whole night had passed. This was a young guy I thought I remembered seeing on patrol in the mall.

'You're Nadina's friend, aren't you?' he said, kneeling in front of me.

It felt wrong to hear him say her name. 'Tell me she isn't dead.'

He gave me a sympathetic look. Oh God, I thought.

'Looks like she's going to be OK,' he said. 'The paramedics radioed my colleague just now. She's badly hurt – I'm not going to lie – but it's not life-threatening. All right?'

All right? Was he joking? 'What did they do to her?'

'I don't know any details, love. Listen, I think it's time you let your mum take you home.'

He meant Tamsin, who was hovering nearby, one manicured hand over her mouth. I had to give it to her for not bailing the hell out.

Tamsin drove me home. I kept apologizing for getting her wound up in this, and she kept saying it was OK. Whether she meant it or not was anyone's guess. But she was a big help with Mum, who wasn't too happy at being woken up. I could tell Tamsin was shocked at that. If she'd been my mum, I bet she'd have been a lot more caring.

I went straight upstairs after Tamsin left. As I closed the door to my room a thought came to me. Nadina's shop could have been randomly attacked. But I'd place money on it being the same people that killed Hamdi Gul. Same street, same kind of shop. If this was true, Sam was key. Most likely he knew who they were.

And I knew something too – that finding him now was on a whole new level. I considered what to do next. I didn't have enough evidence to go to the police. Even if they took my suspicions seriously, I'd be safer without them stirring things up. Was it worth telling Tamsin? No, I decided, not yet. She'd probably just freak out and want to tell the police. For the moment, I was in this by myself.

The next morning I phoned Nadina's house right away. Her brother answered and told me what had happened in more detail.

At half ten last night Nads and her dad had been in the shop. Three young guys had burst in. Two had knives. The third guy, apparently unarmed, had gone to the door, acting as lookout. Nadina and her dad hadn't got a good look at him. The other two had been dressed anonymously, scarves over their faces. They'd demanded the money from the till. As Nadina's dad had been opening it up one of them had shouted at him to hurry up and the other had struck Nadina in the jaw and broken it. I could only guess she'd been giving them lip. Despite everything, I almost smiled. Big mouth, getting into trouble. That was very Nadina.

As if that hadn't been enough, the guys had given her dad a roughing up too. Godssake! I felt heat rise inside me. They gave you the money! They weren't fighting you! How bad can your lives be that you kick people when they're down?

'I'm not sure they're going to let you see her,' Mum said when I told her I was going to the hospital. I was standing in the hall, zipping up my body warmer and trying to find my gloves.

'Why not?' I said. 'Her brother said she's awake and she and her dad are going to be in for several days. Even if she can't talk, I want to see her.'

'That's very nice of you.'

I'm not doing it to be nice, I thought, irritated. 'See you later.'

'Are you going out like that?'

I looked down at myself. Underneath the body warmer I'd slung on yesterday's jeans and my volleyball T-shirt over a long-sleeved top. My trainers were mud-flecked. 'Last I checked, hospitals were for treating sick people, not strutting your stuff.'

'Don't be silly,' Mum was wearing a printed dress, leggings and several bangles. As far as I knew, she wasn't going anywhere special. Not with Dad anyway. He was upstairs, either sleeping or on the computer. 'All I meant was, you don't need to dress like you've come off the track all the time. You're a pretty girl. Make more of yourself.'

'Not helpful.' My hand connected with my gloves in the pocket of another of my coats and I pulled them out. 'Criticize my style, fine, but not now. It's not like I'm going out wearing a bin liner, is it? And hello! I have a boyfriend. I can't be getting it too badly wrong.'

'Ollie lives in sports gear too,' Mum began, but stopped when I glared at her. 'All right, sorry, I know this isn't the time. Look, why don't I drive you over? Have a word with the nurses and see if we can find out more about what's going on.'

'Can do that myself, thanks.'

'I'm only trying to help.'

Something about the way she said it made me see red. Before I could think better of it, I said, 'That makes a change.'

Mum went quiet. 'What do you mean?'

'Oh come on, Mum! You weren't too concerned about how upset I was last night. You're only being nice now cos it's convenient. Let's face it – you never notice anything to do with me or Benno unless it suits. When was the last time you said, "Well done," to either of us?'

'That's not true,' Mum began, but I carried on.

'When we have problems, they're not "important". You don't have the time, you're tired, we should take care of ourselves. Fine, I can, but Benno's only eleven. I'm more of a mum to him than you are!'

Mum's expression showed no hint of emotion. The only sign that I'd got through was her hand. It moved from the banister to smooth down her dress. 'What exactly are you trying to say, Imogen?'

'Think about it. It's not that hard. On top of this, you're a hypocrite. Dad too, though he's practically the invisible man these days. We all know what happened back in Kent, when Dad went away for a few months. You're not these perfect people you pretend you are.'

'I'm going to ignore this,' Mum said, very slowly. 'You're upset, and when you're upset it's very easy to lash out at those closest to you –'

Stop talking to me like you're a counsellor! I thought. I'm telling you what's wrong and you're not hearing. Even as I spoke, I knew what I was saying would really hurt her. 'That would be you? Sure.'

'I think you should go before this gets worse,' Mum said. 'When you come back, you can apologize, and we can talk like grown-ups. I don't expect stroppy, immature behaviour from you, Imogen.'

Yeah, that's right, I thought. I'm just throwing a silly strop. Forget that I'm pretty much a model daughter who never complains, who'd never act like this unless she meant it.

Dad appeared at the top of the stairs. 'What's going on?'

'Nothing you need to get involved with, Andrew,' Mum snapped. 'Imogen's just leaving.'

Dad looked between us. 'Do you want to talk, Immy? Would that help?'

I shook my head. I was too mad to talk and I doubted Dad would understand. Mum really didn't know me at all. I could have said all this, but sometimes you reach a level of anger where the only thing you can do is leave.

By the time I got to Whipps Cross Hospital it was early afternoon. The wards were confusing and it took me a while to find Nadina. I felt awkward as the nurse showed me to her bed.

Nads was lying propped up by pillows with her mum holding her hand. I'd seen loads of other members of her vast family in one of the waiting rooms. I managed not to wince. I'd known she'd look bad but this was proper rough. Her face was bloated and swollen. I could tell there'd been blood around her mouth and one ear. Her jaw was heavily bandaged.

Nadina's eyes met mine. I waved. Nads raised her free hand and pointed to her mouth, shaking her head.

'Change to see you speechless,' I said. 'Better make the most of it while it lasts, eh?'

Nadina flipped her finger at me.

'Enough, no jokes,' Nadina's mother scolded. She explained that laughing was the worst thing Nadina could do right now. The surgeons had placed wires in her jaw and bound it in place. The bandages would be off in a day or two, and the wires in six weeks – but laughing or chewing or shouting might cause problems.

She went out to get a hot drink, leaving us alone.

I settled into her chair and cleared my throat. 'Gutted this has happened to you, babe,' I said in a low voice. I wasn't sure why I was whispering. Because I felt weird being this touchy-feely? 'Us being friends is really important to me, y'know? I'm so glad it didn't end up worse. Frankly it's a miracle you've got a sense of humour after this. Sometimes I guess things are so crap all you can do is laugh, right?'

Nadina gave a thumbs-up. I moved to hug her, then stopped as I realized I'd knock the bandages. Nads rolled her eyes and I laughed. Suddenly things felt a lot more comfortable between us. Weird, I thought. Right now we couldn't communicate properly. And yet somehow I'd managed to say more to her than I ever had before.

Nadina mimed. I realized she was pretending to speak on a phone.

'Want your mobile?'

She pointed at me. I took mine out of my pocket. Nadina held out her hand. I gave it over and she started pressing buttons. I realized she was texting.

'Nads . . .' I said, suddenly wary. She ignored me. After about a minute, she handed my phone back. She'd written me a message on the New Text screen.

Gotta say sorry 2 u. I did something really crap that makes me a bad mate. Forgive me Im?

She was looking away. Moisture glistened in her eyes. So she *had* blabbed to Ollie about me going to Sam's!

My insides knotted in hurt. Yet despite that, I couldn't bring myself to let rip. I cared more about Nads than I was mad right now.

'It's OK,' I said, meeting her eyes. 'It's happened, I can deal with it, and I don't want you stressing. I'm not mad.'

Nadina seemed to sag in relief. She traced a smile over the bandage. To show I meant it, I smiled myself.

I was just handing her my mobile so she could type something else when her mum returned. It was fine though. We'd said what we needed. I left. Outside it was beginning to drizzle. As I headed back the way I'd come I felt my mobile vibrate.

Slowly and uneasily I took it out. But it was only Ollie, asking how Nadina was. I'd texted him earlier, telling him what had happened and that I was going to the hospital to see her and might not be able to see him until the afternoon.

She's battered but OK, I texted back.

When I got out on to the main road I saw the bus I needed just leaving the stop. It would be a good fifteen minutes until the next one, knowing what Sunday service was like. Might as well walk instead. It would give me thinking time.

Two weeks ago Sam had seen the attack on Hamdi Gul. He'd been close enough to be recognized. Mia, who was maybe a cousin, had been there too but hadn't been part of the action. For whatever reason, Sam hadn't gone to the police. The week after, he'd stayed in the house as much as possible, scared. He'd come out on Saturday night though – to find me. To tell me something, and not that he fancied me. Before we could talk, the accident had happened.

The people who tried to run him down are the ones Sam saw in the shop, I thought. Murder didn't seem such a far-fetched explanation now Hamdi was dead.

And after Sam disappeared I'd been chased and started getting those texts. Was what had been happening to me connected to Sam? If I could understand that, I might be able to do something.

I turned the corner on to a quieter street and right into a gust of wind. Man, I could do with another layer. I decided to cut down another small road, a more direct route home. It was only further along that I realized I was being followed.

This wasn't me being jumpy. Out on the main road it had been less noticeable, but here it was obvious. What was more, the guy wore khaki. A coat I recognized from the park.

Once again I felt my pulse race.

Perhaps they'd come from the skatepark. It was just round the corner, a well-known spot for trouble to hang out. I should have been more cautious. Could I run? Or would it be better to pretend I hadn't noticed? No, then he'd follow me home. If he didn't already know where I lived, I wasn't about to show him.

Should I give over the phone? I could get another. It was just a thing after all. But would that be the end of it? And did I want to let him get close, down this quiet back street?

That decided it.

I broke into a run along the pavement towards a back alley that snaked behind the houses to the next street. If I sprinted through there, hopefully I could lose him on the other side. But he didn't speed up. I looked back. No, I wasn't wrong. He was walking. Had I got it wrong? Was I seeing things?

Someone stepped directly into my path. I ran straight

into him and would have gone flying if he hadn't grabbed me.

'Thanks,' I said breathlessly. 'That was –'

He grabbed my other wrist and dragged me towards him. Realizing the danger I was in, I stamped on his foot, trying to free myself. I work out enough to have muscle power, but this guy was strong. I couldn't see much of him. He was wearing a hoody. A black hoody, with his face covered. The other guy from the park!

Out of the corner of my eye I saw the guy in khaki jogging up to join us. I kicked, trying as hard as I could to wriggle free. He let one of my arms go. Then his free hand punched me in the stomach. My body doubled up. Somehow the impact sent my glasses flying and I heard them clatter on the pavement. I stopped fighting. The other guy drew near.

This is it, I thought.

'It's in my bag,' I said. 'Go on, take it.'

The guy in khaki pulled the bag from my shoulder and turned it upside down. My purse, Oyster card, phone and all the other stuff I kept in there tumbled out. He grabbed the phone and flipped it open. I wanted to ask what it was he hoped to find. But even more I wanted to get out of this in one piece. So I stayed quiet.

After what seemed ages, he chucked the phone away. It skidded across the pavement and over the kerb.

'Yep. She's not got it.' he said. He sounded young, local.

Rather like everyone at school. The only difference to his voice was a hard edge. One that said, *Don't mess*.

The other guy pushed me against the alley wall. Pain whammed up my back.

'Your mate. Where is he?'

'Which mate?'

That earned me another jab to the stomach.

'No jokes. You know.'

They could only mean Sam. 'Don't know. No one does. Honest to God. He's taken off.'

'Don't lie. Where's he gone?'

'If I knew, I'd tell you!'

I sounded scared. Scared enough for them to exchange a glance. Then the guy in front of me leaned in close. I caught a snatch of blue eyes above the scarf covering his face. A stale smell clung to his clothes, the kind that hit you when you passed a grimy pub.

'Listen up, Imogen Maxwell,' he said. 'You want to avoid trouble, you keep quiet. Same goes for your posh little mate. Tell him to give over what he's got on us, fast. Cos wherever he is, he ain't gonna be able to hide forever.' He drew back, letting me go. 'Wanna know why?'

He paused. Realizing what he wanted, I said, 'Why?'

'Cos if he don't play along – you're the one who's gonna get it. And your little brother. And one more thing . . .' The guy leaned in again, even closer. 'There are a lot of things we could do to ruin the life of a pretty girl like you. Know what I mean?'

I nodded. His face was almost touching mine. Very quietly, he said, '*Good.*'

For a second I thought worse was coming. But after a tense moment they swaggered off. They didn't even look back. They knew I was no threat to them. I slid down the wall, my bruised stomach throbbing.

After a while I felt together enough to feel around for my glasses. One lens was shattered and the other had a huge crack across the centre. I realized that one of the arms had bent too. It would be easier to buy a new pair than get these repaired. These frames were fashionable ones – they'd been expensive. I didn't want to go back to wearing my grotty old pair. The fact that they'd broken something so essential, that meant something to me . . .

Fighting tears, I gathered my other belongings. Apart from a scratched screen my phone was still working. 'She's not got it,' the guy had said. I could have told them that. What had they thought was there?

I had a new text – Ollie's reply from earlier.

Come over. I want to see you. x

I texted yes and ran. It hurt, and I could barely see where I was going, but I didn't want to stay in this place a moment longer.

★

Ollie and his mum lived on the edge of an estate twenty minutes from the station on the ground floor of a grey terrace. It looked like something out of a dystopian movie. The front yard got used as a dustbin by whoever passed by. Keeping it clean was a losing battle. Judging by the people I'd seen hanging around here, I could understand why the house had a cage over the front door and windows. And this was the nicer end of the estate.

Ollie's mum had been given the flat by the council when she'd come to England. Ollie had been ten – the same age I'd been when I moved here. Exactly why she'd left Colombia so quickly was something Ollie was cagey about. Given how unemotional he usually was, I guessed it was bad.

Ollie only ever invited people round when his mum wasn't in so I wasn't surprised when he opened up. I gave him a smile that felt strained. Inside I was still jittery. I'd gone home and picked up my old glasses and tidied myself up. I felt stupidly self-conscious on top of everything else.

'Hey.'

'Jesus Christ!' Ollie cried. 'You look raw, babe. What happened? Has someone roughed you up?'

'I look that bad?' It wasn't funny, but I started laughing, just as I had the last time I'd been this freaked out, at the bus station last Thursday. Ollie looked alarmed. He pulled me inside. Something about his hand on my arm brought back the guy in the alley. I shook him off.

'Don't!'

He backed away, holding up his hands. 'Im, stop this. You're creeping me out. Tell me what exactly happened? Please. I need to know, because all kinds of stuff's going through my head right now.'

How did I begin explaining? Did I even want to? I took a few deep breaths. 'It's fine. I'm fine, Ollie. Gimme a moment.'

Ollie swore under his breath, half turning to the wall, running a hand through his hair. He'd gone very pale. He then did something he'd never done before. He gave me a hug, a proper one. Not an arm slung round a shoulder, or a hello/goodbye one, or cuddling when we were making out. This wasn't me and Ollie at all. I could even feel his heart beating, very quickly. Half embarrassed, half uncomfortable, I just stood there. After he let go, there was an awkward silence. When it stretched past the point of OK, I said, 'Wow. Who are you and what have you done with Ollie?'

'Jeez! Can't I get anything right? I'm trying to comfort you. Don't fling it in my face. Anyway, that's not important! You need to tell me what happened.'

What was wrong with me? He was being nice. Why wasn't I letting him?

Ollie took my hand and led me through into the living room. The telly was on, showing a footie match. He turned it off and perched on the arm of the sofa, a big cushy patterned one his mum had picked up at the market.

He folded his arms, very head prefect all of a sudden. 'I'm not going to mess about, Im. You've got to talk to me. If you want to lie and say you're fine, you might as well just leave. I can help if you give me a chance.'

This direct no-nonsense approach was much more in my comfort zone. Yet I hesitated. I wasn't sure why. Ollie was my boyfriend. I should be able to talk to him, right?

'Give me a moment.'

'What's there to think about? C'mon, Im. I'm scared for you, OK!'

There was no one else I could turn to. I'd had enough of going it alone and I didn't know what to do. Screw Ollie being jealous of Sam. He wanted to listen and I wanted to let him.

Ollie didn't say much as I explained. His expression didn't shift when I admitted I'd been over to Sam's. I had the feeling he wasn't surprised, and that made me sad. He looked shocked when I described how I'd been beaten up, and his face creased into a deep frown when he heard that they'd threatened to hurt Benno.

'God.' He said flatly. 'This is . . . I don't know. I don't know what to say.'

'If Sam doesn't come back soon, they said they can think of a lot of ways to ruin my life. So I'd better do my best not to piss them off, hadn't I?' I choked back a sob. Suddenly it all seemed very real.

Ollie seemed to snap back to life. 'Where did they hit you? They didn't break anything, did they? Shit, I should get you some painkillers and stuff –'

'I took some at home. Not that they've done much good.' I placed a hand on my stomach, wincing. It was beginning to throb badly now. God knows what a lovely bruise I'd have tomorrow. Ollie insisted on taking a look at where I'd been hit, pressing his fingers to my stomach.

'Good old sports science A level,' I said humourlessly. 'You've clearly been paying attention in the injury-treatment module. Let's ring the teachers and tell them.'

Ollie ignored me. He was being very through. After a few minutes he said, 'Far as I can tell there's no real damage. You should see a doctor though, just in case.'

'Yeah, yeah, later. So what do you think I should do?'

Ollie rubbed the side of his nose, muttering, 'This is a bloody nightmare,' under his breath.

'I wish it was just a nightmare,' I replied. 'Unfortunately it's real.'

He sighed and looked at me. He hadn't mentioned my ugly old glasses. I wasn't sure he'd even noticed. 'D'you ever think about how things just seemed easier when we were in Year 11? Just a few months ago. Yet it's like we're in a different world. It was safe then. Sorted, no questions, all black and white. D'you ever miss knowing exactly who you were?'

All the time, I thought. Back then my life, and Ollie's, had revolved around school. Being head prefects had suited us. It was weird that I'd never realized that Ollie felt exactly as I did.

'I still need to decide what to do next,' I said.

'That's simple, right? You gotta find Sam. He needs to bloody well man up and sort it out rather than leaving you to deal with his crap.'

'I don't think he intended me to get it in the neck,' I said with an exhausted sigh. 'Will you help me?'

Ollie hesitated, just for a second. 'Of course.'

I started by doing something obvious. I rang Sam's mobile.

'Hello, you're through to Sam's phone,' the voicemail said. 'Leave a message. I'll try to get back to you.'

'This is Imogen,' I said after the bleep. 'Sam, you've landed me in it. I've been getting threatening texts and I've been shoved about by whoever these guys are and there's only so much flack I can take, given that I know basically nothing about what's going on. I get that you're scared, and that this hiding-out thing is great for keeping *you* safe, but it drops me right in it. I need to talk to you. Urgently. Ring me back.'

I ended the call. 'How was that?'

'To the point and very you,' Ollie said, putting away his own phone. 'He'd better ring after that.'

'Yeah.' There was a silence. Ollie seemed to be out of words and so was I. It was a bit of a relief when he said, 'Im, this is crap timing, but I gotta go. It's kind of important.'

'Sure,' I said. 'I'll be OK.'

Ollie laced up his trainers, grabbed a coat and we went to the door together. While I'd never thought twice about walking through this estate before, suddenly I wasn't so confident. I was half hoping he would walk me to the main street, but over the last five minutes he'd become anxious, constantly checking his phone.

'Talk tomorrow,' he said, brushing my cheek with his lips. 'This'll get sorted, Im, promise. Sam's the one who has it coming.'

I didn't want Sam to get hurt. I just wanted out of this mess. However I thought it better to say nothing about that. Not to Ollie anyway.

SAM

I was sitting in the park–cum–green–cum–whatever it was again when I picked up Imogen's voicemail. It felt weirdly intimate to hear her voice coming out of my phone, even if she did sound pissed off. Given what had happened, I guessed she had every right to be.

How had I got everything so wrong? I'd thought things would be easier with me gone. But then, I'd only really been thinking about me, hadn't I? Not other people. I'd never imagined they'd start on Imogen. Why on earth had she even been targeted?

There was one thing I was sure of. There was no way I could leave Imogen on her own to deal with trouble that was meant for me. I couldn't ignore the fact that what she was going through was my fault.

I dialled her number.

She picked up instantly.

'About time.'

I could hear chatter in the background, the high-pitched scream of a child, a whirring. 'Where are you?'

'You're the one who should be answering that question, Sam.' Her voice sounded cold. 'If you *really* need to know, I'm in a park and I'm alone. And if you give me a good enough reason, I won't instantly run to your stepmum and tell her where you are.'

I sort of hated that she'd read me so well and sort of liked her for it too. 'I never meant for you to get into trouble. honest. Are you all right, Imogen? They haven't really hurt you, have they?'

'Depends on your definition of hurt. I've been chased, threatened, pushed against a wall and punched in the stomach. Aside from that I'm feeling great.'

She spoke so breezily that it was hard for me to take it in. 'I don't know what to say,' I said, stunned. How could so much change in just a day? 'I . . . Imogen, I'm so sorry. I had no idea you'd get targeted! If I'd have known, I'd never have—'

'Save that for later,' she said curtly. She lowered her voice. 'What the hell is going on?'

'I'll tell you everything,' I said, still reeling from the news. 'But not over the phone. I'm not convinced it's safe. Could you . . . I mean, if it's not too much bother, could you meet me where I am?'

'Which I assume isn't Walthamstow. Scared of coming back?'

'They tried to kill me! You'd be frightened too!'

'Who says I'm not?'

There was a pause.

'I've been staying with Harrison,' I said. 'We grew up next door to each other. I guess he's the closest thing I have to an older brother. Anyway, he's at uni in Essex. Colchester. If you come up, I'll meet you. Then we can talk.'

'Colchester's miles away. I don't have cash for train fares.'

That was one thing I didn't understand about people in Walthamstow; they seemed to think even other areas of London were halfway across the country. Apparently some kids had never been out of Waltham Forest borough. It shocked me that people who were so sorted in some ways could be so unsorted in others.

'I'll pay you back for your ticket. Please, Imogen.'

Imogen sighed. For a moment I thought she was going to lash out.

'Sure,' she said. 'A trip to Colchester. Perfect way to spend Sunday afternoon. How long does it take?'

'About an hour once you're on the train. Please, don't tell anyone about this.'

'Whatever, Sam. I'll come now.'

'Stay safe, OK?'

'Can't promise you that,' Imogen said wryly, and ended the call. I groaned. Of all the stupid things to say! But she was coming, and part of me was glad that I'd finally be able to share this hell.

IMOGEN
SUNDAY 17 NOVEMBER

Immediately after speaking to Sam I rang Ollie. He didn't pick up. I couldn't wait so I went straight to the nearest tube station. In under forty-five minutes I was on an overground train heading out to Colchester. Ten minutes into the journey, Ollie called back.

'I know where he is,' I said, not bothering to say hi.

'No way!' Ollie's voice was breaking up a little; was it my imagination or did it sound a little uneven? 'So where's he hiding out?'

I told him, adding, 'We're meeting at Colchester station.'

'When – now? Isn't that out of London somewhere?'

'Yeah, Essex, and yeah, now. I was going to ask you to come with me when I rang. I'll be there in about forty.'

Ollie's voice cut out entirely. I frowned, removing my phone from my ear to see if the call had died. Then I heard Ollie muttering and quickly put it back. 'You OK, Ollie? You sound frazzled.'

'I'm fine. Don't stress. Good luck, Im, OK?'

'Thanks. Nice to know you care,' I said. It was only half a joke. Ollie had been part of my life for months, but I'd never really trusted him with something this important before. At least bad stuff, crap though it was to deal with, taught you who your friends really were.

SAM
SUNDAY 17 NOVEMBER

I looked up a taxi number on my phone – the university campus was too far from Colchester to walk, and the buses were infrequent on Sundays. As I waited for it to arrive I felt nervous. I'd told Imogen that I'd tell her everything, and I really wanted to do just that. I was so sick of keeping it to myself. But that would involve letting out the part of this I was sure would tear her up. She'd been hurt enough already. Things would have been so much easier if I'd been able to get it out that night at the chicken shop and now I wouldn't have this horrible dilemma.

My taxi arrived and took me to the station. I got myself a coffee from the shop on the platform and sat in the waiting room, drinking it slowly.

I was on my second by the time the London train drew in. I saw Imogen get out and felt a deep sense of dread. She looked less well turned out than she did at sixth form, all layered up and without any make-up. I immediately noticed that she was wearing her old glasses, the ones she'd had when I'd first joined the school. She wasn't smiling. Not that I'd expected her to be pleased to see me.

She opened the glass door. It creaked and swung shut behind her. She sat next to me on the wooden bench, folding her arms.

'Right,' she said. 'Where do you want to start?'

IMOGEN
SUNDAY 17 NOVEMBER

Sam rubbed the side of his nose, looking at me wearily. He was bundled up in a heavy coat and scarf. He still had stitches in his chin. Raw-looking scabs had formed around the cut. It wasn't a pretty sight.

'I could try the start,' he said.

'Hello, Captain Obvious!' I met his eyes. 'No fibs or dodging questions, OK?'

Sam sighed. 'I guess you've figured by now that I was there the night that guy in the shop got attacked. Hamdi, not that I knew his name then. I didn't intend on being there. We were only in the area because Mia wanted to eat out.'

'She's your cousin, right?'

He nodded. 'Little cousin, though she looks older. Before we go on, was it you IMing her yesterday?'

I nodded. Outside there was a rumble as another train drew in. It felt peculiar to be having this conversation somewhere so public. 'Did I freak her out?'

'A little. Were you on my computer?'

I explained about house-sitting and waited for Sam to carry on.

'I don't really like Walthamstow,' he said. 'I hate all those takeaway chicken joints. You know they use cheap meat and pump it full of water and fat to make it look good?

It's gross. The American Diner's all right though, so that's where we went.'

The diner opposite the Guls' shop. It would have been packed on a Saturday night. 'Mia said you told her to get a table while you went into the shop.'

'I only wanted to break a note and get some change for the jukebox. I went in and looked for something cheap to buy. I was at the opposite end to the till when I heard shouting and three guys ran in. They had hoodies and scarves on – I couldn't see much of them.' He swallowed, and I felt sorry for him despite myself. 'They had knives and I was so absolutely freaked out you would not believe. They started threatening Hamdi, telling him to hand over the cash.'

'What did you do?'

Sam didn't answer. I leaned forward.

'Sam. What did you do?'

'What do you think?' Sam yelled, so loudly that I drew back. 'I hid in the photo booth at the back of the shop. And I did *nothing!*'

Now I understood why he'd been so reluctant to open up. 'You mean you didn't try to get help?' I said. 'That shop has a back door. You could have slipped out and raised the alarm. Or phoned the police. Or helped him.'

Sam covered his face with his hands. 'Believe me, it feels like I killed him, and no, that isn't melodramatic, because I could have made a difference. There must have been a minute, maybe two, before they really laid into him, and I stayed hiding, only thinking about protecting myself! I hate that I did it, but I did and there's no getting away from it. And yes, I saw everything.'

The words came out muffled, but the regret in his voice was clear. I didn't know how to react. Yeah, part of me was disgusted. Hamdi might still be alive if Sam had done something.

But part of me felt awful for him. What shitty luck to have been in the shop. And who could tell how they'd react in a life-and-death situation? What would I have done? I *liked* to think I'd've raised the alarm. But I might have frozen too. I'd turned to putty when those guys laid into me, and I'd screamed at the police when I saw Nadina on the stretcher. I hadn't reacted to either of those situations in the way I'd've thought.

Can't judge Sam for this, I told myself. I can't like him for it, but I can't be unfair.

'Look,' I said, 'a lot less of us would have played hero than you think.'

Sam lowered his palms from his face. 'It shows what I'm made of, that's for sure,' he said in a small voice. 'I wish I could go back and change it, but I'm not Doctor Who.'

'They saw you. Right?'

'Yes, when I finally got it together enough to run. When they got violent with Hamdi I was terrified they'd realize I was there and turn on me. It was really lucky that the high road was busy, else they'd have chased after me. I dragged Mia out of the diner and we ran. I think she got away with it. They probably only saw her from behind.'

I wondered how they'd worked out who Sam was. There must be any number of kids fitting his description in the local area. 'So this is why they tried to run you down.'

'I'm a witness and this is a murder. That's a pretty good motive, isn't it?'

'Sure, but . . .' I pushed my glasses up the bridge of my nose, frowning. 'It's pretty damn drastic, Sam. Didn't they try threatening you first? "Keep your mouth shut else we'll beat you up" kind of thing. Come to that, how did they even work out who you were?'

'Guess they must've got a good look at me, even though I thought they hadn't. As for threatening me, that wasn't much of an option.' Sam's voice shook. I sensed we were getting to the crux of it all. 'You see, I wasn't just an eyewitness. I did manage to get it together in one sense . . .'

I snapped my fingers. 'You videoed the attack on your phone!'

He nodded, patting his pocket. 'The phone's here. Proper evidence. I mean, it's not great quality, but it shows most of the attack. The drawback is, they know I filmed them.'

'Does the video show who they are? Is there CCTV to back it up?'

'From what I've heard, the CCTV was down and they were waiting for someone to come and fix it. And with the video . . . sort of yes and no.'

'Can I see it?'

From outside I heard an announcement that the next train from London was due. I couldn't believe we'd been sat in this freezing waiting room for well over an hour. The rest of the world seemed a long way away. I held out my hand for Sam's mobile – then stopped. I'd realized something.

'They wanted *my* phone. Those guys – the ones who hit me. For some reason they think *I* was there too. Or that you shared the video with me. Or something.'

'I haven't shared it with anyone,' Sam said – then stopped, looking dumbstruck. 'Oh. Imo, they must have thought Mia was you.'

I shut my eyes, remembering the photo I'd seen in Sam's room. 'That explains a lot. You weren't around to threaten so they turned on me. That night outside the chicken shop would have backed up their belief that we're mates. Bloody hell! In some twisted way it's almost funny.'

'Hilarious.' Sam sounded wretched.

I frowned. 'What?'

'We're probably right about the mistaken identity and I'm really sorry about that. But there's one other thing I need to say . . .'

This must be what Sam had come to tell me at the chicken

shop. The thing he'd lied about when I'd gone to his house and been sidetracked by hearing about Benno being bullied.

'Go on,' I said.

Sam took out his phone and held it towards me. His hands were white and shaking. I heard a rumble as a train rolled in.

'This is how the gang knew who I was,' he said very quietly as a video loaded on-screen. And then my mobile buzzed. Annoyed, I took it out, pressing the button to cut the call.

'The screen said Ollie,' Sam snapped. 'Why is he calling?'

'Because he's my boyfriend.'

'Yes, but –' Sam jumped up, grabbing my arm and pulling me towards the door. I was so surprised that I didn't resist.

'What the hell?'

'We've got to get out!' Sam shouted. Confused and disorientated, I found myself on the platform. People were heading towards the exit. Everything was normal.

'I don't understand . . .' I started to say – and then at the furthest end of the platform, I caught sight of someone very familiar. Ollie! He must have come here to find me. Then I saw that he wasn't alone. He had two guys with him. Two guys I recognized. Two guys that made me freeze.

One wore a black hoody. One wore a khaki coat.

Sam tried to pull me towards the exit, but I was staring at Ollie. Why was he with these guys? Then I saw his face. There was blood under his nose. Even from this distance that was clear. And he was standing awkwardly. As though in pain.

'Let go!' I cried, grappling with Sam. 'We've got to help him. I told Ollie where we were. They've beaten him up! Pumped him for information!'

One of the guys shouted and pointed. They started running towards us.

Sam grabbed my shoulders and forced me to look him in the eye. 'Never mind Ollie now! If they catch us, we're *dead*!'

'Get off me!' I shook him off but Sam grabbed my wrist.

'Don't be stupid!' he shouted. 'They have knives! They beat you up earlier and this time they'll do something worse. Do you want to get stabbed to death?'

Even though I was terrified for Ollie, I knew Sam was right. We bolted, weaving through the people heading towards the exit. The barriers were open and we rushed through, pushing people out of our way. Outside the station I looked from one side to the other.

'Taxi rank!' Sam yelled. There was a cab waiting and we tumbled into it. As Sam spoke to the driver I slammed the door and locked it. The guys had just skidded out on to the pavement. One held Ollie by the arm. It only took them an instant to spot us, but by then our taxi was on the move, and there wasn't another. I pressed my hands against the glass, helpless and desperate as we sped away from the station – and from Ollie. Sam said something but I barely heard.

What have I done?

SAM

I asked the taxi driver to take us to the university campus. I'd've liked to get further away but I didn't know the area; taxis were pricey and the twenty quid I had on me was only going to go so far. I tried not to think about how much the last couple of days had burned into my savings. The university at least was safe. I hadn't told Imogen where Harrison's house was, so there was no way she could have passed that info on to Ollie.

Imogen hadn't spoken since we'd got in the cab. She stared out of the window as we were driven round umpteen roundabouts before passing out of the town centre into the countryside and then dropped off at the edge of the campus.

I cleared my throat. 'There's a student cafe five minutes' walk away. Let's go.'

Imogen took out her phone, pressing a few buttons. Then she shook her head in frustration. 'He's not picking up.'

'There was nothing we could have done,' I said. 'They tried to kill me, remember, and they beat you up.'

'We abandoned him!'

'We wouldn't win in a fight, Imo. They'd have killed us. You know that. Let's go somewhere safe where there are lots of people and work out what to do next.'

Imogen just shook her head, staring at her phone. I led her

through the green-cum-park area, past tall blocks of student halls and into the quad where the food places seemed to be. Despite it being Sunday, they were all open and quite busy, which didn't surprise me. Judging by what Harrison shoved down his throat, students were always hungry.

I went into a cafe that reminded me of the greasy spoons back in Yorkshire, holding open the door for Imogen and craning my neck to read the menu on the display board above the till.

'Are you thirsty? Hungry?'

'Whatever.' Imogen went over to a vacant table. I ordered a plate of chips and two Cokes. The man serving didn't bat an eyelid, though I clearly wasn't old enough to pass as a student. Perhaps he had me down as a child prodigy. When I brought the tray over, Imogen narrowed her eyes at me.

'Question: Why didn't you go to the police?'

I unbuttoned my coat. The air in the cafe was muggy and my heavy coat was making me overheat. 'Guess.'

'Just tell me.'

I sighed, looking round at all these happy, ordinary people tucking into food with friends and wished I was one of them. If only we were normal.

'You know it as well as I do – guys like that never get done. Justice doesn't happen. I didn't want to report them and then get killed in a revenge attack. I was scared. Before Hamdi died it was just a robbery. If I'd gone to the police, what was I going to achieve? The guys that did it might get cautioned, even put inside for a few months. Then what? They'd be out and coming after me. It was safer to keep my mouth shut.'

'It's murder now,' Imogen said flatly. 'You've hard evidence. The police will be able to put them away long term.'

'That doesn't rule out their friends coming round and punching my face in.'

'How's that any different from living in fear right now?'

'I don't know. I didn't think about that.'

'You didn't think about this running-away plan either, did you?'

'It seemed a good idea at the time.' I lapsed into silence.

'There's no sitting-on-the-fence option any more. You'd better make your mind up, fast.'

For the first time her borderline-aggressive manner got on my nerves. 'You don't seem to be terribly upset about your boyfriend being in the hands of these guys,' I said. I'd intended to be mean and I got my reaction. Imogen jerked upright, scowling at me.

'Shut up! Course I'm worried. I'm just trying to get my head round your total stupidity!'

'I bet you wouldn't have bloody gone to the police either. In fact, I *know* so. Think about that before you call me stupid. You didn't report those texts, did you?'

Imogen's gaze flickered downward. 'It's none of your business.'

'Well, like it or not, we're in this together, so if you can bring yourself to get along with me that would be pretty helpful.'

Imogen made a growling noise and grabbed a couple of chips. I opened my can of Coke. My phone was back in my pocket. It felt like it was burning a hole in the coat lining.

'When they said they'd hurt Benno, I believed them. Because they did Nadina's shop too.' Imogen was looking at me. Her lower lip was trembling ever so slightly. 'Did you know that? She's in hospital. Broken jaw.'

This was news. More than ever I felt as if I was drowning in a pool that was steadily getting deeper. True, I found Nadina a bit full on, with her intense attitude and loud, aggressive way of speaking, but she seemed like a nice enough girl. That someone I knew had been so badly hurt really hit home.

'Nadina will be all right, won't she?'

Imogen nodded. She took out her phone. I saw her eyes widen. I leaned in so I could see the screen.

Will call in 1 hour. Make sure u pick up.

'That's from Ollie's number.' Imogen said, unnecessarily, because I could see. 'They must still have him!'

'I guess.'

She slapped her hand on the table. 'Don't sound like that!

You might not give a damn if Ollie's OK but I do. Didn't you see how he looked? They've beaten him up! Used him to get to me so they can get to you! How d'you feel about that, Sam? More and more people getting hurt because of you.'

'Oh, shut up!' I shouted. Imogen looked surprised. A group at the next table glanced over, nudging each other. 'I'm not the enemy here. If you knew what I do . . .'

'Yeah? And what *do* you know, Sam? I'm sick of your bloody secrets!'

I looked away, close to losing my temper. You don't realize how hard I tried to protect you! I wanted to shout. I was so close to telling her what I knew – *so* close. But all of a sudden I was scared of how she'd react now things had changed. Now Ollie was in their hands. What she might try to do – or try to make me do. She was well and truly wound up. I didn't trust her to make the right decisions under these circumstances.

'I'm going to the police,' I told her, standing up. 'Now.'

Imogen suddenly looked afraid.

'Sam, don't. Not now they've got Ollie. Let's at least take that call first. *Please*, Sam.'

Looking back, I don't know why I agreed to wait. I should have known how it would all work out. It wasn't as though I cared about Ollie, and I doubted he was *really* in danger.

'Let's go to Harrison's then,' I said. 'You'll want to be somewhere private when your phone rings.'

IMOGEN
SUNDAY 17 NOVEMBER

We left the cafe. I placed a hand on my stomach. It was beginning to give me hell again. I looked at my watch. Forty minutes. 'Is this house far?'

Sam shook his head. He took me up a long flight of steps. We passed through another square, which seemed to be a student village area with a bank and a bookshop, and along a path with ugly buildings I guessed were either halls or lecture blocks on either side. It led through a green and an area with two-storey houses. Sam was saying something about the houses being designed to look like an ordinary street, and how someone in Harrison's house had moved out and he'd been staying in their room. I wasn't really listening. We arrived at a house with a blue door. Sam rang the bell. A blond guy with a body like a rugby player's opened up.

'Hi, Harry,' Sam blurted before Harrison could say anything. 'This is Imogen. Imogen, this is Harrison. Do you have any painkillers?'

Sam must've noticed me wincing. Harrison looked me up and down, grinning, and raised an eyebrow at Sam. I groaned.

'Whatever you're thinking, don't. I am *not* his girlfriend.'

'Got it.' Chuckling to himself, he went inside. We followed

him into a bare hallway with a faded carpet. Harrison went into the nearest room and started rifling around. If there were painkillers to be found, we might be waiting a while, time I didn't have – the room was titchy but it was an utter tip. Dirty clothes and loose paper littered the floor, and the desk was piled high with dirty cups and plates. There were even takeaway boxes on the bed. I put my hands in my pockets, feeling increasingly tense. I couldn't afford to miss this call. Ollie's safety was on the line. I was doing my best to block it out, but each time I pictured his bloodied face on the platform, guilt kicked in.

'While I love your company and all that, I feel the need to point out that you're here under false pretences,' Harrison was saying. He was moving so slowly I had to grind my teeth together to stop myself from shouting at him to hurry up. 'You said one night. It's been four already. While I'm OK helping you out and all, you've got to patch things up at home sometime, y'know.'

Sam smiled wryly. 'Come on, Harry. I did make you lot that chilli yesterday. Your housemate said it was the best thing he'd ever eaten.'

'Ricky's from Glasgow. He doesn't know any better. Aha!' Harrison took out a packet from the bedside drawer. Sam washed out one of the mugs in the grubby kitchen and filled it with water so I could take the tablets. I shook my head when he asked if I wanted to lie down.

'Wouldn't want to impose on your mate's hospitality any longer than I need to.'

'Hey, I don't mind. Neither will the other guys,' Harrison said, winking. 'This house needs a woman's touch. It's just Sam I object to.'

Sam rolled his eyes. 'Imogen, let's go.'

'Have fun!' Harrison called after us. Sam mouthed an apology and took me upstairs to a room very like Harrison's. Excepting the duvet on the bed, it appeared unlived in. Sam closed the door.

'This is where I've been staying. We can wait here till they call. Are you sure you don't want to lie down? At least until the painkillers kick in? There's half an hour yet.'

'Twenty-five minutes.' Now that there was a bed in front of me, lying flat seemed a good idea. After checking that my phone had decent reception, I eased myself down. The mattress was surprisingly comfy. I closed my eyes. I could hear the thump of music from below us, and a different beat from the side. Something gurgled; water pipes, maybe the shower. Sam shifted on the plastic chair by the desk. When you just listened, I thought, it was amazing what you could hear.

'What do you think they'll say?' Sam asked.

'They'll threaten to hurt Ollie. That's a given. As if they needed new material for threats.'

Sam didn't say anything to that. After a silence that

seemed to last forever, there was a creak as he rose from the desk chair.

'I'm going to get us something to eat. Might make you feel better. I'll be back in time, OK?'

I didn't reply.

His feet padded on the carpet. The door swooshed open and shut. Alone, I unbuttoned my jeans and pulled down the zip, easing the pressure on my bruised stomach. Sam said he felt bad that I'd got beaten up because of him. I now knew exactly how that guilt felt. Ollie had been so concerned – insistent on helping, despite the rocky patch we'd been through. I wished I hadn't let him. Good deeds give you naff all, I thought. Ollie trying to be a good boyfriend, me saving Sam that night – both had exploded in our faces. Big time.

By the time Sam returned the painkillers had kicked in and I was sitting on the bed, trousers zipped up and feeling less uncomfortable. I tore my eyes from my silent phone and looked up at him as he laid a bowl on the bedside table.

'There wasn't much worth having in that kitchen. Made a sort of minestrone from some frozen veggies and pasta and tinned tomatoes and stuff. Hopefully not too gross.'

I took the bowl and closed my hands round it. I wasn't hungry, but the warmth was comforting.

SAM

SUNDAY 17 NOVEMBER

It was five minutes past eight when the call finally came.

Imogen carefully put her uneaten bowl of soup on the bedside table. She let the phone ring six times before picking up. She said this would show them we weren't total putty in their hands.

'Are you alone?' The gravelly voice on the other end made me shiver. We'd agreed that she'd put the call on to speakerphone straight away.

'I'm with Sam,' Imogen said. 'Is that a problem?'

The way she said it was like the problem was all theirs. Like a challenge. I couldn't help admiring her cool.

'We've got your boyfriend. He ain't very comfortable. And he ain't gonna get any more comfortable unless you cooperate.'

'What do you want?'

'Put your mate on the line.'

Imogen looked at me. Don't blow it, her expression said. I leaned towards the phone. My voice came out sounding shaky.

'Sam here.'

'We're not gonna piss about, and neither are you, got it?' The voice was suddenly very sharp, noticeably aggressive, the kind of voice that belonged to someone who'd beat you to pulp and laugh about it afterwards. 'We know exactly what you saw and we know that you got a video. Who've you sent it to? No lying or smart games, cos we *will* find out. And *then* you'll be dead.'

'I've not sent it to anyone. It's just on my phone. I'm the only person who's seen it.'

'You expect us to believe that?'

Imogen placed a hand on my shoulder. Whether she was warning or encouraging me I couldn't tell.

'Yeah. That is, I mean, I was too scared to do anything with it . . .'

The laughter on the other end of the phone was so loud that Imogen and I both flinched.

'So there's just the one copy? You've not backed it up anywhere?'

'No. Just the one.'

'You'd better be sure about that.'

There was a very clear threat in those words. 'Just the one,' I repeated. There was a tense moment as I waited to see if they would believe me.

'Good boy,' the voice mocked. 'And now you're gonna delete it. Right here, right now, when I say so.'

Imogen sucked her breath in sharply. I knew what she was thinking. The only evidence of the attack on Hamdi Gul – gone.

'Need a few moments to think about whether you're

gonna cooperate?' The voice said teasingly. 'Want us to persuade you?'

There was a scuffling and then Ollie's voice came on the line. 'He's really not joking. If you don't delete that video, they're going to kick my head in.'

'Jesus Christ!' Imogen cried. Ollie didn't sound that different to me, but she'd paled the instant he'd spoken. 'Ollie, what happened? Are you OK?'

'Tell them,' someone said in the background. There was a heavy thud followed by the muffled sound of Ollie crying out. Imogen made a hissing noise. I stared at the opposite wall. The terrified look on her face freaked me out.

'They cornered me.' Ollie growled from the handset. 'They knew I was your boyfriend. They made me tell them what you'd told me.'

'And how did we make you?' hissed the voice.

Ollie paused. 'Forcefully.'

Imogen dug her fingers into the mattress we were sitting on, her lips pressed together tightly. If those guys had been here now, I wasn't so sure she'd have been holding her anger in so well. I had a feeling she'd have gone for them.

'You've got to delete it, Sam,' she said.

I hesitated.

'It won't just be Ollie's good looks we ruin if you don't play ball,' the voice went on. 'We know where you live,

Sammy. You can't hide indoors forever. First we'll grab your skinny dog and cut it up in front of you. Then we'll make you wish you'd never been born. As for your pretty blonde mate . . . she knows the score. Bad things can happen in the back streets of Walthamstow. Especially to kids like you . . .' A pause. 'If we find out you've lied to us . . .'

'Sam!' Imogen hissed, giving me a shove. 'Just delete the bloody thing!' To the guy on the phone, she said, 'You promise that you'll let Ollie go? That you won't hurt my brother? I'll film Sam deleting the video on my phone and send it through to you as proof.'

There was a pause. Then the guy's voice came over, sounding amused. 'You do that. Top marks, Head Girl.'

'Head *prefect*,' Imogen muttered. More clearly she said, 'How do we know you're going to release Ollie if we do this?'

'Just trust me, baby.'

Imogen swore under her breath. 'Ollie, call the moment you get released, OK?'

'Think we understand each other now,' the guy said. 'Now, I'm gonna put the phone down so you can make your video. I want you to send it through to your boyfriend. You've got five minutes.'

The line went dead.

Imogen and I looked at each other for a long time. I realized we were both shaking. Gradually I became aware of the everyday things I'd blanked out – the beat of music, how warm it was in here . . .

'Well,' Imogen said, her voice noticeably more wobbly, 'that went well.'

'Yeah. Brilliantly.'

'They're not kidding, Sam.' She pushed her hair back, then raised her phone. 'Let's do this. Don't think we need five minutes, do you?'

'You care about Ollie,' I said softly. 'Right?'

'Sam, don't give me this now. Just do it!'

I looked at the screen. It had the video loaded. I turned my phone over in my hand, thinking. Imogen hadn't seen the video. If she had, would she still be acting this way? Should I show it to her? Change everything?

But then I pictured the spark of terror I'd seen in her eyes when her brother had been mentioned. Imogen really loved Benno. I could go to the police and we might get these guys locked up, but then what? They'd just send someone else to attack Benno and Jessie and us. They were proper nutters. They didn't care about anyone or anything.

'It's not the right thing to do though, is it?' I said. I couldn't help myself. I was thinking of Mum and what she'd say about what I was about to do. 'Letting the bad guys get away with murder – it's wrong. People like that don't stop. They'll go on to hurt other people. They hurt Nadina. Who's next?'

'Maybe they'll get caught! I don't like letting them win, but I have to protect my family. If that makes me a rubbish human being, fine, I am. I don't *care* any more.' Imogen's cheeks flushed. 'Right and wrong – they don't matter now. It's too complicated. From where I'm sitting, all I see is grey. And a shedload of reasons for you to just press delete!'

I gazed at Imogen and thought about how much I'd respected her for all the things she'd done at school. How calm and collected she was. That almost robotic, unemotional manner of hers. Putting down the people who'd cyber-bullied me, trying to welcome the strange new ungrateful northern kid. A leader. A good person.

She didn't look so cool now. She looked panicked.

For a second I felt slightly disappointed in her.

'All right,' I said. 'But just so you know, I don't agree when you say that right and wrong don't matter any more. They always matter. Especially when things aren't black and white. Maybe that makes me weird? I don't know.'

'And I don't care,' Imogen said softly.

I paused. 'Are you ready to start recording?'

IMOGEN
SUNDAY 17 NOVEMBER

We did it.

'There's no going back now,' I said as the video I'd made of Sam deleting the footage pinged through to Ollie's email account. Sam said nothing. He'd surprised me during the last half-hour. I'd expected him to really freak out. As for all that about right and wrong . . . I felt my throat tighten. It's fine to lecture me, Sam. There's not as much at stake for you. I didn't like selling out. But I had no choice.

Sam had taken off his coat but not his scarf. It was half falling off, trailing on the floor. It struck me that I didn't know any other boys like Sam. The ones I'd grown up with were all swagger and mouth, trying to prove how tough they were. It was interesting to get to know someone more sensitive, even if he was harder to figure out.

'You're a funny one.'

Sam gave me a small smile which had very little warmth to it. 'I'm very ordinary, Imo.'

No else called me Imo. Im or Immy, but never Imo. I picked up my bowl of uneaten soup. It was still slightly warm. I started eating. Now that the adrenalin of the call had worn off, my body was sagging.

We'd sent the video ten minutes ago. What was keeping them?

My thoughts slipped back to the start of Year 11, when I'd first got to know Ollie. We'd had a Coke together after our first school-council meeting. I hadn't known him before then, but I knew who he was. A lot of my mates fancied him, including Nadina. Funnily enough, I hadn't. Maybe it was his haircut that had put me off. It had been longer then, with a stupid fringe he kept flicking out of his eyes. Over our drinks I'd told him he ought to cut it. He'd laughed and said he ought to turn cutting it off into a sponsored charity event. Later on he'd done just that.

I soon discovered we had lots in common.

'Listening to you two is like two blokes,' Nadina had huffed. 'You must be the only girl in the school who forgets she's female around Ollie.'

She and the other girls kept asking about us. It was clear that no one believed that we were just chatting. 'Prefect meetings' even became code for making out for a while. 'My boyfriend and I are having a *prefect meeting* tonight,' girls would say, nudging their friends.

I also tended to run into Ollie after school on Mondays, when the nearby sports centre admitted kids from our school for free. After a while I learned to ignore the constant questions.

When had things moved to another level? I had to think for a second. It had been right at the end of the year, almost four months ago now. We'd been chatting in the sports-centre foyer when a mate of Ollie's passed by.

'When are you getting together?' he'd yelled. 'Perfect match, smooch smooch!'

He was gone before we could retaliate.

'Your mates too, huh?' I asked.

Ollie rolled his eyes. 'They've been at it all year. So old now.'

'Maybe we should give it a go and shut everyone up.' I'd meant it as a joke, but as soon as it was out we both paused.

Ollie broke the silence. 'It's not the worst idea. Why not?' He grinned. 'I mean, you're no Rihanna, but you're all right, y'know.'

'Charming!' I gave him a shove. It developed into play-fight that ended with him pinning me against the side of the vending machine.

I pretended to huff and look annoyed. 'OK, you win. I'll let that insult slide. But next time you'd better describe me as more than all right. Got it?'

'Got it.' Ollie let me go. 'Wanna come to my game tomorrow then? Could stop by the diner afterwards.'

After that, we'd never looked back. No one seemed surprised that we'd become an item. Having a boyfriend turned out to be fun, sort of like having a good friend you also made out with. We weren't all over each other, but that wasn't our style. Nadina wanted the lowdown on Ollie. Was he a good kisser? Did he give me that excited feeling in my stomach? I avoided answering because I didn't really know. He was better than the couple of other guys I'd kissed. He didn't set my world on fire, but did that ever actually happen apart from in films?

I put the now empty bowl of soup down, feeling anxious. 'Why hasn't he called?'

'There could be loads of reasons. Maybe they made him promise not to until he's well away. Or maybe they've taken his phone. It's got the video you made on it, after all. They might want it.'

Sam had a point. 'Do you think I should call him?'

'If they have his phone then that's probably not the best idea. Wait for him to call you,' Sam said firmly. 'I'm sure he's OK. Ollie's a tough guy.'

'You're doing a pathetic job of reassuring me,' I said with a tiny smile.

Sam smiled back. 'It'll be OK.'

I sighed, glancing at my phone. Sam said something about being back in a moment. Just one call, I thought. Then this nightmare would be over.

SAM

Downstairs Harrison and his housemates were heading out. When I told him that Imogen might end up staying over as well as me, they fell about laughing. Was the idea that I had a friend who was a girl really such a tremendous joke?

In the kitchen I found a pile of dirty plates on the counter. More because I needed something to do than because I wanted to be helpful, I shifted everything on to the draining board and turned on the hot tap. The washing-up liquid bottle made a hiccupping noise as I squirted it into the water. So mundane. So normal. So outside what I'd known for the past two weeks.

I could see my reflection faintly in the tiles behind the taps. I stared at my face. This was me. An ordinary-looking guy, a loner – someone not entirely sure who he was any more.

A bit of a waste of space.

I picked up the first plate, then put it down again.

I don't want to be a waste of space any more, I thought.

It suddenly seemed deadly intense in the kitchen. Now had become one of those very important moments.

There was a choice I needed to make. An important one. I knew something no one else did. And it would change everything.

IMOGEN
SUNDAY 17 NOVEMBER

Nine turned to half nine to ten. Finally my phone rang. I grabbed it.

'Ollie!'

'No,' Mum said. 'Where are you, Imogen?'

I realized there was no way I was going to be back in London tonight, or going to school tomorrow. For a second I wondered why Mum sounded so miffed. Then I remembered our argument. Man, had that really only been a few hours back?

'I've been worried.' Mum's tone switched to concern. 'It's not like you to blow up like that. Maybe I was a bit harsh. Look, come home and we can talk . . . sort things out.' She paused; I heard mumbling in the background and Mum said, 'No, I'll deal with this, Andrew. OK?'

Poor Dad, getting flack from Mum that was meant for me. But Dad interrupting had given me a moment to think. 'I'm not going to be back tonight. I'm staying at Kimmie's.' I lied. Kimmie was a mate Mum had met, but she didn't know where she lived. 'Maybe we can talk tomorrow.'

There was a silence. Then Mum made a huffing noise. 'I could insist that you come back, but I won't, if that's the way you want it. But please, Imogen, try to be more mature next time. I can't be dealing with you being silly as well as everything else. If you're staying at a friend's house, let me know. Don't you care about your family?'

'More than you'll sodding ever know!' I said, and cut the call. I felt tears in my eyes. She had absolutely no idea!

The door creaked. Sam appeared, drying his hands on a tea towel. I shook my head before he asked.

'I guess you'd better stay then.' He tossed me a packet. 'I brought the rest of Harry's painkillers in case you need them.'

'Thanks,' I said, weirdly touched. I wasn't used to people thinking of me.

'We can head back tomorrow morning. It should be safe to return. Given we've deleted the video.'

'We had good reasons.' I realized that my eyes were still wet. Annoyed he'd seen me this way, I wiped them dry. 'It's done now.'

'You don't have to be so prickly. I'm not your enemy.' Sam paused. 'I might be able to help. If the idea of me giving *you* a hand isn't too crazy. We should get some sleep. It'll be better tomorrow, I promise.'

Despite myself, I laughed, though it was a sniffly, joyless kind of laugh. 'Sleep? Fat chance.'

Sam picked up his coat from the chair, spreading it out on the floor. 'You've got to try. Can you pass me one of those pillows?'

'You can't sleep on the floor,' I said. I shifted across on

the bed. 'Come on. There's space for two here. No funny business though, OK?'

Sam stared at me. 'What? No.'

'I'm not arguing about this,' I said softly. 'I don't mind.'

He hesitated a long moment. 'If it's really OK.'

'It's OK.'

He came over, gingerly lying down beside me before reaching across and turning off the bedside lamp. We lay side by side, staring into the darkness.

After a while I started to cry. I couldn't help it. Every time I closed my eyes I saw Ollie at the station as we escaped. Leaving him in the hands of two murderers.

I felt Sam shift beside me. I wasn't sure how long it had been since we'd turned off the lights, but he'd been almost unnaturally still. 'Imo, it's going to work out.'

'If they let Ollie go, he'd be home by now. Even if they took his phone and he hasn't got my number written down anywhere, he could get it from one of our mates. Why hasn't he called?'

'I don't know, but there's no reason they'd hurt him, not now. They're thugs, but I don't think they're total psychos. They've got what they wanted. He'll be OK, Imo.'

'They're murderers! And I left him with them! All Ollie wanted was to help me.' It was impossible to control myself. I was sobbing properly now, all the fear and anxiety of the evening taking over. Sam said stuff – about how it was going to be fine and how Ollie was tough and how tomorrow we'd know exactly what was going on. How long I cried into the pillow – or was it Sam's shoulder? – I didn't know. Somewhere along the line exhaustion caught up with me. Incredibly, I fell asleep.

The next morning I awoke to find that my phone showed no messages. As Sam and I trudged out of Harrison's house, I said, 'They must still have him. It's the only explanation. We did what they said, and they double-crossed us!'

Sam had shadows under his eyes. I hadn't slept well, but he looked wrecked. We were both shabby and untidy in yesterday's clothes. People on the bus and the train were going to think we were living rough. 'Let's get back to Walthamstow,' he said. 'If Ollie's not at his house, we'll know it was a lie. And then we really will need to go to the police.'

I felt stupid when I thought of how eager I'd been to surrender our only evidence. Why had I believed what those thugs had said? Sam probably couldn't stand me for 'making the wrong decision' now. Somehow he seemed less friendly this morning, more wrapped up in his own thoughts. Like I cared what he thought. We weren't mates, never had been, and after this was all over and done, we'd probably never speak again.

But I did care. I hated being thought badly of. Even by

Sam. I couldn't put my finger on why his opinion mattered to me. Maybe it was those odd little moments we'd shared. Like when he'd offered to help. Who knew?

We got the bus to Colchester station and then the London train. We didn't say much. Today was the first day I'd ever skipped school.

Was it safe to go home? They'd got what they wanted from me and Sam. But then there was Ollie. I had a nasty feeling that this was far from over.

When we finally reached Walthamstow tube and came up the escalators into the bus station I stood for a moment, taking in the sights and sounds and smells around me. One day. Yet it felt as if I'd been gone forever. After checking my phone – no messages – I looked at Sam.

'Are you coming with me to Ollie's?'

'I have somewhere to go.' Sam gave me an apologetic smile. Then he turned and walked away, turning left by McDonalds.

I frowned. Wherever he was going, it clearly wasn't home. Oh hell, I thought, feeling exhausted all of a sudden. Sam Costello and his funny ways had always been a mystery to me.

SAM

I felt exhausted, physically and mentally. As I walked along the high street I thought about how it had made me feel last night, lying there next to Imogen, uncomfortably aware of how close our bodies were. She'd fallen asleep with her head on my shoulder, the warmth of her breath on my neck. If I'd known how distracting sharing the bed would be, I'd have slept on the floor – no, that was a lie. Despite everything, it had felt good to be so close to another person – good to be so close to *her*.

I only had a vague idea where Nadina's family shop was, so it took me a while to find it. It was one of those stores that seemed to be thick on the ground round here, the crowded grocery-cum-minimart-cum-newsagent that sold a bit of everything. To my surprise it was open. I guess the police must have finished doing their stuff. The family probably can't afford for it to be closed too long.

Nervously I stepped inside. The interior reminded me uncomfortably of the shop Hamdi Gul worked in – same packed shelves, long aisles and a similar section of Turkish specialities. I wondered if anyone had been shopping here when the break-in had happened. Had they stuck up for Nadina's family? Or had they been just as scared as I had?

A guy I guessed was Nadina's brother was at the till. He

didn't seem to think it strange when I asked to see her and texted Nadina to come down from the flat above the shop. Can't be hurt too badly if she's home, I thought, reassured.

When Nadina came through the door behind the till she raised her eyebrows but didn't ask why I'd come. She took me up a narrow staircase and into a sitting room. It was one of the most stuffed rooms I'd ever seen, three long sofas covered by colourful throws and cushions squashed between heaving cupboards and cabinets. Most of the wall space was crammed with enlarged photos of people I guessed were family. Nadina flopped down on one of the couches, muting the telly.

'What d'you want?'

The words came out sounding raspy and considerably quieter than Nadina's usual voice, which was loud enough to hear from the other side of Walthamstow. Although it was less obvious than I'd expected, I could tell that her jaw was wired up.

'Yeah, I can talk,' Nadina said, picking up on my surprise. 'Poor everyone else, eh?'

I smiled self-consciously; I didn't know Nadina well enough to feel comfortable about laughing. 'I'm glad you're back home.'

'Yeah, well, beats hospital, but I ain't staying in with daytime telly tomorrow. I wanna see how everyone at school is gonna take the mick out of me. You coming in too? We can be a club or something. Walking wounded united, innit.'

I realized she was talking about the injuries I'd picked up from the car incident. Neither had given me much trouble at all. I really had been lucky. 'I guess so. I can't skip school forever.'

Nadina picked up a glass from the table by the couch and sucked in a mouthful of the gloopy-looking contents through a thick straw. 'Mmmmm, lunch. Mashed banana and milk. It's like being a baby with this wired-up jaw, I'm telling you. I don't even like sodding milkshakes.'

I thought about it. 'You could always mash up veg and potatoes with stock to make a thick soup. Or you could make a bean chilli and blend it?'

Nadina's eyes lit up. 'Nice one! You got some tricks up your sleeve. Starting to see why Im finds you so strangely intriguing. Not that she'd admit it.' I wasn't sure how to respond to that. 'Now look, Sam, not being rude or nothing, but why're you here? We're not mates, right, so this ain't a social call.'

I was beginning to understand why Nadina and Imogen got on.

'I wanted to ask how much you and your dad saw of the attack on your shop. I mean, would you be able to identify who did it? How many people were there? Did the police find any evidence they seemed to think was useful?'

Nadina gave me a searching look. 'Haven't got a clue why you're asking, but I don't mind. This is what you're meant to do with trauma. Talk about it, innit.'

That wasn't what I'd done, but then there wasn't really anyone I trusted enough to open up to. I ignored the fact that Nadina was talking to me, someone she had no reason to trust.

She explained that three guys had robbed the shop. All were young, around a similar height, but beyond that pretty unidentifiable, especially the one who'd acted as lookout. Nadina had barely got a glance of him. The others had worn hoodies and scarves over their faces. Knowing what had happened to Hamdi, Nadina and her dad hadn't put up much resistance when they were told to open the till, but they'd still been roughed up before the guys had legged it.

It sounded exactly like what I'd witnessed – enough for me to be fairly sure it was the same people. I sighed. I'd been hoping Nadina might have given the police enough information to put them well on the way to catching these lowlifes, but it was too vague.

As I got up to leave, Nadina said, 'What's all this to you anyway?'

I swallowed. 'The difference between doing something and not doing it.'

IMOGEN
MONDAY 18 NOVEMBER

Both buses I needed to get to Ollie's took forever to come. I tried ringing, but my calls went straight to voicemail. Either his battery was dead or something had happened to the phone.

What can I do? I thought. Apart from going to the police after seeing if he was home, I couldn't think of anything else. Not after we'd wiped the video.

It occurred to me that I'd never asked Sam if the video identified the gang. He'd not even got round to showing it to me. Had that been deliberate? He'd been so cagey with information that I was beginning to wonder . . .

When I reached Ollie's estate it was drizzling. Some kids were hanging by a block's stairwell about a hundred metres away, kicking a football to one another. Going to school clearly wasn't something they'd fancied today – or most days, according to Ollie. He sometimes jokingly called this place No Hoper Homes. 'Getting in's easy. It's getting out that's tough.'

Ollie would move on to better things one day though. He'd been putting in the work for it the whole way through secondary school. I desperately hoped his future wasn't going to be messed up because he'd tried to help me.

They wouldn't have harmed him, would they? They'd been prepared to kill Sam, but that was different. He really was a threat. Ollie didn't know anything.

I wasn't expecting the door to Ollie's flat to be opened when I pressed the bell, but it was, by Maria Paula, Ollie's mum. At first I couldn't work out what she was doing here early afternoon on a Monday. Then I clocked that she was wearing a blue and white uniform and remembered that she worked part-time at Boots. She must be about to leave.

'Hi,' I blurted. I'd only met Maria Paula a few times. Ollie was funny about his friends talking to his mum. I got the impression he was ashamed of her. He'd once said something about her accent being embarrassing. Trying to control my shaking voice, I asked, 'Don't suppose Ollie's in?'

Maria Paula smiled. She was quite a young mum and pretty in a petite, doll-like way. The only thing about her that was never neat was her hair, which was thick and curly and a little wild. 'Of course, please come in. He's watching TV.'

I gaped at her. After all the fear and worry I'd been through, Ollie was home in front of the telly! I'd thought he was still in the gang's clutches. I'd been terrified he might even be dead! Had that even been him on the phone last night at all? It was starting to feel like I was going insane.

'Is he all right?'

Ollie's mum chuckled. 'A bit sore, but his arm is not badly hurt. These things happen. He won't be playing the good guy like that again – I made him promise. Still, I'm proud of him. Osvaldo!' she called. 'Imogen's here.'

What the hell was she talking about? I closed the front door behind me just as Ollie appeared at the doorway to the front room. I stared at him. Apart from the bruise around his eye and having a bandage round his arm, he looked fine. When he saw me, Ollie went very pale.

Maria Paula glanced between us, looking amused. 'Have you fallen out? Need me to referee?'

'Not funny,' Ollie snapped. 'Can you leave us alone?'

Maria Paula raised an eyebrow, but she went into the kitchen, humming under her breath. Ollie grabbed my arm with his good hand and pulled me into the living room, kicking the door shut.

'Told Mum I broke up some kids fighting,' he hissed. 'Don't tell her how this really happened, all right?'

I shook him off. 'Ollie! Why didn't you call me? I was majorly freaking out!'

There was something guarded about the way he was standing, something tense, as though he thought something would happen at any moment. 'Couldn't. They took my phone.'

'Why didn't you get my number off somebody else? I

was terrified for you – oh, never mind. Just glad you're OK. Tell me everything.'

I moved to sit on the couch, then stopped when I realized Ollie hadn't shifted. 'What?'

'Mum will be able to hear. Thin walls.'

'Jeez!' I didn't mean to sound angry, but I'd been on a total roller coaster of emotions and I just wanted answers. 'Why are you so down on your mum the whole time?'

'Shut up!' Ollie's eyes blazed. 'You don't know anything about me and my mum. I know what you're going to start saying and it'll upset her. So just keep a lid on it until she heads to work. Talk about volleyball or whatever. OK?'

I'd never seen him this wound up. A little afraid of Ollie for the first time ever, I shuffled backwards. Then Maria Paula opened the door.

'Work is calling,' she said in a breezy tone that told me she'd overheard at least some of what we'd been saying. She stood on tiptoes and gave Ollie a hug. 'You hope the school fixes the boiler for tomorrow, Osvaldo. Else I've lots of nice household things you can be busy with.'

I tuned Maria Paula out. Another lie. I couldn't think of anything to say. Luckily the doorbell shrilled. Maria Paula went to answer it.

'What's going on?' I demanded.

Ollie stared at me. Slowly he said, 'He really didn't tell you . . . show you . . . anything? You don't know?'

'Ollie, can you start talking to me in a language I understand!'

From the hallway I heard the front door click. Maria Paula started to say hello – then stopped. A male voice said, 'Are you Maria Paula Moreno? Is your son Osvaldo here?'

'Yes. What's happened?'

'Can we come in please, madam?'

There was a shuffling and the sound of footsteps. I glanced at Ollie. From the look on his face I knew immediately that something terrible was about to happen.

Maria Paula came through. Behind her were two uniformed police officers. They looked like twins, both strapping guys with very short hair. Neither was smiling. But Maria Paula was, in a fluttery, hopeful kind of way.

'You are here about the fight my son broke up perhaps?' she said, a bit too brightly. 'I'm not sure there is too much we can tell you.'

'I'm afraid that's not the reason for our visit, Ms Moreno,' one officer said.

'Is it a burglary on the estate? Always someone has their flat broken into.'

The other man stepped forward. 'Ms Moreno, I'm sorry to inform you that we're here because of your son.' He cleared his throat and turned to Ollie. 'Osvaldo Moreno, I am arresting you on suspicion of participating in the murder of Hamdi Gul. You do not have to say anything, but it may harm your defence if you do not mention when questioned something which you later rely on in court. Anything you do say may be given in evidence. Do you understand?'

I blanked out. I was vaguely aware that the officer was running through what would happen down at the station, and the other standard spiel. Ollie had gone very pale. He made no effort to argue, or run. He didn't make any effort to do *anything*.

Maria Paula went to Ollie and grasped his hand, squeezing it hard. She was shaking her head violently. 'This is a mistake!' she cried. 'My son would never be involved in violence. Never! You have the wrong boy. This is a horrible mistake and I want you to leave, now!'

'Ms Moreno, you'll need to accompany your son to the station. We can't talk to him without an adult present. If you'd like a solicitor, we can supply one.'

'I don't need to accompany him. He *isn't* going.' Maria Paula looked at Ollie, her face pathetically hopeful. 'Osvaldo. Swear to me this is wrong. I know you didn't do anything. You're a good boy.'

Ollie swallowed. His eyes flickered to me, but it was his mum he looked at as he whispered, 'Sorry.'

SAM

I felt peculiarly calm as I left Nadina's. I noticed far more of what was around me than usual – the smell of frying, the different languages spoken by people I passed, the bluish grey of the clouds. Maybe that was what happened when you finally decided to face the world.

I walked straight into the police station, took out a memory stick from my pocket and laid it on the counter where the officer on reception duty was sitting. I cleared my throat.

'There's something on here you need to see.'

Explaining everything to the police wasn't as straightforward as I expected. For starters, they wouldn't speak to me without calling Tamsin. She sort of deserved to hear this from me, not in the police station, I thought, feeling bad that I hadn't even rung to let her know I was back. I felt even worse when she started to cry the moment she came through the doors.

'Where were you?' she cried. 'I was worried! I was this close to reporting you missing!'

'Didn't think you'd really care.' Yet again I wished that I'd thought things through, but I hadn't, and as Imogen might say, I had to deal with that now.

When Tamsin had calmed down we were invited into an interview room. It was cold and dimly lit, with uncomfortable plastic chairs either side of a table that wobbled. I could tell from the expressions of the two officers waiting for us that they were taking this very seriously. Not a surprise, considering what was on the memory stick.

'*So there's just the one copy? You've not backed it up anywhere?*' the guy with the gravelly voice had said on the phone. He'd sounded amused. Thinking what a loser I was, no doubt. And believing me when I said I hadn't.

The joke's on you, I thought, and I almost felt good. Of *course* I'd backed the video up. I might have been terrified, but I wasn't stupid. Speaking to Nadina had finally persuaded me to do what I was doing now. I couldn't carry on living my life in fear. Hamdi was dead, but I could at least see that he got some justice. I knew it was dangerous to accuse people, but I'd been overlooking the fact that I had hard evidence in the video. This was the best chance anyone was ever going to get to see that these thugs got what they deserved. The police wanted to know everything. They remained poker-faced when I described how I'd filmed the attack, but I did wonder how much they judged me for hiding when a man was being pummelled to death just metres away, especially as I'd stayed long enough to film most of it.

I also filled them in on what had happened since. This meant I had no choice but to bring Imogen into it. Sorry, I thought. I hope you can understand why it has to be this way.

'Thanks, Sam,' one officer said when I was done. 'I know it takes guts to speak up. This is very valuable evidence. It would have been more valuable still had you come to us earlier. There was another attack on a shop on Saturday night and we believe it's the same group responsible. If you'd spoken up, we might have been able to prevent that incident.'

I squirmed. 'I know that now. Sorry.'

'However,' the other officer flashed me a smile, 'thanks to this footage, we should be able to crack this. Just to double check — you say you can definitely identify one of the three young men you filmed in the shop.'

'Yes. I wasn't sure at first, but I recognized his scarf and a bangle, and his body language, and then I knew.' I drew a breath. 'You see, I go to school with him. His name's Ollie Moreno.'

As Tamsin drove home — and as the police set off to haul Ollie in and speak to Imogen — I wondered how different my decisions would have been if Ollie hadn't been involved. Somehow, when you had the power to shop someone you knew, it felt like there was more at stake, which when you thought about it was totally illogical. This was murder, whichever way you looked at it.

Ever since what had happened at Colchester station, I'd

played an unfair game with Imogen. She'd leaped to the conclusion that the gang had got to us through Ollie; that he was their captive and we needed to save him. Whereas I'd known all along that it was just an elaborate stage piece designed to manipulate her. It wasn't very smart – I could have blown the act at any point by telling Imogen that Ollie was one of them. I guessed the gang had been banking on me being scared enough to keep my mouth shut.

Well, it was out now. Imogen would discover through the police rather than me what her boyfriend had done. I felt strangely deflated about that. All the times I'd got cold feet and all the lies I'd told to hide what it really was I couldn't say – bad decisions at every turn. I still wasn't even sure why I'd felt quite so awful about breaking the news to her. In a weird way, I supposed it was as simple as this: I liked Imogen and hadn't wanted her to hate me because of what I'd seen, because of what my evidence would mean. And stupidly I'd felt like it was my problem, something I should sort out on my own. I'd been scared and had convinced myself that shutting up was the best solution. I'd made one wrong call after another. When I looked back now, it all seemed so stupid. I shouldn't have been a coward. I should never have got Imogen involved. And I should have gone to the police straight away.

Would Imogen turn against me for what I'd done? Would her heart be broken and she'd never forgive me?

I hoped not. I'd watched Imogen and Ollie a lot over the past couple of weeks, and despite what Imogen said, their relationship seemed more friendly than romantic. Maybe I'd read too many books, but I did wonder if they'd just fallen into going out. Maybe once she got over the shock she'd be more OK without him than she thought.

Maybe I was just thinking these things because deep down I wanted there to be nothing there.

Tamsin braked sharply, jolting us both forward. I saw that we were at a red light.

'Sorry,' she said. 'I should pay more attention.'

I peered at her. Tamsin was still as pale as she'd been in the police station. She'd placed a hand on her forehead, and despite the sweater she was wearing, she was shivering. 'Are you feeling OK?'

'No, not really. And that horrible video hasn't made me feel any better.'

'Shall I make you a cup of something when we get in? I mean . . .' I struggled for the words. 'I have a bit of making up to do.'

I couldn't quite bring myself to apologize. Somehow I felt as if apologizing would drag up all the bigger things I never talked about to Tamsin or Dad. Like how I felt about slotting into their lives, and how they really felt about me being here. I wasn't ready to go there.

'Thanks.' Tamsin sniffed, and I opened the glove

compartment to find her a tissue. She had just enough time to blow her nose before the light changed.

My thoughts turned back to the video. Would I ever forget that sickening sequence of events? It had been just two guys who'd run into the shop to start with. My film didn't show them very clearly – they were dressed to rob, anonymously. They'd both gone straight to Hamdi and started threatening him. He was opening up the till when they first laid into him. Was he not doing it quickly enough or had they just wanted to hurt someone? Their mindset was too far from my own for me to even begin to imagine.

It was at this point that Ollie had appeared. He was wearing his usual jeans and sports sweater. He'd made an effort to disguise himself by putting his scarf over his face, but I'd got a good look at him. Perhaps Ollie hadn't known about his friends' plans. The others shouted at him to take the cash as they continued to beat Hamdi. Unless he'd joined in after I'd got out, Ollie hadn't laid a finger on Hamdi himself.

I guessed this meant that the police would be more lenient on Ollie, especially if he gave over the others' names. Would he wind up in prison, or the teenage equivalent, because I'd come forward? Even though I knew I couldn't really be held to blame, I still felt uncomfortable. I mean, this was Ollie Moreno here, Mr Perfect, whom I'd never really liked because he was cooler and better-looking than me. How narrow my world had been before this had happened.

IMOGEN

MONDAY 18 NOVEMBER

When I got home the front door was locked. Relieved that I was alone, I collapsed on the sofa. The last thing I felt like was facing Mum. Not just because she'd still be pissed off, but because pretty soon either she or Dad was going to need to accompany me to the police station. That's what the officers who'd taken Ollie and Maria Paula off had said. They seemed to know I was involved. There was only one person I could think of who would have been able to tell them that.

This was doing my head in. I went upstairs to change into my trackies and trainers. Soon I was outside again and running to the park, hoping that crisp air and the feeling of my soles bouncing off tarmac would help me to make sense of things.

Ollie had been arrested, for God's sake! He'd crumbled when the police had come. As though he'd been expecting it. He hadn't said he was innocent. He hadn't said anything at all. Apart from 'sorry'.

It was the way he'd looked at his mum that told me without a shadow of a doubt that there was no mistake.

My frustration mounting, I put on a burst of speed. How could Ollie do this? How could he take part in a murder? He wasn't a killer, he wasn't a criminal. He'd never even been violent, for God's sake! He was supposed to be one of the good guys!

It began to drizzle again. I looked at the grey, heavy skyline. Even in the park, I could see buildings all around me. For the first time I felt like Walthamstow was a sealed glass tank and I was struggling to breathe.

I didn't want to think about Ollie. Instead I thought about Sam. He'd known about Ollie all along. That must have been what he'd shied away from telling me. Maybe he wanted to get me on his side in some weird way, before he went to the police. Right now I was too angry at him for letting me go through the stress of yesterday to begin to try to work out what might have gone on in his head. Why hadn't he just told me the truth? Who had he been trying to protect? Himself, or me?

When I reached home the lights were on. I unlocked the door and went through to the kitchen. Mum was sitting at the table with a coffee, on the phone. When she saw me she covered the receiver.

'Stay right there. Sorry, Immy just came in. Yes, just rearrange my 4 p.m. appointment. Thanks, Sandra. Bye.' She placed the phone back in the receiver and gave me a look. 'What's going on, Imogen? And what's happened to your glasses?'

I hadn't expected Mum to notice I was wearing my old pair. Much bigger things passed her by, such as the fact that I clearly hadn't gone to sixth form today. I sat down, unzipping my tracksuit top. 'The police have called, obviously. So you don't need to ask me, do you?'

'All I've been told is that the police want to speak to you in relation to these break-ins and the death of that poor young man. They made it clear you weren't involved directly.' Mum took a sip of coffee. The tightness of her body language told me she was annoyed but she clearly wasn't going to let rip until she'd heard me out. 'We're not going down to the station until you tell me everything, so you'd better start talking. I'm not angry, but I want the full story.'

There was no point staying silent so I did as she said. Mum started off interrupting constantly, but after I snapped at her she listened silently – well, silently apart from when I mentioned I'd been roughed up. She made a huge fuss and demanded to look at my stomach. I felt a weird sense of satisfaction as she exclaimed at the large bruise.

When I was done, Mum said, 'I can barely believe this – God, Immy! Are you sure you're not in pain? We should get a doctor to look at that bruise. You should have done it yesterday. You were right by the hospital when it happened, for goodness sake.'

'Well, I didn't. Shoot me.'

'That isn't funny. What a mess!'

'Sorry,' I said in an offhand voice. 'All this just happened and I couldn't stop it.'

'Imogen –' Mum folded her arms, face troubled – 'I still don't understand. Why on earth didn't you tell anyone you were being threatened? You know how serious cyber-bullying is. For God's sake, they *beat you up*!'

She stressed each of the last three words. I stared at the table in front of me. I could see a ring from a coffee cup in the reflection. I concentrated very hard on how the light fell on the table, and how it made it shine. I heard Mum sigh.

'I'm your mother. You're –' Mum's voice dipped a little. 'Well, you're my baby, though you're not so little any more. This shouldn't be happening to you. Not by yourself. I'm here for you. I wish you'd told me. I wish you'd told the police. Why didn't you?'

'I just didn't,' I said, softly but firmly.

I felt Mum's stare. She looked as though she was either going to burst into tears or come down on me like a ton of bricks and say how much I'd disappointed her. I waited to see which it would be. Instead I heard her chair squeak, and then the splash of water. Looking up, I saw that she was filling the kettle.

'Coffee?'

I nodded. Mum took two fresh mugs from the cupboard. Gently she said, 'I'm having a tough time believing your Ollie is involved in this. He seems such a dependable young man. Focused, with his head screwed on.'

'He's not "my" Ollie.' I snapped. I didn't want to talk to Mum about this, but I couldn't help it. I'd suddenly realized how angry I was. 'I don't want anything to do with someone who's done what he has! How could he do something so totally out of order? We ran an anti-bullying campaign together, Mum. He hated gangs and violence then. Clearly not any more! God – it's like he was leading a double life!'

'People go along with things for lots of reasons, Immy. Ollie may have got pressured into a situation he then couldn't get out of.'

He should've been strong enough to say no, I thought. He should have known what was right. 'Yeah, well, shoulda thought about that before he started hanging round with violent killers.'

'So you think he's guilty then.'

'I saw his face when the police came for him, Mum.'

The kettle clicked. 'Let's have these, calm down, then go to the police. And the doctor. No arguing.'

'I want this sorted,' I said. 'I want to get on with my life without all this crap.'

'Crap happens. Get used to it.' If there hadn't been softness in Mum's voice she'd have sounded like she was on her high horse again. I took the coffee she handed me. This hadn't been as bad as I'd feared. Mum was being calm and reasonable rather than complaining how I'd disrupted her day. There had even, if I wasn't mistaken, been a hint of sympathy there too. I hadn't even been grilled about our argument yesterday. Perhaps she realized this wasn't the moment. Or perhaps my injury had shocked her into caring for once. Either way, for the first time in a while, I was grateful she was there.

SAM
TUESDAY 19 NOVEMBER

Being back at sixth form after everything I'd been through felt surreal. I sat in English literature feeling even more out of the loop than usual. I couldn't bring myself to care about the novel we were studying. It was just a story and seemed silly. For a change I was preoccupied with real life. So much could happen in a week.

I didn't feel like reading in a classroom at lunchtime. Before I knew where I was going I was in the canteen at one of the vending machines. As I picked up my can of Pepsi Max, I heard Imogen's voice behind me.

'And here I was thinking I was going to have to trawl all the hidey-holes this school has to offer to find you.'

'Oh. Hi there.' I turned, hands automatically smoothing down my shirt. I never knew why I did that – an automatic response from when I'd been bigger maybe.

It felt weird to be talking to Imogen so publicly. I couldn't help remembering what Nadina had said about Imogen finding me 'strangely intriguing'. Maybe she'd wanted to speak to me at school in the past but my unfriendliness had put her off.

Encouragingly, Imogen didn't appear to be too mad at me over yesterday. She suggested we went somewhere away from the crowd. 'Figure you're the expert,' she said. We ended up sitting by the radiator in one of the fourth-floor English rooms.

'You had your stitches out,' Imogen said, taking a banana and a muesli bar out of her bag. I nodded.

'I had an appointment first thing. The nurse said the scar's healing well, my wrist too, though that never really gave me any trouble at all. No Nadina today?'

'Nah, her mum wanted her to rest up. Nads was all set to argue but then she remembered she had a mock exam.' She sighed. 'I need to go over. Still don't feel I apologized properly.'

When I looked quizzical, Imogen explained that she and Nadina had fallen out because she'd accused Nadina of telling Ollie that she'd been to see me. I'd known Ollie had been scared of the hold I'd had over him, but I hadn't really clocked before that he'd been jealous too. After all, it must have looked to him like I'd been seeing his girlfriend behind his back.

'If Nadina says she didn't, you have to believe her,' I said. 'She's your best friend. There are tons of other ways Ollie could have found out – one of the other girls you were with at lunch could have mentioned it maybe.'

Imogen swore. 'Why didn't I think this through? And why d'you have to be right all the time?'

'Don't know about right. Just trying to be logical, which normally I'm not.'

Imogen watched as I opened up my lunch, a ham-and-tomato sandwich and some crisps. 'Talking of Nads, I hear you paid her a visit.'

I hesitated. 'I thought that if Nadina or her dad had seen the guys I might not need to show the police the video.' I took a deep breath and looked her in the eye. 'About that . . . I'm sorry I lied to you about not backing it up. And I'm sorry you had to hear about, you know, Ollie, from the police rather than me. That can't have been easy.'

She nodded. 'It wasn't.'

Unnerved by how calm she was I said, 'Why aren't you chewing me out about everything?'

'Chewing on something else, that's why,' Imogen said, toasting me with her banana. When I just stared, she sighed. 'That was a joke. Sometimes when everything's completely crap all you can do is laugh, y'know? In that hysterical fake happy kind of way.'

'You're a bit scary like this. I think I prefer being yelled at.' I opened the crisps. She took a couple when I offered.

'More seriously, I don't know what to think.'

'That makes two of us. Aren't you . . .' I hesitated, 'upset? About Ollie?'

Imogen shrugged. 'I don't want to talk about him.'

'Sometimes it's the people around us that help us know who we really are. When they go, you end up in a kind of crisis.'

'Sounds like you're speaking from experience.'

It suddenly struck me that never in a million years could I have believed I'd be having a conversation like this with Imogen Maxwell, with her asking questions and actually sounding interested.

'I suppose I am,' I went on, and told her about Mum, and how since the age of thirteen I'd had to come to terms with the fact that sooner or later she'd be leaving me forever. About Dad, and how it had felt to move in with him and Tamsin. About how alien school had felt to me. When I got to that part, Imogen laughed.

'You like to make life hard for yourself. So basically, you flung friendliness back in my face because you were being a judgemental jerk.'

I felt my cheeks colour. 'That's not fair! It was different. I was a total outsider, no one was into the same stuff as me . . . making friends was always going to be impossible –'

'How is that not being a judgemental jerk?'

It took me a moment to realize that her tone had been teasing.

'Sorry,' I huffed. 'It was just hard for me, settling in somewhere new. I suppose . . . I suppose I wasn't confident enough to try. After Mum died, I sort of didn't really know who I was any more. I'd been so focused on looking after her, I guess I lost sight of me. It was easier to avoid everyone and not have to deal with it.'

She smiled. 'It was a bit like that for me when we first moved here from Kent. I guess it was so long ago I'd forgotten about how weird it was. And there was me thinking you were just trying to act all superior and mysterious!'

The idea of me being mysterious was funny enough to make me laugh. 'Isn't it only brooding vampires who are mysterious?'

Imogen grinned. 'For all I knew, you could've been a vampire. It's not like you let anyone get to know you. Just so you know, we're really not so different from you northerners. We're all human. We feel the same things. And actually? We can be OK when you give us a chance.'

'Well, I'm all right too when you give me a chance,' I replied.

Imogen gave me one of the wry *yeah, right* looks that I was beginning to like. 'Seriously, Sam – you've been through a lot. But that's then, this is now, and now doesn't need to be bad if you don't let it. Your mum would want you to make the best of things, right?'

'I'm not sure Mum would like me buddying up with my young, pretty stepmum.'

Imogen made a face. 'C'mon, Tamsin seems OK. What's she do for a living, anyway? Always seems to be at home.'

'She's an actress, but she's taking some time out before the next job. Actually she's really under the weather right now. I made pancakes this morning and she couldn't face them.'

'Think she's pregnant?'

The thought hadn't remotely crossed my mind.

Imogen laughed at my dumbstruck expression. 'Anyone would think you didn't know what that meant. I bet she is; she told me she was off booze too.'

Oh, help, I thought. A little brother or sister? That would be a massive change. My reply was cut off by the buzzer. I realized I'd been talking so much that I hadn't even started on my sandwich.

IMOGEN

It was Benno's reading-club day with Sam, so I was able to go straight to Nadina's. I realized as I walked that I was constantly checking my phone. No news was good news right now.

When I arrived Nads was sprawled on the couch in front of the telly drinking a lumpy brown concoction. When I asked what it was, she told me it was bean chilli.

'Sam's suggestion. Beats bananas, that's for sure.'

It was so odd; the words were Nadina, but the husky voice wasn't. I handed her the hairspray I'd picked up in Superdrug on the way over.

'Guessed you might be running low on stock,' I said. 'Can't have a disaster like that happening. And, I guess it's a bit of a peace offering. Look, babe, I hate bringing this up, cos it makes me feel like crap, but I owe you an apology. That argument we had about someone telling Ollie I'd been to Sam's? I'm proper sorry I didn't believe it wasn't you. Not the kind of thing a best mate does, eh?'

'It's all right.' Nads shrugged. Somehow, something about the action made me pause . . . I was remembering something. Nadina, in the hospital. Unable to talk, but using my phone to text an apology.

I did something really crap that makes me a bad mate.

At the time I'd taken that as confirmation that I'd been right to get mad at her for telling Ollie what I'd been up to. But if that *wasn't* her, then what was it she'd done?

I asked what she'd meant. Nadina groaned. 'Don't make me tell you. Really not what you're gonna want to hear right now. It *is* to do with Ollie, but not in the way you thought.'

'I don't want anything to do with Ollie any more,' I snapped. 'So rock on. I don't care.'

When she saw that I wasn't budging, Nadina shifted her position on the couch, putting aside the bean drink. Reluctantly she said, 'The Monday after the chicken–shop thing, I went round Kimmie's. She lives on the same estate as Ollie. A guy Kimmie knows came over and said there was a party going on a few flats down. I know.' She caught my sceptical look. 'Party on a school night, right? The guy throwing it was older than us, out of work. Unplanned birthday thing or something. Anyway, wasn't much of a party. Just a few people and bottles and loud music, but . . .'

'But?' I prompted.

Nads looked away. 'Ollie was there. He was in a right mood. Angry and upset and acting plain weird. He'd had a bit to drink. A bit too much, y'know?'

That wasn't the Ollie I knew. But then, I hadn't really known him at all, had I? 'Go on.'

'I went over to say hi. Ollie went off on one about how

he'd seen you and Sam together and how you were lying to him about it . . .'

Suddenly it made sense. Ollie had never believed me about not liking Sam, even before I'd been round his house. He'd seemed to think there was something going on. Now I knew that Ollie had been in the Gul's shop that night. He'd have seen Sam running away with Mia. A tall, blonde girl with glasses. He must've assumed Mia was me! It was an easy mistake. Hell, even I'd thought that photo of her was me for a moment. And when Sam came to the chicken shop, wanting to speak to me, any suspicions Ollie had would've been confirmed.

No wonder he'd been convinced I'd lied about Sam. God, he would have been scared I knew he'd done the robbery, though it must've become clear I didn't. He'd even checked out my phone to see if I had the video . . .

Hang on. The other guys . . . They'd texted me on that phone. They had my number. And they'd known where I was when they'd beaten me up near the hospital.

Only Ollie could have given them this information!

Nadina was still talking. 'Didn't get what Ollie was going on about, to be honest. Thought it was the booze talking. I told him he oughta go home. We left the party together. Then, when we were outside . . . He made a move on me, Im.'

She spoke over my exclamation. 'It was just a snog. A

clumsy drunk snog at that. And, well, this is why I'm such a crap mate . . . I let him. I felt bloody awful afterwards. I'm so sorry, Im. It was such a sucky thing to do.' She looked so small and ashamed of herself that weirdly, instead of anger I almost felt sorry for her.

Nadina had fancied Ollie long before we'd got together, only he hadn't been interested. Why had I assumed those feelings would go away just because I started going out with him? 'Did anything else happen?' I said. It came out sounding colder than I meant it to.

'No! Honest! It was obvious straight away he only did it cos I was there and he was drunk and in a really weird mood. And I felt a bit upset after too. Used, y'know? Like he'd just done it to see if he could. He texted as soon as I'd left asking me not to tell you. I wanted to, but . . . I was just so ashamed . . . And then the stuff with Hamdi blew up and I guess I thought maybe it'd be better for everyone if I just kept quiet. So that's it. Can you forgive me, Immy?'

I stretched my arms behind my head. I should feel hurt and betrayed, but instead I just felt empty.

'Please don't hate me,' whispered Nadina, her eyes shiny with tears. 'I couldn't deal with any of this crap without you.'

I shut my eyes and took a slow, deep breath. 'It's not your fault, Nads. And I get why you never said anything. Yeah, maybe if things were different I'd be angry, but as I said, I don't want anything to do with Ollie any more. I hope he gets what he deserves. Just be truthful with me in future, OK? You're my best mate and I want to trust you.'

There was a silence. I looked away. Out of the corner of my eye I saw Nadina wipe her eyes.

'Im,' she said, 'you *can* trust me. I promise. And I get that you're upset that Ollie was in on this robbery crap. Imagine how I feel. I mean, he did over my effing shop! His mates broke my jaw and beat up my dad, an old man! But he was just the lookout. And from what the police said to me this morning, he didn't touch Hamdi either. This is Ollie we're talking about. We've known him for years. Do you seriously believe he'd happily go along with robbery and assault and *murder*?'

I'd seen Sam's video. The police had showed it to me. I hoped one day I could forget how awful it'd made me feel. At least the fact that Ollie hadn't touched Hamdi was a silver lining, I supposed.

'I bet he didn't want to be there, Im. Even tough people get pressured into things. There's more to this – there's gotta be.'

'If he was unwilling, then why didn't he tell the police that? He's taking all the blame himself!'

She gave me a knowing look. 'World's not black and white, Im. Sometimes I think that's something you don't get. Remember what I said when we had our bust-up?'

I felt a twinge inside me. 'To listen to my heart.'

'Exactly. And what's your heart telling you about Ollie? Forget your head. Forget evidence! What's your gut instinct saying?'

I thought about the Ollie I'd known before everything had turned upside down. He had his tough side, sure, but that only ever came out at the right moments. Like when he needed to be firm with bullies, or sort out a fight. He had great judgement and knew right from wrong. The rest of the time . . . he was hardworking. Certain. Fun. He knew what he wanted from life. When he talked about getting out of the rat race, going to university, earning enough money to make a decent life for him and his mum, there was something different about him.

That was the real Ollie. Why had I ever doubted it?

SAM

I left home earlier than usual, hoping to catch Imogen. I knew she often got into sixth form well before lessons began and sure enough I found her sitting on the common-room sofa with a cup of tea and a packet of custard creams, finishing off a worksheet. There were a few others in the kitchen, but they were deep in conversation and didn't notice when I joined Imogen.

'The police called to update us yesterday,' I said in a low voice. 'Ollie's the only identifiable one. You can't tell who the others are. This means the only real link is if Ollie names them.'

Imogen pursed her lips. 'So whoever they are, they could say he's lying? That's not very comforting.'

She offered me a biscuit.

'I love custard creams, but no thanks.'

'If you love them, what harm's one going to do? One biscuit won't make you balloon. You're a good-looking guy, Sam; stop beating yourself up.'

I felt my cheeks burn. The fact that Imogen thought I was good-looking had completely thrown me. I'd been overweight so long that it was still hard not to see myself as a big guy — even with all these sharp-fitting new clothes. I really needed to come to terms with who I was now — not with who I'd been before.

SAM

As I took a biscuit the buzzer went for class. Imogen and I cleared the table and headed off to begin the day. I passed Nadina as I was going into history. She gave me a small smile and a wave and I took my seat feeling like sixth form had suddenly become a much friendlier place.

IMOGEN

I don't know what I expected to find outside Ollie's house. A police cordon? An officer? A big sign saying 'Do not pass'? But it was the same as usual, apart from that this time Maria Paula had no smile for me when she opened the door. It was clear she'd been crying. I guessed she'd not been at work. I looked round at the bare hallway and thought of the mismatched charity-shop furniture in the main room. All Ollie's mum has is him, I thought. Her son, who, according to the script, should soon get out of this place and have a brilliant life. And it has all come crashing down.

There weren't too many places Ollie could hide in a flat this size. I found him in his room, lying on the bed with his arms behind his head. I squeezed round the door. There wasn't a chair so I leaned against the wall. Ollie's bedroom was, literally, a room with a bed in it. Last I'd seen, there'd been basketball and football posters on the wall. This time they were scrunched up in the bin.

I cleared my throat. All last night and all today I'd thought about how to do this, but now I was here finding words was hard. 'I shouldn't be here. Police expressly told me not to — conflict of interests and all. But guess what, I am.'

Ollie didn't move. I waited. After a long moment he shifted into a sitting position, back to the wall. His face wasn't giving much away but something about the way his shoulders were hunched made him look haunted. It had been all very well to say those things about him being guilty and deserving what he got. Now he was in front of me, it wasn't so easy to feel that way.

'What?' he asked.

'I want to know why you got involved in this.'

He shrugged. From nearby I heard Maria Paula talking. On the phone I guessed. She was speaking Spanish, but her tone sounded on the edge of hysteria. I closed the door.

Another silence. I folded my arms behind my back. Ollie stared down at the mattress. He was wearing a T-shirt and what looked like pyjama trousers. His feet were bare. When had he last gone out? Was he even allowed to? The police might have told him to stay in. For an active guy it must feel like being in hell.

Eventually he said, 'No point you being here, Im. There's nothing to say.'

'Your mum knows everything, I'm guessing.'

'All my mum knows,' Ollie said, 'is that I helped some guys hold up a newsagents' and while they were beating the bloke to death, I was raiding the till, and then a week later we did another shop.'

'Nadina's shop.'

'Yeah.'

He was being so matter of fact. I hadn't expected him to

be sobbing, but I'd expected some feeling. 'She must have asked how this began.'

'Best she thinks I just fell into it.'

'So there *is* a reason.'

Ollie drew the duvet over his knees. 'Leave it.'

No chance, I thought. 'You never say much about your mum. You're certainly her world.'

Ollie flinched. 'I let her down. Don't need you to tell me that.'

'If you explained—'

'Did what I did. End of.'

He wasn't making eye contact but at least he was talking. 'You didn't just fall in with this,' I said. 'That's not you. I don't know why you're protecting these lowlifes by not telling the police who they are, but I'm willing to guess they've some hold on you, or you're scared, or something that makes sense. Because I know you'd never willingly do something that'd hurt your mum.'

I perched on the side of the bed. Ollie immediately turned away.

'I'm not going till you tell me,' I said.

After a silence that seemed to last a long time, Ollie put his hand on his forehead. In a voice that suddenly sounded choked up, he said, 'I'm never gonna get past this. This is my life down the drain, just like that. We came here to escape this stuff.'

He was talking about when he and his mum had left Colombia, I realized. Feeling like I was a broken record, I said, 'Why did you get into this?'

Outside, Maria Paula's voice was getting louder. Ollie gripped the duvet. 'I wanted to be better than this. Now I'll be a sodding statistic. Just another immigrant kid with a record.'

'Talk to me. What've you got to lose?'

Ollie drew in a breath. 'Back in August some guy two doors down threw a party. No one sleeps when those go on. People from sixth form were there, so I thought I might as well go too. Wasn't my scene, but then I got talking to this guy Paz.'

It wasn't a name I recognized. 'He lives on the next estate,' Ollie said. 'He's a mechanic, couple of years older. Great footballer too. He came over from Colombia like me. We were so similar it was unreal. He just got stuff without me spelling it out, y'know? Proper deep things no one else could understand.'

Having the same background counted, I guessed. Maybe Colombia was a bigger part of Ollie than I'd realized. He never really talked about it. All I knew was that he and Maria Paula had come over as refugees several years back and been granted political asylum.

He continued. 'It was like, I dunno, having this older brother suddenly. Paz remembers what it was like in

Colombia better than I do. He could tell me things. My mum doesn't talk about stuff from before. I get it – she wants to forget. Dunno, used to be OK with that. Now it bugs me. I don't really know why we had to run away. I know it was because of violence. Someone Mum knew got shot dead, maybe even a family member, but that's it. Don't even know who my dad is or if he's still out there. Those are big things I've a right to know, Im. It's my life too. But there's no point asking Mum. She won't tell. So meeting Paz was like finding a bit of me I didn't know. Man.' Ollie made a noise that was almost a laugh.

Now I'd got him talking, I didn't want to break his flow. 'So if Paz was so great, why did you never mention him?'

Ollie rubbed his forehead. 'Felt disloyal, like I was going behind Mum's back, asking 'bout things she wants dead and buried. Paz ain't on the straight and narrow either. He's got stolen goods he sells on. Nothing major, just small stuff. And he carries a knife. Not that that's unusual, but one time we were out, he used it to threaten some mouthy kids. I don't act like that and I don't do weapons. I didn't like that he did. But when you're, I dunno, holding someone up to be something great, you make excuses for them. Didn't want him to think less of me either. So the other things he did that didn't sit right I ignored too. A few weeks back . . .'

He hesitated, dark eyes fleeting to mine. He's afraid, I realized.

'What?' I prompted.

Ollie took a breath and blew it out slowly. Almost inaudibly he muttered, 'A few weeks back Paz introduced me to the McAllister twins.'

I felt the colour drain from my face. This was worse than I could possibly have imagined.

I knew who the McAllister twins were. Everyone did. Josh and Dale McAllister were brutal scumbags who didn't give a damn, and if you cared about your life you bloody well didn't get on the wrong side of them.

I'd only ever seen the twins from a distance, but they were practically identical. Pale, almost transparent complexions, close-cropped fair hair, long faces and rangy all-arms-and-legs build that I'd heard was deceptively strong. These guys were seriously mean. They were only a year older than us but already notorious. Their patch was the next estate to Ollie's. Both had been cautioned but never charged. Everyone knew what they'd got away with though – assaults, break-ins, a couple of stabbings. I'd heard a particularly nasty story of what Josh McAllister had done to a guy who'd hit on his girlfriend.

Now I understood why Ollie wasn't speaking up. A chill ran through me.

Then I realized something worse. The McAllisters knew who I was.

'We are totally in the shit,' I said.

Ollie gave me a humourless smile. 'Understatement.'

I took a moment to work through this new information. God! How lucky had I been that time they'd gone through my phone? They'd only hit me a few times. By McAllister standards, that was getting off very lightly.

Anger surged through me at the thought that Ollie had given them my number, my location, told them that threatening Benno would be a good way to get to me. With effort, I held it in. If I had a go at him now I would never get to the bottom of this. 'Why didn't you get the hell out before things even began, Ollie? You recognized them, right?'

'Of course! But we were on a patch I didn't know. I was freaked by what they might do if I left. And y'know, it wasn't so bad. I acted hard. Almost felt like I was hanging out with regular dudes. Then Paz left.' He drew a breath. 'I should've left too, but I couldn't think how without pissing them off. So I stayed. Guess which night this was.'

'When the Guls' shop was done?'

'You got it,' he spat with a humourless laugh. 'It was the first time I'd bloody met them! They'd drunk a bit and were in a dodgy mood, but I had no idea they were going to do a job until we were there and then I couldn't get out. They told me to be lookout. Didn't even think of not doing what they said. I was shitting myself.' Ollie shook his head. 'I never wanted to help them do Nadina's shop! I tried to get out of it – I even tried to warn Nads – but Josh and Dale blackmailed me. I felt trapped.'

'What about Sam?' I asked.

Ollie made a noise that if I hadn't known better was almost a sob. 'That was the worst. I saw him in the Guls' shop. But I didn't rat on him. And he didn't rat on me. He didn't even tell you what I'd done, and you were with him that night! I thought he'd want to turn you against me. But then . . . that night at the chicken shop . . . when I saw him with you *again*, I knew he'd changed his mind.'

'Ollie, it was never like that at all! I wasn't with him the night of the Guls' shop. It was Sam's bloody cousin.'

'Well, she sure looked like you.'

'It's true, Ollie. It wasn't me.'

With a sigh he finally looked me in the eye. 'Put yourself in my shoes, the night at the chicken shop. The guy you know has seen you committing a crime comes along wanting to speak to your girlfriend in private. You seemed pretty keen to go with him. I don't care what you say – you've always had a soft spot for Sam. The idea that someone like him . . . not only knew this stuff about me, but was seeing my girl behind my back . . . it just made me see red! I phoned Josh and Dale. Tipped them off about Sam. Told them where he was.'

He spoke over my exclamation. 'I swear, Im, if I'd known they were gonna try to kill him and you'd get involved, I'd never've said anything! They were right round the corner; I had no idea.' He leaned back. 'That's all. The whole sodding sorry story. Now tell me how you knowing this makes it better.'

I ran a hand through my hair. It felt in need of a wash. Out of the corner of my eye I caught sight of the bin again. I wondered if Ollie had torn up his posters because they reminded him of the old him, the squeaky-clean prefect who wanted to be a sports star.

'You put me in danger,' I said. 'And Benno. My *little* brother!' I was surprised by how well I'd kept my anger under wraps. 'You told them where I was, gave them my number, told them the best way to get under my skin. To threaten me. They beat me up! How could you do that to me?'

Ollie looked miserable. 'They made me. I'm sorry, OK? I didn't think they were going to be that brutal.' More softly he went on, 'Believe me, I feel bad enough already. I really didn't want you or Benno to ever get hurt. And I never wanted to worry you like that during that whole stupid Essex trip either, but by that point they had me in it and I had no choice but to play along. I thought, if they can get the video off Sam, then maybe this'll finally stop.'

'Why didn't you dump me if you thought I was cheating on you?' I thought aloud.

'Immy. You were all I had left.'

It was a confused reason. But in an odd way it made sense. Ollie hadn't intended me to be in the accident by the chicken shop. Now I looked back I realized that buying me chocolates and taking me out the day after had been his guilty conscious speaking. He'd been angry and upset with me, thinking I might have something going on with Sam, but never quite sure enough to break it off. The rest of the time he'd been scared witless by the McAllisters. Enough to make a whole chain of seriously bad calls.

I wasn't furious any more. Instead I just felt sorry for him.

'This is such a mess,' I said. 'Look, Ollie, you didn't want this. You've never done anything like this before. You have to play that up to the police. You might get off lightly. Please . . .' I met his gaze, 'don't protect the McAllisters. I don't care if they've threatened you or me or your mum if you speak up. Tell the police. It's your only chance, Ollie. You need to get out of this. For your mum, and for you. Hell, if you won't speak up, I bloody will!'

Ollie gave me a funny kind of smile. 'Guess you've made the decision for me, huh? You're gonna give evidence.' He didn't need to add *against me*.

'Have to, Ols.' Suddenly I felt a bit choked up myself. 'But this isn't me against you. It's us against the McAllisters. We've got to get Josh and Dale locked up else they'll come after me, Sam, you. Benno. Your mum even. You know how things work round here. You don't speak out unless you're brave, stupid or you're bloody sure a trial's gonna go your way. There's no wussing out now.'

'Else we're dead.' Ollie stated it like a fact. 'Some threats are empty. Josh and Dale's ain't.'

I ignored the shiver that went down my back. 'It won't come to that.'

I realized that Maria Paula's phone call had ended. Hesitating just one moment, I leaned forward and gave Ollie a brief hug. To my surprise, he returned it.

'We were good for a while, weren't we, Im?' he murmured.

I opened my mouth to ask what he meant. But then I realized I already knew.

'Yeah. We were. Don't you forget it.' I managed a smile. 'Good luck, OK, Ollie?'

I got up, the spring of the mattress sounding very loud in the sudden silence. As I crept out of Ollie's room and then through the front door, half of me felt like I'd learned an awful lot. The other half felt like I knew nothing at all.

SAM

NOVEMBER AND DECEMBER

In English literature this term we were doing *A Tale of Two Cities*. It was a Charles Dickens novel and I wasn't too keen on it, if I'm honest, but it opened with a famous line that really said something to me: *It was the best of times, it was the worst of times*. That summed up perfectly the weird limbo period before the McAllisters' trial. Unlike Ollie, they were being kept in custody. So for the meantime we had every reason to feel safe.

He'd given their names to the police the day Imogen had gone round. She didn't say much about how she'd got Ollie to speak up, but she did fill me in so that I knew exactly who we were dealing with.

Dad came back from Copenhagen the same day I received the youth-court summons with the date of when I was expected to give evidence. I was upstairs with Jessie doing homework when I heard his voice downstairs. Tamsin can explain, I thought, and waited for the inevitable. Sure enough, I heard him bellow, 'Sam!'

Slowly I went downstairs. Dad was leaning against the counter in the kitchen, tie loosened. He looked tired and frazzled from his journey. He also looked furious. But when he gave me a hug, I realized that it wasn't at me.

'You brave kid!' he said. 'Tammy's filled me in; I'm

proud of you for coming forward, Sam, dead proud! Tons of kids wouldn't. Do you realize that?'

I wasn't sure what I was supposed to say to that. 'Um, I guess. How was your trip?'

'It's all this fear of retribution,' Dad carried on. Tamsin, who was sitting at the table, made a letter *T* with her fingers. I nodded, and she got up to fill the kettle. 'That's why law and order's gone to pot round here – everyone's so bloody scared that they just let scum get away scot-free. If more people spoke up, the police could make a start on cleaning up our streets. As it is, gang crime's out of control. Didn't used to be this way when I was growing up here. Well, enough is enough. The turnabout starts here!'

He banged his fist against the counter. Then he started talking about beefing up the house security system and how we were going to go into that hearing all guns blazing. This wasn't unusual – Dad liked to talk big and often got ahead of himself – but as Tamsin handed me my tea I began to wonder if he had missed the point.

I finally managed to get a word in. 'Don't you mind that I might have put us in danger?'

'We shall laugh in the face of danger,' Dad said, half humorously. 'You did what you had to, kiddo, and we're behind you all the way.'

Tamsin cleared her throat. 'Yes. Both of us.'

There was something loaded in the way she said that.

Suddenly having an inkling of what was coming, I started to gabble about very important homework. Dad shushed me. Then, with a big grin on his face, he revealed that from next year I wasn't going to be the only kid in the house.

So Imogen was right! I looked at Tamsin. She didn't seem to be any bigger than usual, but then she had started wearing baggy sweaters so I probably wouldn't have noticed even if she was. She gave me a nervous smile. I realized I'd been staring and went red.

'I hope you don't mind, Sam.'

I didn't know what to say. Was Tamsin so afraid of upsetting me she had to ask? What could she do if I did? Maybe best not to answer. For the first time I realized – she wanted me to like her. It was stupid, but I'd never clocked how hard she was trying, what with giving me lifts, never asking awkward questions, even not telling Dad about my vanishing trick when really she ought to have done.

And I never gave anything back. I had to be honest with myself. I ignored how nice she was because it was too difficult to deal with. I'd assumed before I even met her that she'd want me out of the way. Even though it was clear she didn't, I still acted that way. It was exactly like I'd written everyone at school off without giving them a chance, something I now knew was definitely a mistake.

I made myself smile. To my surprise it wasn't so hard. 'Of course I don't mind!'

'See!' Dad said. 'Ready-made babysitter there! Let's toast that.'

He went to the wine rack. Tamsin shook her head. 'Phil, come on. I just made tea anyway.'

'One tiny glass, Tammy. C'mon. The baby won't complain, I'm sure. Sam, you have one too, go on.'

It suddenly struck me that Dad was going to be a bit useless with all this. I couldn't imagine him around a baby. He had plenty of energy and enthusiasm, but he wasn't patient enough. Perhaps this was an opportunity for me to get to know Tamsin better. Helping her out while she was pregnant couldn't be so different from being there for Mum when she'd been ill.

'Do you really not mind?' Tamsin whispered. 'Because I know you'd say you didn't even if you did.'

I thought about it and suddenly realized that I really, genuinely, didn't.

It was weird to suddenly be getting on better with Dad and Tamsin. I began spending more time downstairs with them in the evenings. Not too much, because I did still feel self-conscious about it, but we watched the odd programme together, and perhaps it was my imagination, but Dad paid me a lot more attention. In the evenings if he was home early enough he even tried some of my cooking. (His verdict on my chicken jalfrezi was that it was 'bloody brilliant' and I ought to be on *MasterChef*.) I couldn't help but feel chuffed. I'd avoided cooking much since moving here. It brought back too many memories of those last months with Mum. I could see now that that was silly. I couldn't stop being reminded of Mum any more than I could stop the sun from rising. Mum wouldn't want me to give up something I enjoyed. And Imogen had been right; I didn't need to worry about my weight any more. When I was looking after mum, exercising and sticking to a healthy diet weren't exactly top of my list of priorities. I was at home all the time; I cooked whatever she felt in the mood for and always ate with her to keep her company, even when I wasn't hungry. Now I was in a very different situation.

'I've overlooked you, Sam,' Dad said one evening as he was helping me load the dishwasher. 'All this has made me realize how much I leave you to get on with things, assuming you're OK. You'd say if you were unhappy, wouldn't you? If you wanted to leave?'

It took me a moment to realize what Dad meant.

'I'm fine,' I said. 'And it's OK. Here, I mean. I don't want to go back to my aunt and uncle, or my grandparents.'

'OK? Or more than OK?' Dad half smiled. Suddenly I realized how awkward this kind of thing was for him and felt a bit more at ease.

'Maybe a bit more than OK,' I said, and Dad laughed. Then he started reminiscing about the time he'd taken me to Ripley Castle when I was seven. He remembered everything in such detail I was surprised.

'Always enjoyed taking you out,' he said. 'There'll be good times to come with the baby, but those trips you and me made, Sam – they were special.'

For all I forgot it, and for all that he was wrapped up in his new life, Dad did love me.

When there were leftovers from my cooking I took them into sixth form and shared them with Imogen and sometimes Nadina, if it was something she could eat. Everyone knew about the youth court by now. The attention could get a bit much so we often hid away at lunchtimes.

'You two are becoming like I was with these hidey-holes,' I joked one day when we were sitting in the English classroom sharing some falafel I'd made.

'Not our fault everyone here is a nosy prat.' Nadina said. 'Think it'll be better or worse when court's done with? If it's worse, I'm out there playing with the traffic.'

Imogen patted Nadina on the arm. 'There are classier ways to go than being pulped by the 123. Resist. More seriously, this mess tells us something, right?'

'What? Don't mess with the bad guys?'

'Nah, 'bout people. When stuff like this happens, it shows you who your mates are. I'm dead disappointed how some of them have reacted.'

We didn't speak about Ollie at all. He wasn't allowed in school until his youth-court date. I guessed he was studying at home.

In a funny way I didn't want this good–bad limbo to end. But of course it did, because it had to, and the day came.

The day that would decide everything.

IMOGEN
TUESDAY 10 DECEMBER

I'd read the leaflet we'd been given about preparing for court thoroughly, and I'd asked Angie, the support officer I'd been assigned, questions too. None of this had quite prepared me for actually being here.

Grim, I thought, looking round at the red brick walls and plain ceilings. And youth courts were supposed to be less formal than the Crown ones! The building we were in had seen better days, with dusty windows and furniture that looked like it had been there forever. Not great for making me feel at ease.

Mum and I had a room of our own to wait in. I'd wanted to find Nadina and Sam, but Angie said it was best if I didn't. 'It's more about how it looks than anything else,' she said. 'I know you three are going to tell it how it is, but we don't want anyone accusing you of conferring and changing your stories.'

Pretty stupid thing to say considering we'd had loads of opportunities to 'confer' at sixth form, but fair enough. I leaned back in my chair and looked at the clock. Court would be in session now. I wondered when − if − they would need me.

'This youth court is basically a *trial* trial, yeah?' I said to Mum. She was sitting next to me with a cup of vending-machine coffee. 'It's a hearing today, and provided they can't prove their innocence it'll be referred to the Crown Court for the proper trial and any sentence.'

She nodded. 'The case can't be resolved here because it's serious crime and there are multiple charges involved. Armed robbery is a big thing, obviously, but murder's in a different league. This is a big case.'

'I get that, but as it's going to go to the Crown Court anyway, why do they faff about having a hearing here beforehand? Isn't it a massive waste of time?'

'Procedure,' Mum said. 'The McAllisters are youths, so therefore the youth court must go over the charges before it's referred. And it's *if* rather than *when*. Innocent until proven guilty, remember?'

'Ha ha,' I said. She did have a point though. That was what made me nervous. All being well, the McAllisters had it coming once this hearing got referred. I was convinced it was them – Ollie wouldn't lie about something like this. But there was always a chance that something unexpected might happen. The case hinged around a few key facts. If they got blown out . . .

Stop thinking that way, I told myself. They did it. It's obvious.

Time dragged. Unable to stay sitting, I paced about. Mum had another coffee. Then, about an hour and a half later, I was summoned.

SAM

TUESDAY 10 DECEMBER

My knees felt weak as I stepped into the witness box. I wished I hadn't let Dad talk me into wearing a suit 'to make a good impression'. The heavy jacket was making me hot. I felt overdressed and fake, as if I looked like I had something to hide.

I already knew that the McAllisters weren't going to be able to see me – because I was a minor special measures had been put in place, meaning that the booth was screened off – but I still felt like I might throw up. While the screens offered protection, they also gave me the surreal feeling that I was there and not there at the same time. I've done the hard thing coming forward already, I kept telling myself. Now I'm just following through what I started.

It didn't get any easier when the questions began. Even though I wasn't asked anything difficult, I still stumbled over basic facts. Once my memory entirely froze. For a place that was meant to be all about the truth, this hearing was doing a good job of making me doubt it.

The questioning seemed to go on forever. When I was finally dismissed I felt ready to collapse. The main thing was, I'd done it. I'd said everything, if not as confidently as I'd wanted. There was no way Josh and Dale could get out of this one.

★

Dad checked his watch. 'Must be near conclusion now. It's gone on longer than I expected.'

I swallowed. 'Is that good or bad?'

'We'll know soon enough. Chin up, son.'

The hearing had been in session several hours now. After doing my bit I'd been shown to a large waiting room, and Imogen and her mum had joined us. To start with we'd discussed the case, everyone talking over everyone else but all saying the same thing: there was only one way this was going. After a while the parents slipped into the kind of small talk people make to kill time. If I wasn't so fretful it would have been funny. Under normal circumstances Dad, with his flash suit and slicked hair and loud opinions, would probably have nothing to do with Imogen's calm and professional mother, who I secretly thought was very like Imogen herself.

'They need to rewrite their fricking "What happens in court" booklet,' Imogen muttered to me. 'This waiting bit wasn't mentioned. Quite important, yeah?'

'They don't mention the "feeling like you're going to throw up any minute" part either.'

'Maybe they're giving Ollie a hard time. A lot of the most important evidence is his.'

'What about Nadina and her dad? Aren't they here today?'

'Yep. Guess they're elsewhere.'

The tall wooden doors opened. Everyone gave a start; I realized we'd fallen silent. Angie and two other liaison officers came in. They wore funny expressions that didn't seem to be any one emotion.

'Would you prefer we spoke to you separately, or are you OK with this?' Angie asked.

Dad waved his hand impatiently. 'Put us out of our misery, Ang. What's the decision?'

Angie cleared her throat. 'I'm afraid the case has collapsed. The McAllisters have been cleared of all charges.'

IMOGEN

Everyone stared at Angie. Time stood still. Then I exclaimed, 'What?'

'You're upset. I understand,' Angie said. 'I know it's not what you were expecting—'

'That's an understatement!' Phil, Sam's dad, interrupted. 'There's a video, for goodness sake. Those losers have been identified – there's no question of what they've done. Has everyone gone completely insane?'

'Hear me out, Mr Costello,' Angie said quickly. She was a willowy woman with a soft voice. She was clearly struggling to assert herself among so many angry people. 'As I said, the case collapsed. It's nothing to do with your evidence—'

'I should hope not!' That was Phil again.

'The case against Josh and Dale McAllister hinged around Osvaldo Moreno identifying them. There's nothing beyond his statement to suggest the guys who committed these crimes are them – no DNA, no fingerprints, no other conclusive witness statements, and they've got rock-solid alibis, at least as far as the court is concerned. Their mother swears the boys were at home with her on the nights of both break-ins, and a family friend backs her up.'

'Yeah, right!' I exclaimed. As if lowlifes like Josh and Dale stayed in watching *Strictly Come Dancing* with their mum on a Saturday night! I wondered if the family friend was Paz, the guy who'd got Ollie into this mess. He hadn't been part of the robberies, so he'd dodged police attention entirely. 'She's lying. That's obvious!'

'Unfortunately unless it's proved otherwise, or there's more powerful evidence, the court has to believe Mrs McAllister,' Mum said.

'Well, that's stupid! Can't they use a bit of common sense?'

'That's the way the law works.' Mum gave me a tight smile.

'So is it a case of Ollie's word against Mrs McAllister's, and they believed her over him?'

Angie shook her head. 'It didn't come to that.' She drew a breath. 'The primary reason that the hearing couldn't refer the case was that Osvaldo Moreno changed his statement. He withdrew everything in it that implicated Josh and Dale.'

For the second time there was silence as we stared at her. Then we all started up again.

'Is he allowed to do that?'

'How does he explain where he was that night?'

'Who's he saying did this now?'

'One at a time!' Angie cried. 'Let me speak, guys, please. Yes, anyone is allowed to withdraw or change their statement. Osvaldo's now saying that he's never met Josh and Dale, which matches what they say about him. He claims he bumped into the guys who committed the robberies on the Brooke Estate. He's given names, and the police will be investigating.'

'Fake names, no doubt.' Phil said. 'Don't the past records of these scumbag brothers come into it? From what I hear, they do this kind of thing for kicks all the time.'

'I'm afraid without positive identification it doesn't matter what the twins have or haven't done before, Phil.' Mum seemed about the only person in the room keeping her cool. Angie looked a bit relieved to have her help. All her colleagues were doing were standing in the background looking apologetic. 'The court may have suspicions, but they can only go on what's presented to them. Ollie isn't the first kid to withdraw a statement, and he won't be the last.'

I glanced at Sam. He looked as if he wanted to die. Catching my gaze, he said in a quiet voice, 'I've put you all in danger.'

'Don't you dare say that.' Phil looked like he was going to explode. 'You did the right thing. It's not your fault this Ollie kid's a bloody weak-willed coward!'

'Hey!' I was reeling from what had happened, but I wasn't about to let Sam's dad disrespect Ollie. 'We don't know why he changed his statement. They could have got their mates to threaten him.'

Phil gave me a look. 'Sorry, kiddo, but the coward

comment stands. You and Sam have come under fire, but you've stood firm.'

I looked away. 'So what's happened to Ollie? Do we know his sentence?'

Out of the corner of my eye I saw Sam shift uncomfortably.

Angie nodded. 'The good news from his point of view is that the video shows he took no part in the assault that resulted in the death of Hamdi Gul. He's got off with a community sentence. A long one, and he'll be closely monitored by liaison officers, but I should imagine he'll be counting his blessings. All the evidence points to him only being an accessory. He admitted everything, showed remorse and the pre-sentence report testified to a good character. The youth-offending team also reported that he has a difficult family background, coming over here as a refugee. These things all count.'

Someone murmured something about justice being served. Sam's dad opened his mouth, probably to blast Ollie and the court some more, then closed it. Even he'd clocked that these comments weren't welcome. Sam must have tipped him off that Ollie had been my boyfriend.

So all that's happened is that Ollie's got a criminal record for life and the real rats walk free, I thought, realizing just how angry I was. All we've gone through, everything we've risked – for this?

Josh and Dale McAllister would have walked by now.

I bet they'd been laughing their heads off. They'd made a mockery of justice and knew it. Who would they hurt next?

'Are we . . . ?' Sam trailed off. Angie gave him an encouraging smile.

'Ask me anything, Sam. I'm here for you.'

And that makes us all feel so much better. I rolled my eyes. I was rapidly losing respect for so-called support officers.

Sam said, 'Are we going to get any kind of protection? I mean, we're in a pretty bad position now. They might want payback.'

'Josh and Dale have been acquitted. We can't continue to treat them like suspects.'

'Oh.' Sam looked at his feet.

His dad slapped him on the shoulder. In a businesslike voice he said, 'Looks like we're done here, aren't we? Best go home and batten down the hatches. It's clear that no one's on our side here.'

This drama wasn't helping. Thank goodness Mum was being sensible.

'They'll get done for something eventually,' I whispered to Sam as we all left. 'This isn't the end.'

He gave me an unhappy look. It reminded me for a second of how anxious he'd been that night outside the chicken shop, when all this had begun.

'You're right,' he said. 'The question is whether they'll get done before we do.'

SAM

Dad ranted the entire drive home, about the hearing, how easily scumbags could make a mockery of justice, how the system always fleeced off decent hard-working people like us. I'd heard him say things like this before but only now did I actually understand what he meant. We were nearly home when his mobile rang. Seeing that it was one of the numbers we had saved for the police, he told me to take the call.

'They're coming round in about an hour, to talk through how they can help us,' I said.

'Help us through the part where we live in fear because we dared to stand up for what's right?' Dad practically yelled. 'Thank God we're in a well-protected house. I might seriously consider that US transfer.'

US transfer? This was the first I'd heard of that, but what was the point of planning a future here with the McAllisters breathing down my neck? My imagination was full of the horrible things they might do to me, and I couldn't even tell myself I was being melodramatic. They'd tried to kill me already. You didn't get worse than that.

When we got in Tamsin met us in the hall and Dad filled her in. Jessie ran down the stairs, tail wagging. I knelt down and buried my face in her warm neck, closing my eyes and trying to pretend this wasn't happening.

'I'm calling my solicitor,' Dad said, striding towards the room he used as an office. 'And the press! Someone must be able to help.'

'Let him burn off his rage,' Tamsin said as the door slammed. She brushed the back of my head. 'He's not mad at you.'

I got up, letting Jessie go. In a small voice I said, 'My worst nightmare was my life going back to how it was the week after I saw the attack. Not wanting to go outside, looking over my shoulder. But that's reality now.'

Tamsin folded her arms, looking pained. 'It might not be that way, Sam . . .'

'Life was finally getting better. It's not fair.' My voice was a whisper.

'I know.' Tamsin's voice was wobbly too. Probably thinking of what this means for the baby, I thought, hoping that this would be over by the time my little brother or sister came into the world. 'But look at it this way: the case is done and dusted, and it can't go to a retrial unless new evidence comes to light, so you and the others are no longer a threat to these yobs. The only reason for them to come after you is revenge, and that's more of a TV drama thing than something that happens in real life.'

I wasn't so sure. 'Seems like a pretty good reason to me.'

'These boys know they got away with murder. They'll be keeping their heads down – they won't want to attract attention. At least, that's what I'd do if I was them.' Tamsin gave me a reassuring look. Unfortunately her words were far from reassuring, though it was nice of her to try. Imogen had said that Josh and Dale McAllister had walked from youth court three times before this. They wouldn't see the police as any kind of threat now. Or anyone else, for that matter. I didn't know how they'd got Ollie to change his statement, but I was sure they had. When you could control what people said and did like that, you were never, ever going to get anything nailed on you.

They're invincible, I realized. Nothing can touch them. Josh and Dale can do what they want. Worse, they know it.

IMOGEN

Mum said something that surprised me when we got home. I'd asked her if she thought the McAllister twins would ever change. Perfectly calmly she said, 'I believe there's hope for most of us, but I also believe that some people are just evil. They will continue to wreck lives for as long as they have the freedom to do so because they've become inhuman.'

I watched her put the kettle on. It felt I'd spent a lot of time with her in our tiny kitchen recently. Dad knew what was going on too and had drifted in and out of our discussions, but he didn't seem to grasp the full implications of what was going on as well as Mum did.

'I don't suppose you'll want me to come to court with you too,' he'd said a few days earlier. 'I can be there, but I'm not sure I'll be very helpful.'

Thanks for the half-hearted offer, I thought. I told Dad not to bother. He didn't look surprised.

Mum hadn't complained about the time she'd taken out of work, though she must have resented it. Perhaps she was trying to make up for not being there for me. Perhaps she'd been shaken to discover how little trust there was between us.

A little later a police officer visited us. Dad and Benno were home by then. Benno joined us without being asked, and that made me feel sad. My kid brother knew that this involved him now.

'Where's Dad?' I asked.

'Upstairs. We can fill him in later,' Mum said, as though Dad wasn't important.

'Oh, so he's not part of this family? What is he then? Some dude who just happens to live with us?'

Mum shot me a disapproving look, nodding her head at the police officer. Suddenly we were back to old Mum, the parent who cared so much about appearances.

As it turned out, all the police could do was provide a special number for us to call if we suspected we might be in danger. As Angie had warned, the officer wasn't really in a position to admit that there might be a revenge attack.

Can't admit that the youth court got it wrong even though everyone with half a brain knows the score, I thought scornfully. My mood was rapidly turning from bad to worse. All the officer would say was that the McAllisters were among a number of young people the police kept a close eye on.

'Where were those "close eyes" when they tried to run Sam down and when they beat me up?' I said when the officer had gone. 'Never mind when they were robbing the shops.'

Mum shrugged. 'They know as well as we do that those two did it. But without enough evidence they couldn't prove anything. They'll want to get something else on them as soon as possible.'

Benno was hunched opposite the couch on his beanbag. Before the meeting he'd looked serious and curious. Now he looked plain scared. Feeling sorry for him, I made him shove up so I could sit next to him.

'Sorry, soldier,' I said, slinging an arm round his shoulder.

'They're worse than school bullies, right?' Benno muttered.

I grimaced. ''Fraid so.'

'We should decide on precautions,' said Mum. 'I know it's a pain, but we've got to be smart about this. Particularly you, Immy.'

I felt anger boil inside but I knew she was right. Reluctantly, I said, 'I'll keep to public areas when I'm out, even when it means going a longer way round. And I'll avoid streets and estates we know are dodgeville.'

'Parks too,' Mum said. 'It's so easy for someone to hide in the bushes. When you run I'd be much happier if you stuck to open spaces like the green, and went in daylight.'

That would mean I'd have to do my running immediately after sixth form. If only it was summer, when the light lasted longer.

'Should Imogen be going out at all?' a voice from the doorway asked.

'So nice of you to join us, Dad,' I said, laying on the

sarcasm thickly. 'I was beginning to think you didn't care. For your information, I am not becoming a hermit because of this. I need a life. OK?'

Dad gave a pathetic sort of shrug. I rolled my eyes.

Rather sharply Mum said, 'Don't take it out on your dad. It's not *his* fault we're in this situation.'

The words stung. Up until this point, Mum had been acting so cool. I'd begun to remember the things I liked about her. 'Don't push guilt at me! I just think Dad ought to have been here earlier.'

'Rather rich coming from the girl who wouldn't tell her parents she was being threatened. You didn't want us involved then.'

The sarcasm in Mum's voice reminded me of myself. I pressed my lips together and looked away.

'Nothing to say?' Mum demanded.

'There's nothing *to* say!'

'Imogen, come on. There's something you're not telling us. I haven't pushed you until now, but this is everyone's safety on the line, and there can't be secrets. Not now.'

I got to my feet. But when I reached the door and saw that Dad was still hovering there like a guest in his own house it suddenly seemed so unfair.

'How about you tell me something,' I heard myself say coldly. 'Why did Dad go away for those months when we lived in Kent? Why did the police come to our house?'

For a second the shock on Mum's face was almost satisfying. When I glanced at Dad my satisfaction died. He was staring miserably at the floor.

'That's not something anyone wants to talk about,' Mum said quietly. 'We've all moved on.'

'What about me? What if I want to talk about it? We were a normal family until that happened! And let me tell you, we're not normal now. Know why I didn't tell anyone I was being threatened? They said they'd hurt Benno. And I knew I had to look after him because there's a fat chance anyone else here will!'

The colour fell from Mum's face. 'That isn't fair! We love you. We work night and day to provide for you—'

'Yeah, and that's the problem. You're never around. And you wonder why I didn't trust you enough to tell you everything!'

Mum was staring at me as though I was a stranger. I tried to push past Dad, but he placed a hand on my shoulder. With a pained look on his face he said, 'I love you, Immy. Do you know that?'

That threw me. I backed away. It was starting to feel as if I was a ball in a pinball machine, being bounced from one point to another.

'I don't know what we've become as a family.' I was horrified to hear that my voice sounded cracked. 'But I don't like it. I don't want this for Benno. I don't want him to grow up feeling as alone as I did.'

I wasn't making sense. Everything I'd bottled up was a jumble. It felt like I was naked all of a sudden. Mum said something to Benno about going upstairs. I shook my head.

'No. If there's anything you're going to explain, he needs to hear it too.'

Benno glanced between the three of us, as though he didn't know whose side to be on. Dad slowly closed the door and leaned against it. For a long moment the only sound in the room was the tick of the clock. Then, sounding defeated, Mum held up her hands.

'It's your call, Andrew.'

Dad placed a hand to his forehead. In a flat voice he said, 'I'd like to talk to Immy alone, if you don't mind, Benno. I have some explaining to do.'

SAM
TUESDAY 10 DECEMBER

The afternoon passed aimlessly. Dad calmed down and apologized if he'd embarrassed me at the hearing.

'I'm just so mad, Sam,' he said. 'I believe in people getting their just desserts. I'm furious you've got to go through this. Being a teenager can be hell enough without this crap.'

'You're not upset I've landed you in this?'

'You have to ask again?' Dad smiled tightly. 'Of course not, Sam. I'm your dad. Look, let's do something to take our minds of this. Would you like a sneak peek of some of the TV scripts we're developing at work?'

Normally I'd be up for this kind of thing, but I just wasn't in the mood. Dad looked a little crestfallen when I said no. I tried to pass the time by getting some homework done, but my mind wasn't on it. At about six I gave up and opened the fridge. Perhaps I'd make something fiddly like lasagne. It always took ages, what with the different layers, and by the time it was made, eaten and cleared up it might be late enough to crawl into bed.

Jessie whined. With a start I realized that I'd totally forgotten her afternoon walk.

'Sorry, girl,' I muttered, patting her head and opening the back door to let her out. 'I'll give you a long one tomorrow to make up for it. Today's been a bit of a write-off.'

Jessie bounded out into the darkness and I left the door ajar and returned to the kitchen. Perhaps my *MasterChef* cookbook would give me a bit of guidance – it was on the counter from yesterday. Sure enough, I found a decent-looking recipe. I'd got out all the ingredients and had onion and garlic frying before I realized that Jessie hadn't come back in.

'Jessie?' I called. There was no response. A shiver of anxiety crept over me as I turned off the hob and put the pan to one side.

Jessie wasn't a disobedient dog. When I called her, she usually came running. She also wasn't a dog that lingered outside for long in wintertime. She wasn't a fan of the cold and the wet.

What if it was the McAllisters . . . I forced myself to stop following that train of thought and to try to be rational. Why would they come here, now, straight off the back of getting off? I called Jessie again. Then whistled.

Nothing.

This time I couldn't stop the anxious thoughts flying through my head. They knew I loved my dog. They'd threatened to cut her up before . . . What if they'd actually done it?

I burst out of the back door and raced down the steps into the garden, squinting into the night as I left the warmth of the kitchen behind me.

I tried calling for a third time.

Silence.

The last thing I wanted was to search the pitch-dark garden. Surely if they'd hurt her I'd have heard something, I told myself. A howl or a yelp. She's probably found a hole in the fence and is having a whale of a time in next door's garden.

A soft crunching noise from the darkness ahead startled me, like two pairs of feet trying to move silently over gravel. Suddenly terrified that the twins were going to jump out at me, I stumbled back into the house and locked the door. As I pulled the blinds shut, there was a heavy crash right outside the window.

I jumped back and ducked down behind the central kitchen counter. Go away, go away, go away, I thought, scrunching my eyes shut. What I ought to be doing was calling the police, said the rational part of my brain. But I couldn't make myself *move*. I was frozen, a useless bundle of nerves.

Any second now I was convinced I'd hear the shattering of glass and Josh and Dale would be in the kitchen with me, Jessie a bloody heap on the steps outside. But the next noise I heard wasn't a smash. It was a bark.

I managed to get it together enough to peer around the edge of the counter.

Through cracks in the blinds I could make out Jessie's

silhouette. Swearing at my own stupidity, I pulled myself together and lurched over to let her in – my legs shaking so badly I could barely walk. Peering out of the back door I realized that one of the big flowerpots on the steps was on its side, in pieces. Jessie must've knocked it over. So much for the McAllisters breaking in!

Even though I knew it was just my mind playing tricks on me, it took me a long time to feel steady enough to get back to cooking dinner. Maybe it would be for the best if Dad did take that US transfer. I wasn't sure how much longer I could handle living like this.

IMOGEN

Dad and I sat facing each other in my room, me cross-legged on the bed, him on the chair by my desk. Awkward did not begin to describe the atmosphere.

I knew he'd step around what he had to say for ages unless I was blunt. 'So, what *really* happened in Kent, Dad?'

'What do you remember?' he asked softly.

Trying to sound like I didn't care, I said, 'Only that things were normal until the police came round wanting to speak to you and Mum. It was about something to do with the place you both worked. That charity, run by that friend of Mum's.' I paused. 'Mum shoved me and Benno off to Laura's. We spent a lot of time there the next few days. No one said why. When we were at home, you weren't there. Just Mum.' I carried on, stumbling a little. I'd blocked ten-year-old me out so efficiently it was hard to go back and even harder to put into words. 'No one told me what was going on, Dad. No explanation, no nothing. Mum was acting like things were normal. Cooking dinner, getting us to school, that kind of thing. On autopilot. I was scared. And angry. Like it wasn't important what I felt! I'd never had anything but, well, love from you two before. Then suddenly I didn't matter any more.'

'You mattered more than anything—'

'Not enough for either of you to take the time to explain what the hell was going on!' I shook my head. 'It was OK for Benno. He was too young to know how wrong everything felt. He noticed you'd vanished though. Mum said you needed to go away. Brilliant lie! Three months, Dad. That's, like, years to a kid! I was starting to forget stuff, like the sound of your voice and what you looked like. You didn't even contact us. It was like you were dead. But then I realized there was only one place you could possibly have gone . . . prison.'

'You thought I was in prison?' Dad's eyes widened.

'It's not such a strange conclusion, is it?' I snapped. 'When you came back it was like you'd had a personality transplant, and then we moved, like we were on the run. Mum was clearly in on it too.'

'Your mother had nothing to do with this. Let me make that very clear.'

'All I know is, I had friends, a nice home and I liked my school. In a few months that was all gone with no explanation. It's not easy to start again. People say it's fine for kids. Bullshit. It's not like I was even a kid any more. What happened made me grow up quickly. No one was on my side any more. Not you. Not Mum. No one. I had to *be* my side myself.' I gave him a sarcastic smile. I knew I was making him feel bad on purpose, but right now I didn't care.

Dad swore under his breath. I folded my arms.

'Over to you. Tell me how wrong I've got everything.'

Dad looked at me. 'You can stop pretending you don't care. I know that's your trick when you're feeling vulnerable, but we're having an honest talk here. I can do without the sarcasm.'

I didn't think Dad paid me enough attention to have noticed my 'trick' as he called it. I let him take a moment to figure out how to start. 'I never wanted to tell you all this,' he said. 'I didn't want you to think less of me. But it's clear you have a pretty poor opinion of me already.'

'Do you blame me?'

Dad ignored me. 'Back in Kent I got in a rut. I didn't enjoy working for the charity, and everything felt static. I was bored. I needed something.'

A horrible idea popped into my mind. 'You didn't have an affair, did you?'

'God, no. Nothing like that.' He cleared his throat. 'Online gambling, that was my vice. A little bit of fun, I told myself. The problem is, it didn't stay just a little bit of fun.'

'Dad! What were you thinking? Gambling never pays. Everyone knows that!'

'You say it like it's obvious, but when you're doing it you don't think like that. You get hooked, Immy. Especially when you win. It's like a drug. You tell yourself it's OK.'

'It's not OK! You hid it from Mum, didn't you?'

'I hid it from everyone. Then I had a losing streak. I lost a lot – and I mean a lot. I panicked.'

'What did you do, Dad? Tell me you didn't start nicking

stuff or something stupid like that . . .'

'Unfortunately I did.' His face looked grey, like he might be sick. 'I started using money that wasn't mine. From work. I convinced myself I could win back what I'd lost. Then I'd stop.'

'You stole from a charity!'

Dad gave a helpless gesture. 'I was always planning to return the money, but as you can guess . . . I got found out. I thought I'd be safe, but the charity was in the middle of a merger and auditors came in. It didn't take long to trace the missing money back to me.'

I could barely bring myself to look at him. I couldn't bear how matter-of-fact he was being about something so wrong. 'How much did you take?'

'Enough to be a big deal.'

'How much, Dad?'

A long silence. 'Fifty thousand pounds.'

More than I had possibly imagined. I felt the bottom drop out of my stomach.

'I paid it back,' Dad said, sounding as though he was in pain. 'We sold our house to raise the money. The trustees of the charity decided not to press charges in the end. They didn't want the negative publicity.'

I thought of our nice house, with the pretty garden, on the well-to-do street. I compared it to where we were living now, with its draughts and creaking floorboards. 'Fifty thousand pounds!' I repeated.

'Your mother gave me hell and I deserved it. Of course I got defensive and blamed her, and . . . well, we needed space, to think about whether to stick together or go our separate ways. That was why I went away, Immy.' I felt his hand on my shoulder. 'It's as simple as that.'

'And no one told me and Benno because you didn't want to frighten us.'

'There was no need for you to worry about us splitting up unless it happened. In the end we decided to ride it out and start again somewhere new.'

Somewhere new being much cheaper Walthamstow.

I thought of all the things I'd wanted and been told we couldn't afford. All of that, and Dad was directly responsible for it. I felt rather than saw his shrug. 'Do you have any questions?'

'Unsurprisingly, yeah.' I looked at him, narrowing my eyes. 'Why didn't you even *try* to explain? You must have realized I'd notice the police coming round.'

'If you were me, would you have told your ten-year-old daughter that her dad was a thief? I don't think so.'

I wasn't going to admit he had a point. 'Didn't you realize how hard it would be for me? I needed you, Dad.'

'It was a difficult time for all of us, Immy. Your mother and I thought you acting tough and shutting off emotionally was just you mimicking the Walthamstow kids because that's how it's done round here.'

I snorted. 'You're terrible parents. What did me and

Benno do to get stuck with you?'

I'd said it without thinking.

Dad seemed to wilt in front of me. All he said was, 'I know.'

What else was there to say? I wasn't going to tell Dad it was OK and I forgave him. I didn't. However much he knew he'd got it wrong, it was me and Benno who'd paid the price. Mum too, I suppose. When he left, I flopped down on my bed and wondered how different things would be if his stupid online-gambling addiction hadn't got out of hand. After a few minutes I gave up. I was who I was — nothing could change that now. At least the truth had made everything clearer. I understood why Dad had become the 'nothing' man. I understood why Mum seemed funny with him sometimes. I understood why my family was more of an illusion of a perfect family than an actual loving home.

But what I didn't understand was why Dad had felt his life was so empty he needed online gambling to spice it up. Weren't his kids enough to make him think twice?

I rolled over. I could see my bedside table. On it was my alarm clock, a novel that had been there ages and a photograph of me holding the volleyball cup my team had won earlier in the year. I'd been feeling proud and happy. One day, I thought, I'll feel proud and happy again. I am not going to be one of those people who gets dragged down. Not by what Dad did. Not by the McAllisters. Not by anyone.

SAM

The next day was almost disturbingly normal. Tamsin dropped me off at sixth form, I ate lunch with Imogen and Nadina, came home, walked Jessie and spent the evening watching a film with Dad and Tamsin from the Alfred Hitchcock box set we'd started making our way through. There was not even the tiniest hint of danger. I was so embarrassed about being such an idiot in the kitchen last night that I'd decided not to mention it to anyone.

Imogen had told me about the precautions her family had decided on. These got me thinking about my own routine. The best time for Josh and Dale to get me would be on my walks with Jessie, when I was by myself. Perhaps I had better stop going to the nature reserve – it would be a brilliant place to spring an attack, as it was usually empty so no one would hear me if I yelled for help.

'If you're coming out with things like that, maybe we shouldn't be watching these creepy Hitchcock movies,' Tamsin said when I told her.

'It's OK. They're old. Everything seems a bit less real when everyone's wearing fifties gear.'

She laughed. Dad wasn't in tonight – apparently he was meeting 'people who could help us'. So far the big noise he'd made to the press and his solicitor hadn't got us anywhere.

Last night as I'd been brushing my teeth I'd overheard him talking to Tamsin. He'd mentioned the American transfer again. Deciding now was a good time, I asked her what it meant.

'It's work. What else?' Tamsin was usually very tolerant of Dad being a workaholic – so it was a surprise to hear her sounding irritated. 'They've offered him a contract that would mean moving to Illinois for five years. It's an amazing opportunity – more money, house provided, all that – but it's a big step, and you know how attached your Dad is to this area, having grown up here.'

'Is he going to take it?'

'I don't want him to. I don't fancy moving to another country, away from my friends and parents, and, heavens, I can't see my career taking off stateside – Illinois is hardly LA. It's hard enough getting any work here! There's the baby to think of too. But now that things are as they are, it might be a good idea.'

So we might leave Walthamstow? I was shocked to find that the thought disturbed me. Things had changed. I had friends. I was beginning to feel for the first time in a long time that my life was going somewhere.

If we went to America I was scared I'd fade back into old Sam who couldn't cope with change. How was I ever going to make a life for myself if everything I had kept being taken away?

I decided to try not to think about it. There were lots of reasons for Dad not to take the US transfer. I'd just have to wait and see what happened.

The rest of the week passed smoothly.

'Perhaps they're waiting until we let our guard down.' I said to Imogen as we left school together on Friday.

'Not sure I credit them with that much brainpower,' Imogen said. 'We're not talking criminal masterminds. They're two thugs. If they come for us, we'll know about it.'

She zipped up her coat in a purposeful manner. It was bitingly cold; I was beginning to forget what it was like to go outside without a billion layers. I thought Imogen seemed distracted. We hadn't had a proper chance to speak at lunch.

'You OK?' I asked. 'Apart from the obvious, I mean.'

She hesitated. 'I was thinking of talking to Ollie.'

Inwardly I groaned. Imogen spoke about Ollie very rarely. Without knowing any details, I gathered that she'd heard his side of the story; perhaps that had changed things. Or perhaps I was still being unfair because this was Ollie, who I still couldn't help being jealous of, despite the awful things he had done. They weren't together any more; from the way Imogen spoke it was clear it was over. Good, I thought. She deserves someone better.

Still, I couldn't help wondering if the possibility of seeing him was why Imogen was wearing her hair loose today. I'd never seen it any way other than pulled back and it was longer than I'd realized, a little way past her shoulders. I found myself staring. It just looked so different — really pretty. She also had a new pair of glasses. They were bigger with black frames, cool in a geeky kind of way — and they really suited her. With her fluffy bobble hat and long hair, she almost looked cute. Not that I would ever say that to her — I didn't want her to kill me.

Curiosity got the better of me. 'You don't seem as mad at him as I thought you would be,' I said. 'He really dropped us in it.'

She shrugged. 'I am mad at him. But I'd like to understand why he did it before I really let rip. I've been thinking of speaking to him for a while actually, but I wanted to wait until I was calm.'

'Do you still have feelings for him?' When I realized it had slipped out, I was so horrified that I almost clamped my hands over my mouth. To my relief, she just shrugged.

'It's weird to say this, but I don't think I ever really did.'

'But he was your boyfriend. And he's, well . . . got that exotic South American thing going on.' For some reason the words 'good-looking' had stuck on my tongue.

'He was never really my type,' she replied unexpectedly. 'Don't think he'll be coming back to Devereux. Everyone knows what he did. He's probably enrolled somewhere else. It's a shame really. He loved this school.'

I wanted to ask if she thought the school would take his face off the prospectus, as it wasn't exactly great to have a criminal for a poster boy, but realized in time how mean that would sound. 'Are you going to go to his house?'

'Promised my parents I'd avoid that estate. Josh and Dale have mates there, plus it's a craphole. No.' She shoved her hands in her pockets. No gloves today, I noticed. 'Part of his community sentence involves cleaning graffiti from the parade of shops at Gate Street. Thought I'd catch him there. Wanna come?'

'Why? Do you need an escort?'

Imogen half smiled. 'The word "escort" has a slightly different meaning round here, Northern boy – take it out of your dictionary. I'm asking cos I fancy the company. All right?'

I found myself saying I'd come. As we waited for the bus, snow began to fall, though it didn't look like it was going to settle. Someone walked by playing a Christmas pop song from their mobile. I hadn't thought about Christmas yet; I ought to make a start buying presents. Should I get something for Imogen? Or would she think that was weird?

By the time we arrived at Gate Street it was dusk. Imogen took me round to the back by the car park. There we found a group of about ten people scrubbing the walls. It didn't look much fun, especially on a freezing cold day like this. I felt a little sorry for them. None of these people here looked like criminals – just like kids who were down on their luck. Ollie was at the end, working robotically. Before Imogen could call out, he spotted us.

'How much longer?' Imogen called. Ollie signalled fifteen minutes. Agreeing that he might find it humiliating if we watched, we had a cup of tea in a nearby Lebanese deli, which seemed to be the only place selling hot drinks around there. I watched shoppers cross the dull grey quadrangle, shuffling from shop to shop. Although the graffiti they were cleaning off wasn't at the more imaginative end of the street-art spectrum, I could follow the thinking of whoever had decided this place needed some colour. All I could see was concrete and faded signs. It was like being in a black-and-white movie.

When a quarter of an hour had passed we found Ollie. Work had clearly finished earlier than anticipated because he was alone.

'Hi.' Imogen stopped a few steps short of him. 'All right?'

Ollie shrugged. There was something different about him and after a moment I placed it; he wasn't wearing sports gear, just jeans and an anonymous-looking sweater and jacket. It made him look less cool, less like a school pin-up.

'Where are you studying now?' Imogen asked.

'Birch House. Bit shit academically, but the sports facilities aren't bad.'

There was a silence. I looked from Imogen to Ollie. 'D'you want me to go?'

Surprisingly it was Ollie who answered. 'Don't bother. This ain't gonna take long. Im's come to ask why I changed my statement. Right?'

'Wrong.' Imogen gave him her wry smile, the smile that I liked so much. 'Came to see how you were first. Asking about the statement second.'

'You can see how I am. I'm cleaning crap off walls.' Ollie glanced over his shoulder, but no one else was around, save a woman with a pushchair a good ten metres away. 'Don't feel sorry for me, all right? Especially not you, OK?'

That last part was directed at me. I guessed part of him was still jealous of me after all.

Imogen rubbed her hands; keeping them in her pockets obviously wasn't doing much to keep them warm. 'They could've stung you with a worse sentence, y'know,' she said. 'You might as well tell us what happened. Trial's over, and it's not going to open up again unless something shifts.'

He rubbed at his chin. Something about the way he moved his hand made him seem very weary. He looked at Imogen. 'Remember Paz?'

She nodded. The name was new to me but I didn't ask.

'He and Josh argued around the time we did the Guls' shop. Dunno what about — but it was bad enough for Josh to want payback. A few days later they pushed him off the balcony of his flat.'

'Christ!' Imogen cried. 'They didn't kill him, did they?'

Ollie shook his head. 'It was only on the first floor. But he broke his leg. Remember I said he was a great footballer? Not any more.' A funny look crossed his face – hurt and angry but also resigned. 'He dropped me, y'know, Paz. So much for being the brother I never had.'

'You thought Josh and Dale might do something to you?' I asked.

Ollie shot me an annoyed look, as though he'd forgotten I was part of the conversation. 'Didn't think. Knew. By then Josh and Dale were in custody, but their mates were more than happy to do the dirty work for them. Told me they were gonna take a hammer to my knees if I didn't withdraw the statement. I'm not like you.' He nodded at me. 'No nice house, no big telly or computer games and all that stuff. But what I have got is basketball and football. Maybe I could make a living playing professionally some day. Or maybe they'll get me a scholarship to some uni. Who knows? But someone breaks my knees . . . that's it, game over.' He paused. 'I told them to get lost. Said I didn't deserve a future any more, not after what I'd done. They didn't scare me. But then . . .'

'Then?' Imogen prompted.

'They started going into a lot of detail about what they'd do to my mum if I didn't play ball. And that . . .' Ollie pulled a face. He was trying to look nonchalant, but he wasn't fooling anyone. 'Well, I've put my mum through enough grief. The thought of her getting hurt, of more trouble because of me . . .'

I realized Imogen had been wrong. The McAllisters weren't thick. They would never be able to think up something like this if they were. A sports injury was bad. They'd be taking everything from Ollie. They must have been surprised when he'd thrown their threats back in their faces. So they'd decided to bring Ollie's poor mum into the equation. It was funny. Somehow I respected Ollie more for caving in because he loved his mum. That was something I could relate to. Imogen too, I suspected. She'd kept quiet to protect her brother, and what Ollie was doing now was no different.

Imogen swore. Ollie looked at his feet. We stood letting the snowflakes fall on our hair. After what seemed like ages Ollie said, 'Gotta go. Not meant to be out after six. They got a tag on me.'

He walked away without saying goodbye. Imogen watched. Almost without thinking I put my arm around her shoulder.

'You OK?'

She nodded. Then she said, 'D'you ever wonder if there's something wrong with you?'

It was such a strange question. Even stranger than me

putting my arm around her and her not shaking it off. 'Not sure what you mean.'

'All the girls fancy Ollie.' Imogen stated it as though it was a fact. 'In Year 11 they went on about me spending time with him. Don't get me wrong – I liked him. He was good company. But he didn't, y'know, *do* anything for me. On paper he should've. Maybe good looks and stuff in common isn't enough to make you go for someone after all. Maybe there needs to be that mysterious X-factor.' She pulled a face. 'Or maybe I'm just weird. I've never been as bothered about boys and having a boyfriend as every other girl I know. Other things just seemed more interesting. More important. It gets to the point where you feel like you're on a different planet.'

I really wished she hadn't picked me to have this conversation with but I was a little hooked to find out where this was leading too. I couldn't help wondering how Imogen really felt about me? Nadina had said she found me 'strangely intriguing'.

I realized that Imogen expected me to say something. I fumbled about for the words. 'So, if you weren't interested in having a boyfriend, how did you end up with Ollie?'

'Shall we make a move?' Imogen looked at me and suddenly I felt as if the situation had become very intense. 'Snow's a right pain when you wear glasses.'

As we began to head towards the bus stop – which meant

removing my arm from her shoulders – she continued, 'Everyone was already treating us as a couple. It was easy to fall into. We got on. Seems obvious now there was nothing really deep there – emotionally, I mean.'

'D'you think it was the same for him?'

She nodded. From how calm and accepting she seemed, I realized she must have thought about this a lot. 'Ollie's just like me, Sam. We're both so focused on getting on in life I guess neither of us realizes stuff like this until it hits us over the head. We're not thinkers.'

I'm the opposite, I thought. I think far too much, about things that haven't happened yet and maybe never will.

Imogen was still talking. 'I didn't feel anything when we, you know . . . acted coupley. Just thought it was all right, then got worried because surely I ought to be thinking it was more than all right. Kissing's like chocolate, you know? You're not allowed to not like it.'

I couldn't help but laugh. Remembering what people said in some of the films I'd watched with Mum, I said, 'Maybe he just wasn't the right person.' Then, because that sounded far too knowing to be taken seriously, I added, 'It's not like I'm an expert, but when you're . . . well, when you're with someone you do like, it'll feel different.'

She made a rude noise. 'I've never even had a proper crush on someone, Sam. I even pretended I had one back in Year 9 cos I wanted to seem normal. How sad is that? I have absolutely no clue why I'm telling you all this, by the way.' She poked me in the ribs. 'You ever fancied anyone? Promise I won't spread it around.'

Her tone was jokey and I really wished it wasn't. I could feel myself start to blush. It wasn't just that it was a personal question; it was also that Imogen was the one asking it, apparently completely innocently.

The answer's yes, I thought. Obviously. I'd taken ages to acknowledge it, but . . . I noticed everything Imogen did. When she wore her hair differently. How patient she was when she spoke to the younger pupils. Her smile. I'd spent far too long wondering exactly what kind of person she was, even way back when we didn't speak. And I really liked hanging out with her, even if it was just walking to the bus stop together. That all pointed to one thing, didn't it?

'Not really.' I avoided her gaze. Then, realizing which direction we were walking in, I said, 'Imo, stop. If we keep going this way, we'll end up at the arcade.'

The arcade was the kind of place gangs of kids with nothing better to do hung out. Most of the shops were deserted or vandalized. It was only a very short walkway, but in the dark, with the McAllisters after our blood, it was somewhere to be avoided.

Imogen gave a start. 'Man, I was so busy talking I went straight past the bus stop. I'm so used to going about without worrying I forgot.'

As we retraced our steps I saw a figure running towards us and tensed. Imogen glanced back and I saw her face freeze. I grabbed her arm, poised to run, though where to I had no idea. But just in time the figure got near enough for us to make him out and I saw it was a man in a long coat, carrying an umbrella – not either of the McAllisters. He pushed past us without a second glance. Just running for the bus, I thought in relief. The sooner we got clear of this place the better.

Imogen started hunting in her bag for her Oyster card. 'Maybe magic things will happen for us at the Christmas party. It's meant to be the season of slush and happiness, right?'

'Party? Whose?'

'Samuel, please. Don't give me that "I haven't been invited look". It's at sixth form, day we break up. It'll just be dancing and music and food in the school hall, nothing to rock your socks, but it'll be a laugh.'

We got on the bus. I didn't want to say that I hadn't been to a party like that for years. At least, not since Mum died. But maybe by the time this party came round I might feel ready to celebrate for once, providing the McAllisters stayed off our backs.

And maybe, just maybe, I would finally manage to say something to Imogen about how I felt.

IMOGEN
WEDNESDAY 18 DECEMBER

Mum opened my door as I was getting ready for the party. I swivelled round on my chair in front of the mirror where I'd been applying mascara.

'Mum, please. Can't you master knocking? I could've been naked or something.'

She ignored the sarcasm. 'I came to see if you wanted a lift.'

'Thanks but Sam's stepmum's giving me a lift. And she's on call to pick us up when the cheesy Christmas songs get too much to handle.'

Mum nodded. I waited for her to go. When she didn't I said, 'Kinda tight schedule here, Mum. If there's nothing else, d'you mind giving me a bit of space?'

But she closed the door and came in and sat on the bed. 'Carry on with your make-up, Immy. I wanted to ask about your dad.'

'What about him?' I turned back to the mirror.

'You two have been funny since your chat. Funnier, that is,' Mum added as I opened my mouth to argue. 'Enough is enough. Your dad's in agony, waiting to see if you can forgive him. He loves you, Immy. He loves all of us. He made a mistake, but he's only human.'

'He doesn't look like a man in agony to me.'

I saw Mum lean forward in the reflection. 'Imogen, he's your dad. What he did was a long time ago. It's Christmas. You can't carry on like this. But because you're exactly like me — and don't argue! — I know that you will. When it comes to things like this, you brush them under the carpet rather than tackling them head-on.'

I laid down my mascara. 'Mum, you really pick your moments. I'm trying to make myself beautiful here.'

'That shouldn't take long.' Mum smiled. I sighed and swivelled round again.

Mum held up her hands. 'Don't worry, I'm going back downstairs. But make up with your dad. Please.'

'Do you forgive him? Sometimes it doesn't seem as though you care.'

I realized I'd been very blunt. Mum raised an eyebrow, but she didn't call me on it.

'I've forgiven him. What he did was bad, but we all make mistakes. Your dad's a good guy really.' She smiled again. 'The last month has been hell for us all, but if one good thing's come out of it, it's made me realize I've been running on autopilot. I'd been neglecting my family.' She paused. 'We've had our wake-up call. All of us. If we're going to mend things, you need to give us a chance. OK?'

She didn't need to say any more. 'Point taken.'

Mum got up. 'Think about it. Let's have a nice Christmas.'

I watched her leave. For a second I felt low, as I always did when something reminded me that my family was basically a big load of fail. But then I thought, Sod it. I wanted to have a good time tonight. Mum was right really. I couldn't hate Dad forever for what he'd done. He was my dad. I only had the one. Perhaps if I gave him a chance, we could start to feel like a proper family again?

I was downstairs five minutes before Sam was due to ring the bell. Benno, who was sitting in front of the telly watching a Christmas film, wrinkled his nose at me.

'You smell.'

'It's called perfume,' I snapped. 'One day it'll drive you wild.'

'Gross. What're you even meant to be? Mum said it was fancy dress.'

I ruffled his hair, mostly because I knew it annoyed him. 'Isn't it obvious, squirt?'

'No.' Benno gave me a look that said I was stupid. 'You're just wearing a black thing with white blobs on it.'

'Those blobs are cotton-wool balls. Promise me you'll never work in fashion. You'll sink.' I smoothed down my top. It was a long one which stopped at the top of my thighs, and I'd paired it with a pair of black leggings. Most of the other girls would probably wear dresses, but that wasn't my style. 'I'm snow! That's Christmassy, right?'

'It's *lame*.'

'Stop teasing your sister.' To my surprise Dad appeared. He smiled at me, rather tentatively. 'You look very nice.'

'Thanks.' Hearing the doorbell, I picked up my bag and slung it over my shoulder. Dad was still looking at me. Taking a breath, I gave him a hug. 'See you later.'

'Be good.' Dad hugged me back. He was smiling properly now. I felt a bit like I was ten years old again.

SAM

I kept looking at Imogen as Tamsin drove us to school. She glared at me.

'Stop it.'

'Sorry,' I said. 'But I'm just not getting the snow thing. I know you told me this is the kind of fancy-dress party where no one really goes in fancy dress – which by the way doesn't make any sense. But your outfit, well, it just looks weird.'

'That's not very polite, Sam,' Tamsin said. 'You're meant to compliment a lady on how she looks.'

'Good job I'm no lady!' Imogen gave me a poke.

I was glad it was dark enough for her to not see me blush. While I might not have realized what the costume was supposed to be, that didn't mean I didn't think Imogen looked great, because I did. What I liked most was that it was so very her. I admired her for being strong-minded enough not to cave into the pressure of competing with the other girls, whom I knew would bling up. The only concession she seemed to have made was that she was wearing heels, which I suspected she'd borrowed from her mum. And her hair was loose again.

The fancy dress had been a bit of a cop out for me. I hadn't wanted to look lame but I also hadn't wanted to stand out. So I'd gone for a Santa hat and a red hoody, which didn't look too bad. I'd never be as good-looking as someone like Ollie – but that was OK. And after spending such a long time feeling negative about myself, feeling OK was enough to make me happy.

'Is Nadina coming?' I said, changing the subject. 'It would be no problem to pick her up too.'

'She's walking with Kimmie. We'll catch her there.' She cocked an eyebrow at me. 'Looking forward to hitting the dance floor?'

'Er, we'll see. My moves are special. I'm not sure the world is ready for them.'

It was so odd. Here we were, on the way to a party, like ordinary teenagers. It was as though the cloud of fear we'd been living under had never existed. Imogen had clearly decided to worry about nothing more than having a good time, and she was right. We would be safe once we reached school. There was no chance of the McAllisters turning up there. I was starting to wonder if they were bothered about revenge at all. Wouldn't they have done something by now?

Maybe I was just letting my guard down because it was almost Christmas and the cheer was catching. It was nice to walk round seeing trees lit-up in windows and happy kids and colourful shop displays. With presents and good food to look forward to, it became harder and harder to believe that pissed-off murderers could be lurking round every corner.

★

My good feeling evaporated almost as soon as we got inside the building. The school hall was draped with tinsel and there was a DJ on the stage pumping out tunes. The dance floor was illuminated by flashing disco lights, and a few groups had already started dancing. It was too dark to see much, but I could tell that some kids were already making out in the darkened corners of the room.

This was more full-on than I'd expected. I'd pictured this as the kind of party where people hung around in groups and no one really hit the dance floor until the night was nearly over.

So much for letting Imo know how I feel, I thought. There was far too much going on for me to make a move here.

'Hey!' Nadina appeared, Kimmie behind her. 'We have Santa and . . . something.'

'Could ask you the same question.' Imogen poked the ribbon Nadina was wearing round her waist. The rest of the outfit seemed to be a loud dress and a denim waistcoat. 'Are you supposed to be a present?'

'Ready to be unwrapped, innit.' Nadina beamed at us.

Imogen groaned. 'By people at our school? Are you insane?'

'Don't be harsh. They're all right, some of 'em.' Nadina nodded her head at a couple of guys who had just come in.

Imogen followed her gaze. 'Mateusz Nowak? Since when did you fancy him?'

'He's OK. He's in my sociology class.' She grinned. 'Said I had the best hair in the school.'

Imogen groaned again. 'He sure knows the right lines to flatter you!'

After a little while Imogen and Kimmie headed off on to the dance floor. I wasn't ready for that yet so I followed Nadina into the canteen, where some festive snacks had been laid out. There were juices and soft drinks too, though Nadina assured me that several people would have sneaked in alcohol.

'Shame I'll be missing out,' she commented, looking wistfully at the stack of mince pies. Her jaw was still wired up. 'Ah well, they probably look better than they taste.'

'D'you think it'll get wild?' I asked.

Nadina laughed. 'You got high expectations. Best we'll get is some dodgy dancing.'

'Nads,' I blurted, suddenly unable to stop myself, 'tell me honestly – d'you think I stand a chance with Imogen?'

Nadina spat out her mouthful of orange juice, which wasn't exactly encouraging. I thumped her on the back as she spluttered and mopped her chin with a napkin, hoping this hadn't hurt her jaw.

'*Ohmadays*,' she said as soon as she could. 'You having me on?'

'Forget it. Just don't tell anyone, OK?' I backtracked.

Nadina chuckled. 'Oh, Sam. Look, I'm not really that surprised. I figured waaaay back you had the hots for her. Was starting to think you was never gonna do anything about it!'

Suddenly hopeful, I said, 'Did she say anything to you about me?'

'Nope. But that don't mean nothing. Im doesn't talk about things like that. God knows I try and make her. Your call, Sammy.' Nadina slapped me on the shoulder. 'Im likes your company and she likes you. What's to lose? Go get her.'

How? I wanted to ask Nadina, but I didn't because that seemed like a stupid thing to say. Should I just tell her? Or should I dance with her? Or maybe there would be some mistletoe about somewhere, though I wasn't sure about that. Kissing in public didn't seem like it would be up Imo's street. The last time I'd kissed a girl had been way back during a game of spin the bottle at a party when I was just thirteen, and I hadn't really known what I was doing. After Mum got sick, well, stuff like that hadn't felt important. It also didn't help that Imogen wasn't exactly a conventional girl – I had no idea what she'd go for.

I picked up a drink and tried to figure out what to do.

IMOGEN

Kimmie leaned across and shouted something.

I mouthed, 'What?' She pointed to the open doors, indicating that she needed air. I shook my head. 'I like this song. Catch you in a bit.'

Kimmie disappeared into the crowd. We were an hour and a half in and the party was in full swing. The floor had really filled up, and the DJ had turned the volume right up. I could see Santa hats, girls in short white dresses and angel wings, and lots of tinsel.

The song ended and a popular rap track started to play. I pushed my hair back from my face and took a swig of the juice Sam had fetched me. Though he'd made a few appearances, he'd spent most of the time avoiding the dance floor. In a few songs, I decided, I'd drag him up here and make him dance.

After I found Nadina, that was. It hadn't taken her long to get together with Mat. He'd come over with a grin and asked her to dance. A few songs later I'd seen them heading off together down the ground-floor corridor. That had been a while ago. I was sure Nads was OK, but I'd definitely be ignoring my best-friend duties if I didn't at least check up on her.

I pushed my way through dancers to the doors and headed

off the way Nadina had gone, passing the boys' loos and the vending machines. No Nads so far. She must have gone all the way to the end. It was a bit eerie in here at night. During the day it was always noisy and busy and well lit. While it was still just light enough to be able to see where I was going, it was more than a little creepy!

I was just wondering whether to text Nads when someone thumped against me from behind.

Before I had time to realize what was happening, both my arms were pinned behind my back in a strong grip. A hand yanked my head back by the hair. A face leaned over me and I felt warm breath on my cheek. It smelt of alcohol.

'Hello again, pretty girl,' a familiar voice said. 'Shame your pretty face ain't gonna be pretty much longer.'

He shoved me against the wall, letting go of my arms. He still had my hair in his other hand, pulling my head back and to the side, throwing me off balance. I saw a knife above me, a glint of light reflecting off the blade as it flashed downward – towards my face. With all my strength I jerked to one side. The knife dug into my shoulder. I screamed in pain. The guy swore. I saw the knife rise again.

Remembering the self-defence classes the school had made me take when I became a prefect, I hit back as hard as I could with both hands. One open palm smacked into his nose and he grunted angrily and slashed down again with the knife. At the same time I moved my hands up and dug my fingers into his eyes.

There was a yell in my ear. Suddenly my hair was free. I broke away and dived along the empty corridor, trying to get back towards the crowded hall. But something had happened, something bad. Pain surged through me, making it hard to move. And it wasn't just coming from my shoulder.

Looking back I saw my attacker clutching one hand to his eyes. The other held the knife. It had blood on it. *My* blood. As I stared, he straightened. An angry face with red eyes met mine.

One of the McAllisters.

Almost in slow motion, he pointed the blade. Towards me.

If one was here, the other couldn't be far away. It didn't take a genius to figure out who he would be after.

Where the hell was Sam?

SAM

It was getting a bit depressing, avoiding the dance floor. I knew I was just putting off the inevitable with Imogen. I *had* to man up and say something tonight. OK, I thought, squaring my shoulders. I could hear the beat of a song I recognized. The time was now.

I left the canteen. I decided to take a detour via the loos — just to check I looked presentable. I stood in front of the mirror. I'd always found it weird that boys' toilets at our school had mirrors, but apparently there'd been a big campaign to have them installed. Guess everyone is image-conscious these days, I thought.

As I adjusted my Santa hat I saw the door of the cubicle behind me slowly opening. Weird, I thought. I hadn't heard anyone come in. As I stared at the reflection, I caught the glimmer of something through the gap.

Something shiny and sharp.

I bolted out of the toilets and into the corridor. I heard a door bang from inside. Someone shouted my name. I looked both ways down the corridor and was shocked to see Imogen at the far end, running in my direction as best she could in her high heels. Without thinking, I rushed towards her.

'Imo!'

'They're here!' she shouted, running to the door that led out to the courtyard. She pulled at the handle and chains rattled from outside. Locked! I reached her, shouting that one of the McAllisters was behind me and she had to run. Then I caught sight of a dark figure lurching towards us from the far end of the corridor and knew instantly that it had to be the other twin. I looked over my shoulder and saw the first one, grinning like a madman behind me, slowly closing the gap between us.

We were trapped. There was nowhere to go! Nowhere except up.

The doors to the stairwell were just opposite. Grabbing Imogen, I slammed open the doors and dashed upward, two steps at a time. Imogen had pulled off her shoes and followed, clutching them in one hand. As we turned the corner on to the next staircase I looked over my shoulder and saw that we were being followed.

We reached the second floor. I started on the next staircase, but Imogen stopped.

'What are you doing?' I cried as the top of our pursuer's head came into view. Imogen gestured at me to carry on. Then she hurled one of her shoes at him. It struck the side of his head. The second throw was even better, hitting in the same place with more force. He cried out in pain and stumbled.

'Now I know why girls wear heels to parties!' Imogen

puffed as she pushed me forward. At the fourth floor we instinctively made for the English classroom where we hang out at break. I kicked open the door and ducked down behind one of the desks. Imogen quickly joined me.

'Imo,' I panted, 'you're hurt! There's blood everywhere.'

'No kidding!' Imogen hugged her knees to her chest. She'd begun to shake. 'He slashed me a couple of times. Got me across the face. I thought I was safe but . . . not going to be pretty any longer, that's what he said –'

'He didn't get your face, Imogen.' I squeezed her arm. 'You're still pretty. More than pretty. It's OK. *This* is where he got you, on your arm. Can't you feel it? I think you'd know if he'd got an artery, but it's really bloody.'

She gave me a wobbly smile. 'It hurts and I can't tell where from, I was so sure he'd slashed my face – Sam! We're making too much noise. They'll find us . . . and . . .'

'Shh,' I said, pulling her into a tight hug. 'It'll be OK. Hang in there.'

Cradling Imogen, I felt in my pockets for my phone. Then I remembered that I'd put it in her bag for safe keeping.

Imogen shook her head when I asked. 'Must've dropped it when he grabbed me. It just happened so fast . . .'

'Let's hope someone's realized what's going on and called the police,' I muttered. I didn't say how scared I was. I didn't want to freak out Imogen any more than she already was.

'Jesus *Christ*, this hurts,' she muttered through gritted teeth. She was shivering. 'It's cold Sam. I'm so cold. I can't feel my hands.'

She needs her arm seen to and fast, I thought, the shoulder too. She was losing a lot of blood and I thought she was going into shock. Terrified for her, and terrified that the McAllisters were going to come crashing in at any second, I took off my Santa hat and knotted it round her arm as tightly as I could. I didn't know if it would help, but it was better than nothing.

'Imo,' I whispered, holding her close and trying to warm her shaking hands with my own. 'I just want to say, I think you were amazing with those shoes.'

She smiled – a panicked, joyless version of the usual smile that I loved.

'I'm always amazing,' she whispered. 'Now shh.'

IMOGEN
WEDNESDAY 18 DECEMBER

Maybe this wasn't the best place to be. Maybe we should have kept moving. Crap! The pain was making it hard for me to concentrate. Think, Imogen! Think for your sake and Sam's.

It felt like we'd been here forever. Even with Sam holding me tight, I felt a deathly kind of cold seeping into my bones. Shock probably. It was silent as the grave. The McAllister twins could be lost. Maybe they'd given up and gone?

I felt Sam shift. 'I think we should see if we can get downstairs. We can use the back staircase. We can't stay here much longer. You need an ambulance.'

That last part was right. 'You stay, Sam. I'll go on my own. If they are out there, there's no point you getting in the line of fire—'

'I'm not letting you go out there on your own! No way. You're too damn important to me!' Sam helped me up and I was woozy enough to let him half carry me towards the door.

Tentatively he put his hand on the handle. 'Are you going to be able to run?' he asked, looking worried. My blood was smeared all over him and my head was spinning.

But there was no point hesitating. We stepped into the corridor.

One of them was waiting just outside the main stairwell doors.

He smiled, waving his knife at us as though he was about to carve a joint of beef. Looking at him face to face, I could see that they were less identical than I'd thought. This one was taller. Slightly broader. And right now, a hell of a lot more dangerous.

'Patience is a virtue,' he said. 'Knew you were here somewhere. I saw what you did to my brother, bitch!'

His words were slurred. He's pissed or doped up, I thought. That could work in our favour. I wondered why the other one wasn't here too. Perhaps he was hiding, or waiting on the stairs. I felt Sam's hand press into my waist.

'We came here to show you no one messes with us,' he carried on. 'We're invincible, me and Dale. We done the service station up the road tonight. You know the one? We'll never get nicked for it. We won't get done for nothing.'

So this was Josh. They're on a high, I thought. This new robbery must have reminded them they had unfinished business.

'We weren't gonna hurt you that bad,' he said, pulling a face. 'Just give you a little something to remember us by. A nice little scar. But now –' he waved the knife – 'you hurt my brother. It's different –'

Without waiting for Josh to finish I pulled at Sam and we ran. Josh shouted and came after us. We had a head start, but Sam wasn't a runner and I was so dizzy from blood loss I could hardly see straight. We finally reached the back stairs. Chancing a backwards look I saw that Josh was gaining on us. As we hit the third floor, hope surged through me. Unless I was hallucinating, I could hear a siren!

We were almost at the first floor when I lost my balance and fell down the rest of the staircase. Winded, I lay at the bottom. If you pass out, you're dead, Imo, I told myself, and with every bit of strength I had left I heaved myself up. Looking over my shoulder I saw with horror that Josh was on top of Sam at the top of the stairs and they were grappling. Sam was lashing out, but Josh had the upper hand. His knife flashed and I screamed. But then I saw it falling. Over the banister, right to the bottom of the stairwell. Sam had knocked it out of his hand!

I had to get help. I could see that in the hall police and teachers were ushering everyone outside. Nadina and Mat were there. So was Dale, being helped out by a paramedic. I sprinted towards them, waving my unhurt arm and screaming.

SAM

Memories are odd. They bring back things you'd rather forget in excruciating detail. When I was finally able to think properly, I realized I remembered very little of the run upstairs, apart from Imogen's incredible shoe throwing. I remembered even less about the final chase. People told me I'd been incredibly brave to fight Josh to save Imogen. They were amazed I'd managed to get the knife off him. They asked how I'd done it. I said I didn't remember.

Actually, I remembered perfectly. The truth was, I hadn't knocked it out of Josh's hand at all. He'd simply lost his grip on it and dropped it. I guess he was more drunk or high than we'd realized.

I wasn't going to tell anyone though. Let people think I was an amazing knife-grappling hero. Why not?

Everything was cleared up pretty quickly after the police got there. It reminded me a lot of the night when Josh and Dale had tried to mow me down outside the chicken shop, only this time it was Imogen who was hurt and me who was doing the explaining. Well, actually it was the police who really did the explaining. Apparently they'd been in the area following up a robbery at a garage. Once they'd been alerted there was trouble at the school they'd come straight over.

'But how did you know?' I'd asked the officers, confused.

Nadina waved her phone at me. 'You ain't the only one doing a bit of heroics.' She explained that she and Mat had been in one of the ground-floor classrooms. She didn't need to say what they were doing. They'd heard shouting and Imogen rattling the door and had peered into the corridor just in time to see us head upstairs, closely followed by Josh. I stared at her, putting everything together.

'Wait – Dale never came after us. Did you take him out?!'

Nadina gave a modest shrug. 'What, like it was hard? Nah.' She grinned. 'We got lucky. He didn't realize me and Mat were there. Don't underestimate the power of surprise, innit.'

I winced, but I was impressed – and grateful. If both brothers had come after us, who knows whether things would have turned out so well.

I rang Dad and Tamsin and they rushed over to the school. After I'd managed to convince them I was fine, Dad said, 'You know what all this means, don't you?'

'No,' I said. 'What?'

Dad smiled. 'It means another court case, of course. That's assault, what those boys did tonight, and they were carrying weapons. And if there's some decent CCTV on our side this time, they could get done for robbing that garage.'

I pulled a face. 'Isn't what Imogen and Nadina did to Dale technically assault?'

'Self-defence! Bit of a difference.' Dad went on: 'There's no hope of them being retried for those previous robberies and the murder – and trying to mow the car into you, more's the pity – but if you don't get 'em for one thing, you get 'em for another—'

'Phil,' Tamsin interrupted, 'Sam's been through a terrible ordeal tonight – yet another one! – and I don't think he needs this right now, do you?'

Dad opened his mouth, then closed it. Gruffly he said, 'Right. I need to think more before I open my gob. Sorry, Sam. Home, eh?'

I smiled at Tamsin and tucked my hands into my pockets. After a few more words with the police, we went to the car.

As we drove home, I leaned my head against the window and watched the lines of Christmas trees and rows of takeaway shops zip by. I was so tired. It was incredible when I thought about what had happened – too incredible. But Dad was right to be upbeat. These weeks of fear, looking over my shoulder every time I went outdoors – they were over. At least for the meanwhile. There was no way Josh and Dale could get out of what had happened tonight.

I took out my phone and started writing a new message.

Imo, I hope you're OK. Pls text and let me know what they say in the hospital. OK?

After a moment's hesitation I added a kiss at the end.

IMOGEN
TUESDAY 24 DECEMBER

I leaned back in the cushions on the sofa, warming my hands on a cup of coffee, half watching the Pixar movie Benno had put on. Across the room Dad was tapping away on his laptop. This was a first. Usually I didn't know where he was in the house. It was nice really. We were doing our own thing, but we were hanging out. Mum was out doing some last-minute shopping, though the heap of wrapped gifts at the base of our tree looked pretty large to me.

Let's have a nice Christmas, she'd said to me the night of the party. It looked like that's what we were going to have. It was weird to be looking forward to it for once. Things weren't sorted, not entirely. But it felt like they were getting there.

The doorbell rang. It was probably Sam. He'd mentioned coming over.

'Nadina, I expect,' Dad said as I put my coffee down and got up.

'Nah, she's got a date with someone else today.' I smiled. 'Turns out knocking out knife-wielding nutters is a pretty bonding experience.'

Dad nodded. He knew the ins and outs of what had happened. As I went past I surreptitiously took a quick peek at his laptop screen, but he was just writing an email.

I opened the front door with my good arm. The one

Dale had cut was a mass of stitches, as was my shoulder. Like Sam had said, they didn't hurt, though they stung like anything if I knocked them. Still, I'd only have to put up with them for a few more days.

'Hey . . .' I started, then blinked. It wasn't Sam. It was Ollie.

'Hey. All right?'

'Mostly,' I said, rather stunned. 'You?'

Ollie shrugged. He was wearing his long stripy scarf and his old basketball hoody. 'Can we talk?'

Realizing he didn't want to come in, I grabbed my coat. I had my slippers on, but after all I'd gone through, I really didn't give a toss how weird it looked. We walked to the road in silence. The 123 trundled past, packed with Christmas shoppers. Ollie cleared his throat.

'Heard what happened. I'm really glad to see you're OK.'

'You know me,' I said, feeling a sense of déjà vu. 'I'm always OK.'

'Yeah. One way or another.' Ollie put his hands in his pockets. 'I've been thinking about everything. Made a decision.' He turned to look at me, and it struck me how much healthier he looked. 'I went to the police and made my statement again.'

After a beat I said, 'As in – the statement you withdrew?'

'Not exactly. See, that was never a full statement. Not as full as it should've been. I held a few things back, like stuff Josh and Dale said to me about other break-ins, people they'd beaten up, that kind of thing. This time round, I didn't leave out nothing. So guess what? It gets classified as new evidence. You know what that means.'

I did. It meant that the case against the McAllisters – the one we'd given evidence at – could be reopened. It was good news. I wasn't looking forward to doing the court thing again, but I knew it was necessary.

'Don't back out this time, OK?' I said.

'Not going to. Want to know what made me change my mind?'

'Christmas miracle?'

To my surprise Ollie laughed. 'No, it was last week. I thought, if someone like Sam can fight Josh McAllister, actually disarm him, what kind of person does that make me? And I don't wanna be a person who shuts up and says nothing. I'm a crime statistic now. I let my mum down. I let you down. But the statement – that's not cut and dried. I could change it. Make a difference. So I have.'

'Proud of you,' I said, half flippantly.

'Oh yeah?'

'Yeah,' I said, giving him a push and thinking how like old times this felt. 'Seriously, I'm glad. Not just cos of what this means, but cos of what this says about you. Always felt you were better than this, Ollie. Now I know you are.'

'Not good enough to get out of cleaning crap off walls,'

Ollie said with a sigh. 'Got months more of that.'

I nodded. We watched the traffic, and Ollie said something about the basketball team at his new school. It felt perfectly comfortable and not at all strange.

After a while Ollie got up. 'Happy Christmas then,' he said. 'Got any new year's resolutions?'

I leaned back, considering. 'To have a great life,' I said after a while. 'And that's not me being sarcastic.'

'Sounds good. I might nick it. See you round, Im.'

'See you,' I said, meaning it. As Ollie walked off, I thought about what having a great life really meant. For me, probably to stop lying to myself and to pay more attention to what others were thinking. I could be really oblivious to that and I didn't like myself for it. And I could be terribly judgemental and harsh, hurting people I cared about. Those weren't nice things, but now I knew I did them, I could work on them.

As for the past? I had scars. Much like I'd have physical scars from Dale's attack. But when you treated them right, scars healed.

If all the stuff with Dad hadn't happened, we'd never have come to Walthamstow. I wouldn't have become head prefect, been introduced to volleyball or met the people who were now my best friends. And while Walthamstow was, as Nads liked to say, no Chelsea, it was home. And it was where I belonged.

Then I caught sight of Sam.

SAM

As I stepped off the bus on to the road that led to Imogen's, I saw Ollie walking towards me. I was half tempted to duck into the bus shelter. But that would be silly, and he'd already seen me. When he was a few metres away, he said, 'Hey. All right?'

'Yeah,' I said, surprised that he was being friendly. 'You?'

'So-so.' Ollie smiled. 'Heard about last week. Nice going.'

It took me a moment to realize he was referring to my fight with Josh – and that he was genuinely complimenting me.

'Right,' I stuttered. Luckily Ollie didn't seem to need anything else. He slapped my shoulder in an almost matey way and carried on the way he was going. I stared after him. What did that all mean? Maybe it didn't mean anything. Or maybe it meant that I had to give it to him, after all, for being big enough to get past disliking me. He seemed to be dealing with the community sentence better than I thought I would. He'd said the last time I saw him that his future was just basketball and football. I wasn't so sure. Ollie would probably be a lot more successful than he thought, because really, despite everything – he was a hardworking guy. A good guy.

As I was psyching myself up for seeing Imogen, I realized to my amusement that she was right in front of me, sitting on her front garden wall in a bizarre combo of outdoor coat, trackies and fluffy slippers.

'What are you doing?' I laughed, suddenly feeling more relaxed.

Imogen shrugged. 'Oh, I do this all the time. You just haven't caught me before.'

'You don't look very warm.'

'I'm not.' Imogen got to her feet. 'Looking forward to tomorrow?'

I was actually. It would be my first Christmas with Dad and Tamsin. Last year I'd been with Mia and her parents, and while I'd had a good time, I knew that I didn't really belong there.

Now I finally had a place to call home. It made me happier than I could remember.

'Next year will be my little brother or sister's first Christmas,' I said. 'It's exciting. I quite like the idea of being a big brother.'

We were nearly at her house, and I noticed Imogen rubbing her hands together. Deciding now was good, I drew out a wrapped gift from my bag. 'Hey. Merry Christmas.'

Imogen's eyes widened. She took the present, pushing a stray lock of hair out of her eyes with her other hand. 'Wow. You didn't have to do this. Can I open it?'

'Go on then.' I grinned.

Imogen ripped it open and took out the pair of gloves inside. 'I noticed you'd lost yours. I don't like the idea of you getting frostbite and your fingers dropping off,' I joked.

'Nice one,' Imogen smiled. 'The colour's great. Thanks! That was really thoughtful.'

We reached Imogen's front door. As she reached into her pocket for keys, we noticed something hanging above our heads. Something which, judging by the way Imogen's jaw dropped, hadn't been there when she left.

'What idiot hung that up?' Imogen broke the silence. We stared at the mistletoe, its fat berries gleaming. I peered over my shoulder, checking that no one was watching from the window.

'Well,' I started, 'you know what they say . . . it's really bad luck to ignore mistletoe.'

'Sam, be serious. We are not having a snog. Not, like, ever, and definitely not, like, here, and most certainly not, like, because of some stupid Christmas tradition. Because that is lame.'

Imogen talked lots when she was wrong-footed, I'd noticed. For once she didn't look so certain. In fact, she was the one that was blushing while I wasn't. I felt weirdly at ease as I said, 'I must be pretty lame then.'

I leaned forward. When our lips met, warmth flowed through me, and there was a pounding feeling in my chest that was brilliant and scary at the same time. I leaned in to kiss her a second time, then felt Imogen's hand on my chest.

'Samuel —' to my delight she was smiling — 'one kiss per berry, remember?' She reached up and plucked off a berry and waved it at me. 'Memento?'

Then the door opened and Imogen's mum appeared.

'Oh, so you found the mistletoe I put up then,' she said smoothly.

I coughed and looked at my feet.

Imogen made a huffing noise. 'Since when were you such a perv, Mum?'

'You were the one who complained there wasn't enough love in the house. I was just trying to create some.' She went back inside, laughing, leaving the door open.

Imogen stepped in, muttering angrily, 'I bet she was watching. Ugh!'

'Hey, Imo.' I caught her arm. 'I do like you, just so you know. More than just friends.'

Imogen looked down at my hand on her arm.

'You might be moving to America,' she said, her expression unreadable.

'I don't think that'll happen,' I said. 'Not now the McAllisters are going down. Tamsin has never been keen on it; she wants her parents around when the baby's born. Dad adores her, so I think she'll get final say on the matter.'

Imogen sighed. 'Look, Sam, so much is going on in my

head right now; I need some time to get through it. You're a great guy and as far as mistletoe kisses go, well, that was a really cheesy thing to do. But I did like it. OK?' She grinned at me shyly.

I beamed. I couldn't help it. 'That's OK. That's very OK.'

Imogen took off the gloves and carefully placed them in her coat pockets. 'Maybe next year you can buy me slippers. These ones are rank!' Then she leaned forward and gave me a very quick kiss on the lips. 'Merry Christmas, Sam,' she said, closing the door.

Next year.

Next year would bring a new court case and new problems. But next year would also bring my new brother or sister and the chance for me to get to know better the new people who'd become so important to me. After years of feeling so anxious and frustrated I could barely breathe, I'd finally started to live again.

Now was good. So good I couldn't wipe the silly grin off my face. But next year?

Next year was going to be incredible.

Turn the page to read an extract from . . .

FORGET ME NEVER

Another suspense-filled thriller from . . .

GINA BLAXILL

SOPHIE

My cousin Danielle was twenty-six when she died. According to the police she jumped from the balcony of her flat, which, in the words of my foster-mother, wasn't a very nice way to go. What a stupid thing to say. Is death ever 'nice'?

My best friend Reece and I were the last people to see Dani alive. We'd been staying the weekend in her Bournemouth flat. I say her flat, but it actually belonged to Danielle's friend Fay, who was backpacking around South America and had said Dani was welcome to use it.

'Come over! It'll be brilliant.' Danielle had sounded so enthusiastic when she rang to invite me. 'Stay for a week, two weeks – I'm right next to the beach. Loads to do. You'll love it.'

'I've got school,' I said. 'They probably wouldn't approve of me taking a week out to splash about in the sea.'

'Oh, yeah, school. Bummer. Well, whatever. Let's make it a weekend.'

Timewise it wasn't ideal – it was just after Easter, and GCSE exams were breathing down my neck – but I went anyway. My foster-mum, Julie, was fine with me going – she said I deserved a break. I hadn't heard from Danielle in ages, even though until recently she'd been working in north London, where I was living.

So after school on Friday afternoon Reece and I got the train from Waterloo and Danielle met us on the platform at the other end, all smiles and carrying an enormous bag of rum-and-raisin fudge. She started chattering about the flat and the beach and her new job, which was a temporary one at an IT consultancy. We had fish and chips in town and then went for a walk along the seafront and tried out the fairground rides on the pier. Danielle knew the people running the air-rifle stand and they let us have a couple of free shots, which they probably regretted when Reece started arguing about the game's rules. Reece had always liked the sound of his own voice – Danielle and I found the whole thing terribly funny and couldn't stop laughing. It's not that remarkable, but I'll always hold on to that moment: a summer night when the light was starting to fade, a warm breeze ruffling my hair, sharing a joke with my cousin.

On Sunday afternoon Reece and I were getting ready to leave when the flat's doorbell buzzed. Danielle went to answer. I was in the other room at the time, so I don't know if she said anything to the caller over the intercom, but the next thing I knew, I could hear footsteps running downstairs.

'Does she always rush about like that?' Reece asked.

I shrugged. 'Pretty much.'

Reece went to the window, pressing his palms to it. 'She's talking to some bloke.'

'He's probably just selling something,' I said. 'Give me a hand with my case, will you? The zip's stuck.'

Half an hour later Danielle still hadn't come back. She wasn't outside the flat or picking up her mobile, so we had no choice but to head to the station. We'd booked two cheap seats on the 4.37 and I couldn't see Julie being happy about forking out for a later train.

'Bit off, Danielle not coming to say goodbye,' Reece said as we left. 'She's a bit of a skitz, your cousin.'

I felt a little disappointed that Danielle hadn't returned, but it wasn't as though it was the first time she'd let me down. She'd probably ring that evening, full of apologies.

Later Reece and I worked out that Danielle must have jumped from the balcony roughly around the time we were changing trains at Southampton. When I got back Julie told me what had happened.

I didn't believe it at first. The idea that Danielle could be gone seemed impossible. But when I began to take it all in — well, it was pretty tough. The next few days were terrible ones I'd give anything to forget. Over the years I'd become very good at blanking out feelings, but I couldn't ignore this. Dani had been the only person in the world who was mine, someone who knew exactly what I'd been through. She never judged me. She *understood*. That was something I could never replace.

The coroner was satisfied it was suicide. Danielle had never been that stable, I knew. She'd threatened to hurt herself before, and depression and mood swings ran in the family. Maybe it had been one of those freak decisions you'd never make if you could go back in time. In the words of the police officer who'd come to tell me the verdict, it was 'terribly sad, but it all made sense'.

The whole thing left me reeling, but very slowly I began to accept that there was nothing left for me to do but try to get on with my life – without Dani.

And maybe that's the way things would have gone if, four months later, I hadn't found the memory stick.

Summer. Weeks and weeks off school. Sunshine, Cornettos and flip-flops. Holidays abroad for the lucky ones. Muggy days that feel endless, hanging out with friends in the park. Fun. That's what summer should be, but this year it just wasn't working for me.

As well as coping with my grief I felt like I was at a crossroads, that everything was in flux. Everyone was waiting for their GCSE results. The exams had gone better than expected in the end, but I still couldn't see myself doing that well – English in particular had been a nightmare. Half of my year at Broom Hill High were leaving to go to colleges rather than staying on for the sixth form, which didn't have a great reputation. Lots of the teachers had gone on about how A levels and BTECs were a huge stepping stone and how the subjects we chose now could determine the rest of our lives. I wasn't sure I bought the idea that we were taking control; everyone still treated us like kids. Especially me – as a foster-kid I wasn't allowed to make my own decisions. I'd had to sit down with my social worker and come up with a 'Pathway Plan', supposedly to help me prepare for independent life when I turned eighteen and left care. Lorraine had strong opinions about what was best for me, and after a frustrated hour of trying to explain I had no idea where I wanted to be in two years, I gave up and let her take over. Biology, geography and law A levels would be as good as anything else.

Apart from helping out in the Save the Animals charity shop, something I'd been doing on-off ever since I'd come to live with Julie almost a year and a half ago, I had very little to do. I'd seen my old classmates down the high street. They'd invited me to join them, but after a couple of long afternoons sunbathing in the park I got restless. I'd rather be *doing* something. Hanging out is kind of empty when the people aren't really your friends; nothing gets said that you remember, and time seems to drag. It was easier for them if I wasn't around, anyway; putting up with someone who'd had a family member die was a real downer. It would have been easier if Dani had been knocked down by a car or had some kind of accident. That it had been suicide seemed to reflect on me somehow – especially as I had a reputation for being a bit crazy myself. The girls were clearly trying to treat me sensitively, but that just smacked home how different I was from them. It made me feel I would never be a normal teenager again.

I kept wondering how the summer break would have been different if Danielle was still here. Maybe we could have spent the summer in Bournemouth, just us – hanging out in town, clothes shopping, watching DVDs, the relaxed kind of stuff we didn't always fit into the weekends and evenings we spent together. Dani could be very inconsistent, sometimes going into moods that meant I wouldn't see her for weeks. But the absent patches had been worth it for the good ones, when she would be incredibly sweet, showering me with gifts and affection.

Instead I had my classmates and lots of school gossip I didn't want to hear. It just reminded me that I'd have to go back to Broom Hill, making me dread the end of the holidays even more than I was already. It was times like these that made me wish Reece hadn't left halfway through Year 10. Paloma, a girl who'd been in my class, had asked after him when I'd joined her gang in the park recently. Everyone still remembered Reece. His run-ins with teachers were legendary. One particular highlight was the time he calmly walked out of a history lesson and returned with an Internet printout that disproved what the teacher had just said about the causes of World War One. Reece had been excluded for that little stunt.

'So,' Paloma said, 'you still talk? You and Reece used to be totally buddy–buddy.'

'Yeah, well, that was before he buggered off to posh school,' I said. I knew I was being a little unfair – Reece had kicked up a huge fuss about being moved to Berkeley School for Boys, threatening his mother with a hunger strike and other ridiculous things. We'd stayed friends for a while, even arranging that Bournemouth trip so we could spend some proper time together. 'I'm fed up with him and his stupid new friends,' I added.

'Didn't seem like he'd changed last time I saw him, a couple of weeks before my party,' Paloma said. 'You were matey enough then.'

I started to make a daisy chain, not meeting her eyes. There was more to our falling-out, but I wasn't confiding in Paloma. I liked her best out of the girls from school because she stuck up for me – Paloma was sometimes teased about her weight, so she knew a thing or two about fighting back – but she did have a big mouth. Eventually she got the message and changed the subject, but I knew she'd try to get the full story later. When she invited me to the cinema the next day, I passed. Julie would have bugged me about that if she'd known. She was worried I didn't seem to have many friends. It wasn't true – there were always people for me to hang out with if I wanted – but I just wasn't close to anyone. Not like I had been to Dani, or to Reece.

I think maybe the reason I don't have many friends is that people are always so curious about my life. In the old days kids wanted to know what it was like to be in care, especially as I sometimes exaggerated the less pleasant bits. More recently I guess people just noticed me because I was different. Once I skived off school and went to Hampstead Heath instead, but I didn't get into trouble. Broom Hill's head teacher thought I was 'troubled', so he just sent me to have a long talk with the school counsellor. The other kids really resented that and said I'd got off easy. I used not to care about gossip, because people said stuff about Reece as well, but it's not so easy putting on a front on your own. Especially as since Paloma's party everyone really did have gossip about me. Horrible, embarrassing, true gossip.

ACKNOWLEDGEMENTS

As usual there are some special people who have helped *Saving Silence* transform from a ragtag manuscript into a proper novel that can sit proudly on a shelf. There are less of them this time, as writing this novel has been a pretty smooth process, but their contributions are no less valuable for it.

My parents, Sheila and David, have once again acted as sounding boards for my ideas and spotted things that don't make sense at an early stage. They are probably very relieved that this book involved less endless 'I'm stuck!' sessions.

My editor, Becky Bagnell, also deserves a tip of the hat for as usual providing me with ongoing support from my initial synopsis to the finished novel.

Both my editors, Rachel Kellehar and Rachel Petty, for doing sterling edits at different stages and making *Saving Silence* into a better book with their suggestions and ideas.

All the other lovely people at Macmillan who have helped with other parts of the book's journey, thank you to you too.

Finally, thanks to all my friends and colleagues who have been interested and encouraging at various stages. Knowing people are on my side is not only cool, but helps keep me motivated — so thank you.